A MATTER OF HEART

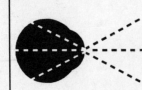

LONE STAR BRIDES, BOOK 3

A Matter of Heart

Tracie Peterson

THORNDIKE PRESS
A part of Gale, Cengage Learning

GALE
Detroit • New York • San Francisco • New York • Waterville, Maine
Meriden, Conn • Mason, Ohio • Chicago

Copyright © 2014 by Peterson Ink, Inc.

Scripture quotations are taken from the King James Version of the Bible.

Thorndike Press, a part of Gale, Cengage Learning.

Thorndike Press® Large Print Christian Romance.

The text of this Large Print edition is unabridged.

Other aspects of the book may vary from the original edition.

Set in 16 pt. Plantin.

LIBRARY OF CONGRESS CATALOGING-IN-PUBLICATION DATA

Peterson, Tracie.
  A matter of heart / Tracie Peterson. — Large print edition.
    pages cm. — (Lone star brides ; 3) (Thorndike Press large print Christian romance)
    ISBN 978-1-4104-7231-1 (hardcover) — ISBN 1-4104-7231-0 (hardcover)
    1. Single women—Fiction. 2. Large type books. I. Title.
  PS3566.E7717M38 2014b
  813'.54—dc23   2014028766

Published in 2014 by arrangement with Bethany House Publishers, a division of Baker Publishing Group

Printed in the United States of America

1 2 3 4 5 6 7 18 17 16 15 14

In memory of Ruth Seamands —
Mama Ruth to writers and believers
near and far —
an incredible woman of God.
Can hardly wait to see you again!
Save me a chair.

CHAPTER 1

TEXAS
LATE AUGUST 1896
They're all talking about me.
Jessica Atherton could feel their furtive glances. *They have their husbands and children, and I'm still unmarried. Me, the one who was always the most beautiful, the most favored.* She frowned and looked back at the paper in her hands. Her thoughts betrayed an unappealing attitude, which Jessica was only beginning to recognize.

I am spoiled. Just as spoiled as everyone says. Shallow and selfish.

She raised her head and forced a smile as she met the gazes of several women. The women had gathered at her parents' home for a meeting of the Texas Cattle Women's Society, so there was no escaping their looks and comments.

They pity me.

The very thought annoyed and vexed Jessica in a way she couldn't ignore. At the age of twenty-one, Jessica had planned for her life to be much different. She'd imagined herself married and living a life of luxury in Houston or perhaps in some large city like Chicago, where she had often visited her grandparents. She had held great plans for her life — travel, wealth, opulence, and of course, a handsome man at her side, lavishing her with gifts and adoration.

"So, Jessica," Aunt Laura whispered, leaning close, "how are you holding up?"

Jessica knew her aunt was sympathetic to the situation. "I feel rather like an animal caught in a trap with no escape. My only choices are to gnaw off my own leg or await the kill."

Laura Reid smiled and patted her niece's hand. "They're soon to depart. With the business end of things complete, most will need to get back to their homes. It's not a good time of year for socializing — too much work needs their attention."

Unfortunately, Jessica knew these particular women were inclined to visit, even with work awaiting. Hannah Barnett was said to be arriving at any moment with her daughter-in-law, Alice, and new grandson. Jessica figured the women were there for the long haul, since this would be Alice's first social appearance since giving birth.

"You know they won't leave before they've seen the new baby," she replied.

A baby that might have been mine.

The very idea gave her a bevy of mixed emotions. On one hand, Jessica wasn't even sure that she wanted children. And on the other, she was still smarting from the fact that the scar-faced Alice Chesterfield had managed to steal away the only man Jessica had ever figured to marry — Robert Barnett. Of course, it hadn't been all that much of a theft. Robert and Jessica weren't in love, and it was only because of people's assumptions that they were linked as a couple. Their so-called romance was something created in the minds of their sentimental mothers, who saw their children as good choices for each other. Still, it bothered Jessica that Robert had so quickly cast her aside.

"Well, perhaps you can slip away," Aunt Laura suggested.

"If the moment presents itself, I will. Until then," Jessica conceded with a heavy sigh, "I must simply endure."

"Jessica, have you settled on any particular young man now that Robert has a wife and child?" Mrs. Pritchard asked from her other side. The woman was a notorious gossip and loved to get the inside scoop on everyone's life. Her husband owned one of the stores in Cedar Springs, and it gave her the perfect conduit for sharing information.

Jess looked to the gray-haired woman with a smile. "Goodness, no. I'm enjoying being able to come and go as I please. I'm not saddled down in any way, and if I want to travel or leave for an extended visit elsewhere, I have only to pack my bags."

"But you must be lonely at times," her friend Beth offered. Beth was Mrs. Pritchard's youngest daughter and Jessica's longtime chum from school. Beth had married at eighteen and already had two children, who were now being cared for with some of the other children in another part of the house. Earlier, she and two other young wives announced they were were having another baby.

Jessica knew that Beth was truly concerned for her well-being, but with all gazes now fixed upon her, Jessica felt completely out of sorts. "Of course I'm not lonely. Goodness, I have people around me all the time and plenty of suitors." She gave a light laugh, as if the entire world knelt at her feet. "I'm perfectly content."

But she could see in the eyes of the other women that they didn't believe her.

Another of her former schoolmates, Constance Watson, piped up. "I don't believe any woman can be completely content until she is wed. I know I wasn't." Several of the women nodded as she continued. "Life completely changes once you marry, and as Mother often says, it will change again when children come along — an event I hope soon to know." She smiled sweetly at Jessica. "I hope that you, too, will know those pleasures for yourself — both marriage and motherhood."

Jessica heard a hint of sarcasm in the woman's tone but smiled in return nevertheless. "Well, bless your heart for sayin' so."

Constance sat back in her chair and nodded soberly. "I will pray for you."

"Yes, we must all pray that God will send Jessica a husband," Mrs. Smith said, smiling at her daughter. "Constance is always so willing to pray for others."

Jessica wanted to flee the room but knew she couldn't without causing a scene. Instead, she folded her hands and thanked the ladies for their concern and prayers.

"I thought Hannah would be here by now," Aunt Laura commented to the group.

Jessica's mother nodded. "Should be anytime now. I can hardly wait to see the new baby."

"What was it they named him?" one of the older ranch wives asked.

"William Robert Barnett," Jessica's mother replied. "After his grandfather and father. Hannah tells me they intend to call him Wills, but her husband has nicknamed the baby Billy Bob."

The women smiled or chuckled and continued to ask questions about the baby and the mother's health. Jessica never thought she'd be glad for the topic to settle on Alice and her child, but at least it took the focus off of her own inadequacies.

Inadequacies. It seemed like such a harsh word, but Jessica could think of no other. These days she was her harshest critic. Others were always commenting on her charm, beauty, and accomplishments. She had finished out at one of the best schools for young ladies that Texas could boast, and she'd done well academically in her earlier school years. Some even commented on her being quite intelligent and in possession of a good wit. Surely a woman with such attributes could not be called lacking. In addition to these qualities, Jessica knew her waist was the smallest in the county, and her face had been compared to those of various Greek goddesses. She had always known of her appealing looks. Her mother, also a woman of great beauty, had warned that she could easily use her appearance to manipulate others. She urged Jessica to draw closer to God and forget about her loveliness.

"God doesn't consider a person's outward appearance, and neither should we," her mother had chided.

Jessica always thought that strange. Why would God have made some things beautiful and others ugly if He hadn't expected folks to notice?

"Oh, that must be them!" her mother announced at the sound of an approaching carriage. Having every window open to allow for the least hint of breeze on this stifling hot day caused the sound to echo throughout the house.

The gathering seemed to rise and move slowly en masse to greet the new arrivals. Happy to see them all exit the house, Jessica sprang to her feet. This made the perfect opportunity for her to slip away unseen. She hoped for at least a few quiet moments to herself and made her way out the back door, past the barn, and toward the horse pen, where her own mare, Peg, stood loyally waiting. The humidity and heat of the day made her feel even more miserable.

"Are you as unhappy as I am, Peg?" Jessica asked, reaching out to stroke the velvety muzzle of the dapple gray. The horse had been a gift from her father and mother six years earlier, along with a very smart sidesaddle. Jessica had been delighted at the time and remained so. She and Peg were the best of friends. "At least you have plenty of shade and water."

The mare lowered her head to search Jessica's hand. "I'm sorry, girl. I didn't think to bring you a treat." Jessica reached up and stroked the black mane. She was a true beauty, standing sixteen hands high. Her dappled body bore an intriguing pattern set against the black mane and tail. Peg was the perfect mount for Jessica. Both horse and owner were beautiful and unusual.

For a moment Jessica allowed the mare to nuzzle her, then stepped back. "Maybe we'll go for a ride later, when it cools down a bit."

"I could escort you" came a familiar voice.

Jessica turned to find Lee Skelly. Lee was shorter than most of the men, but quite muscular. He acted as her father's foreman and right-hand man when her brothers Howard and Isaac were otherwise occupied, as they were now.

"Have you had word from your brothers

about when they're headin' home?" he asked, leaning back against the fence of the pen.

"Mother said they would be home by Christmas."

"They still buildin' new houses for colored people in Corpus Christi?"

Jessica nodded and pulled a handkerchief from her sleeve. Her mother's friends had written to encourage the mission. Howard and Isaac, true humanitarians that they were, eagerly gave up ranch work in favor of construction. Both had a mind for politics, and this was exactly the kind of thing that would speak of their giving characters.

"They are enjoying the change of pace, I think." She dabbed at the perspiration forming on her face and turned to leave.

"So what about that ride?" Lee asked, coming alongside her.

Jessica continued walking. "I don't think my father would approve. It isn't becoming for me to be out with a man my own age without a chaperone."

"I'm completely honorable," he protested. "We can even take old Osage with us."

Jessica thought of the older man who was once her father and grandfather's ranch foreman. Osage was nearing eighty now, but he hadn't slowed down much, despite her father's insistence that he retire. Having no part in lounging around, Osage kept an eye on things around the house and took time to oversee some of the younger cowboys in training.

"I won't make that kind of demand on Osage. He has enough to keep him busy."

"Ah, Jess, you could talk him into it. If not Osage, then maybe your pa would make an exception and let me escort you."

Jessica threw him a glance and shook her head. "He's not likely to agree."

"Why not? I'm a good fella, Jess. I think we could have a right good future together."

At this she stopped. "Are you proposing to me?"

He gave a sheepish grin. "Well, why not? I'm a fella of my word, and you're a beautiful woman. We could have a great life together."

"You don't even know what I want out of life."

"I figure you want the same things every girl wants: security, family, a home." He took on an air of confidence and asked, "Ain't that right?"

Jessica shrugged. "I couldn't say. I don't know what I want."

He laughed. "Jess, you don't need to want for anything if you agree to be my gal."

Turning, she looked hard at the man. "It would hardly be appropriate for me to be your gal. You're my father's foreman." The minute the words came out of her mouth, Jessica thought they sounded terrible. Lee frowned, and Jessica knew he'd taken offense. She hurried to cover her tracks.

"In your position here, the other men might think Father was giving you an unfair advantage if he allowed you to court me." *There. That doesn't sound quite so arrogant.* But from the continued scowl on Lee's face, Jessica wasn't sure he'd even heard her.

"You don't think I'm good enough for you?"

Jessica felt her cheeks warm at the question. "I have no thought of it either way," she lied. "I know it would not meet with my father's approval, and therefore have not contemplated the idea. I do know, however, that a simple thing like that could cause all sorts of problems among a group of men."

She shrugged. "Besides, Lee, I have no desire to marry anyone. I rather like having my freedom. I can come and go as I please. And I very well may do just that. I have cousins who live in Chicago. I got to know them when I spent time up there with my grandparents. They've been begging me to visit."

Lee shook his head. "You don't think I'm serious, do you?"

She put her hands on her hips. "And just what is that supposed to mean?"

It was Lee's turn to shrug. "Just that you don't think of me as a man, as a possible beau. You're the boss's daughter and deserve much better than the hired hand. And why not? Your pa owns this place. It's like he's king over this ranch, and that makes you his little princess. Can't have the princess marryin' the pauper."

Jessica hated his analogy. God had already been pricking her conscience about the way she acted and the times she'd made other people feel ill at ease. For a moment she felt completely defenseless.

"I'm . . . I don't know what to say." Jessica shook her head and fixed her gaze on his face. "I really wasn't thinking any of that, Lee. You're a fine man. My father thinks highly of you, and I don't have any reason to believe you wouldn't be a proper suitor."

"Then why won't you step out with me?"

She knew the reason but worried he would take it wrong. "I don't see a future in it." She held up her hand. "Before you go off thinking I'm being uppity or believe myself too good for you, let me tell you the exact

18

opposite is true."

He frowned. "Whadd'ya mean?"

"It has nothing to do with whether you are good enough for me. It has to do with me." She shook her head. "This isn't coming out right. I don't mean it's all about me and what I want out of life . . . or need. It's about me . . . being . . . a mess."

He laughed. "Oh, Jess, you ain't no mess. You're the purtiest gal in these parts. Now, if you wanna see a mess, you ought to see my little sister. Grief, but that gal can't hardly turn around without breakin' something or causin' disaster. Ma says she puts her foot in her mouth more often than she puts on her shoes."

Jessica wanted to shout that he had no idea what she was saying, but she held her tongue. Maybe part of maturity was recognizing when to fight your battles.

Lee sobered, as if realizing he'd acted inappropriately. "Sorry, Jess. I didn't mean no disrespect."

"I know," she said, and the sadness in her voice hung in the air. She turned and made her way to the house, hoping Lee wouldn't follow her and press for more. He didn't, and Jessica let out the breath she'd been holding.

Poor Lee. He truly was a nice young man,

but Jess had never seen him as anything more than one of the workers. Not because he was of a lower station, but because she simply only saw him in that capacity. She'd not dealt with him much at social events, and he wasn't really one to attend church.

"There you are," Beth said, thrusting a bundle at Jessica as soon as she entered the kitchen. "We're all taking turns holding little Wills. It's your turn."

Jessica looked down at the dark blue eyes of Robert's son. Something akin to deep regret washed over her.

He might have been mine. If I had been a different woman — with a different heart — I might be the one sharing my son with family and friends.

"He's beautiful," she whispered, almost afraid to say anything more.

"We all thought so," her mother said, coming alongside. "Hannah says he's the spitting image of Robert."

Jessica nodded. "Yes, I think she's right."

The baby started to fuss, and Jessica feared she'd done something wrong. She looked to her mother with a questioning expression. Alice stepped in just then and took Wills.

"He's just hungry. I hope you don't mind if I take a few moments to feed him." She said it more to the group than to Jessica.

Free of the baby, Jessica hurried away from the gathering and sought the solitude of her room. The women might talk about her abrupt departure, but unlike times before, Jessica didn't care.

"Let them talk," she said, pacing her bedroom floor. "Those old biddies are always gossiping about someone. It doesn't need to ruin my day. If they have nothing better to do than pick apart my actions, then so be it."

She plopped down on the carefully made bed and sighed. She didn't like people thinking poorly of her. She wanted them to like her, to desire her company. She wanted them to be impressed with her knowledge and abilities. Folks felt that way about her mother and her aunt, and it was only natural that Jessica should want the same.

"Is that just more of my self-centered ways?" she asked aloud. "Worrying about what people think of me?"

She looked around her room and couldn't help remembering Lee's earlier comment. This was the room of a princess. From her feather mattress and beautifully crafted canopy bed swathed in pink tulle to the wardrobe filled with expensive, intricately designed gowns, Jessica was living the life of royalty. At least Texas royalty.

"But does that have to be bad?" she asked the empty room. "Is it wrong to enjoy fine things?"

Getting to her feet, Jessica crossed to the window, where new drapes of the finest damask had been placed only the week before. She had told her mother how tiresome the other drapery had become, and her mother had arranged for replacements. Toying with the fringed edges of the cream-and-gold material, Jessica knew that it had been an additional expense that could have been better spent. There had been nothing wrong with the other curtains. In fact, Mother had placed them in one of the other bedrooms.

Jessica turned and spied her reflection in the mirror. Soft brown curls had been carefully arranged atop her head. They spilled down the back to just cover her neck. She wore a gown of sheer white muslin with a lining of pale pink silk. Six-inch-wide lace in a V shape gave the bodice a narrowing appearance and made Jessica's waist appear even smaller than it was. And with the full leg-o'-mutton lace sleeves, the gown seemed most ethereal — fairy-tale like. She always received compliments when she wore it.

Jessica touched a finger to the glass. Was

that all there was to her? Was she just a pretty bauble designed to turn heads and fascinate suitors? Nothing more than a story-book princess?

She glanced back at the door to her room. Just on the other side and downstairs, a collection of women gathered. Women who had husbands and children, whose lives meant something, who had people who loved them.

"What do I have? What do I offer? Robert married Alice rather than be saddled with me."

Knowing in her heart that Robert and Alice genuinely loved each other didn't ease her momentary self-ridicule.

"Of course Robert would marry someone sweet and quiet like Alice. Even with her scarred face. I say what I think, and often I'm loud and insist on my own way. No one wants those qualities in a wife."

She sat down once again, this time at her dressing table. Yet another mirror reflected her pensive countenance. Picking up one of a dozen ornamental hatpins, she studied it a moment, then stuck it in a pin cushion. One by one she did the same for the others. The action seemed to calm her.

Maybe I should marry someone like Lee. Maybe that's what I deserve — a loveless marriage to a poor man.

A light knock sounded on her door. "Come in." She leaned back as her mother entered the room.

"Are you feeling all right?"

"Physically? Yes, I'm fine. Emotionally? I'm not sure."

Mother smiled sympathetically, and Jessica vacillated between wanting to scream at the implied pity and needing her mother's embrace.

"Is this about Alice and the baby?"

"I don't know. I think it's about everything. I'm starting to see some things about myself and my life that I don't really like. Things that need to be improved."

"Nonsense. You are perfect the way you are. Don't fret. One day the right man will come into your life, and he will sweep you off your feet and become the love of your life." Mother's expression became quite soft. "I know, because it happened that way for me. I thought I knew love with my first husband. Soon enough I learned there was no love between us. After he died, I was certain I would never find true love. Then your father came into my life, and everything changed."

Jessica knew her mother was trying to help, but her words rang hollow. "Everyone has things about them that need changing," she said in a barely audible voice.

"I suppose that's true; however, I know that you have a good heart and a wonderful nature. I don't want you thinking yourself hopeless or without value because Robert married another." Mother patted her shoulder. "You are my daughter, my baby. You have great value in my eyes and in those of your father. But more important, you have great value in the eyes of God. Remember that."

Jessica nodded, but the words didn't help. She hadn't been as focused on God and spiritual matters as she knew her parents wished. Religiosity and showing up for the Sunday pew warming seemed more hypocritical than spiritual, and Jessica found reading the Bible to be a bore. She looked in the mirror and found her mother looking at her with an expression that suggested she wanted to hear her daughter affirm her willingness.

"I'll try to remember it, Mother. I'll try."

"Good. Now why don't you come downstairs and rejoin us. There are only a few people still here, and Hannah has taken Alice and the baby home. It shouldn't be so painful for you now."

Jessica gave a heavy sigh. Mother simply didn't understand. Apparently, no one did.

CHAPTER 2

Sunday brought cooler temperatures, which was unusual for Texas at this time of the year. Nevertheless, Austin Todd had taken advantage of the less oppressive afternoon to snag a much-needed nap.

He'd barely closed his eyes, however, when he found himself caught up in the age-old nightmare. Why could he not lay the past to rest? Would he always be haunted by the ghosts of those he'd failed?

So many people had counted on him, and he'd let them down. The nightmare only served to remind him of their disappointment in him. Austin tossed restlessly atop his narrow bed as images of his brother, mother, and father passed before his eyes. His brother looked at him with the same stunned expression Austin had last seen on his face. Mother and Father fixed Austin with looks of disapproval and accusation.

And then there was Grace.

27

Austin awoke with a start. Soaked in sweat, he all but jumped from the bed as though it were afire. With hands trembling, he reached for the pitcher of water. He poured the tepid liquid onto a cloth and wiped his face. Why couldn't the past just die?

He replaced the pitcher and threw down the cloth, not caring where it landed. Stalking from the room, Austin fought against a lifetime of regret and unmistakable feelings of failure, especially when it came to family relationships.

Outside, Austin leaned his lanky frame against the house's front wall and breathed in deeply of the air. It was nearly evening and a new week would soon begin. He had obligations in Dallas on Monday and had no idea how long he would have to remain. As a cattle inspector — part of the Texas Rangers — Austin kept busy upholding law and order on the range.

It was a world of difference from his previous job in Washington, D.C., a job he'd shared with his brother, Houston, until that fateful night nearly six years ago. A picture of his brother's face came to mind. With laughing eyes, a strong jaw, and a perfect smile, Houston was three years Austin's junior. The brothers had been inseparable, even going into the same career of working for the Treasury Department's Secret Service.

They had worked side by side, feeling they knew each other's moods and moves better than anyone else ever would. Their job entailed ferreting out counterfeiters — something they did quite well. Austin had a keen nose for the business. Often with nothing more than the tiniest hunch, he had been able to expose criminals and put an end to their plots. Once, he'd even thwarted an attack on a top government official. Houston had teased him unmercifully when their boss had presented Austin with an award meriting his service.

"Your head will swell too big for you to get out the door," Houston had said. He joked about the matter but clearly was proud of his older brother. His parents had been proud, too. At least until that dreadful night when Austin killed his brother.

"Be sure and tell Austin that he can eat with us anytime he likes," Robert Barnett's mother announced as he made plans to ride over to the small cabin where the Texas Ranger lived. "He certainly doesn't need to wait for an invitation."

Robert glanced to where his mother sat

happily holding his son. Alice was getting a much-needed rest while baby William's grandmother fussed over him. "I'll tell him again, Mother, but I can't force the man to eat with us."

"Well, at least take him some sugar cookies. Rosita made a fresh batch yesterday."

"I'll do that," Robert promised. He lost no time in getting to the kitchen, lest his mother stop him again. He wrapped a dozen or so cookies in a dish towel and made his way out the back door, munching on one of the treats as he went.

Manuel already had Robert's horse saddled and ready to go. The sorrel seemed happy to see his master and bobbed his head up and down at Robert's approach. As soon as the horse realized there was food involved, he made certain to get part of it. Robert allowed the animal a piece of cookie then finished it off himself. He tucked the bundled cookies into his saddlebag, then took the reins from Manuel and mounted.

"Gracias, Manuel."

The fourteen-year-old boy smiled and nodded. A younger brother to one of the ranch's cowboys, Manuel had proven himself a hard worker. Robert gave him a quick nod, then urged the horse into a trot.

The Barnett property had grown considerably over the years, and while it was no rival to the King Ranch in South Texas, it was garnering attention in its own right for quality livestock and trustworthy dealings. Robert was proud to bear the name Barnett. Prouder still that he could follow in his father's footsteps.

The ride to Austin Todd's cabin was several miles. Perched on the edge of what had formerly been Barnett land, the small house was perfectly suited for one man. Austin seemed to appreciate the solitude, but Robert wasn't sure that he would have much positive to say about the news he was bringing today.

When the cabin finally came in sight, Robert paused to wipe his brow and offer up a prayer. "Lord, you know what I'm here to say. Help me to say it right and for Austin to receive it well. Amen."

Robert caught sight of Austin chopping wood and gave a wave. Reaching the house, Robert quickly tied off his horse and made his way to where Austin continued to work.

"I see you're taking advantage of the cooler weather."

Austin looked up and gave a brief nod. "I figured it was a good time to stock up a little. I appreciated your pa havin' that dead tree dragged here for me. I've been whittling away on it." He motioned to the stack of leafless limbs. "I try to trim off a little every night I'm home."

"Sounds like a plan," Robert declared. "I was hopin', though, that we could have a little talk. My pa sent me."

"Problems?" Austin asked, setting the ax aside.

"No, not really. You're invited, in fact, to a gathering at our place. Night after next."

"Not sure I'll be back from Dallas. What's the occasion?"

Robert smiled. "Well, you know my pa wants to get a railroad spur built out here."

"He wants to start a whole town, as I recall."

"Well, he figures if there's a spur for the ranchers to use, the town will just form naturally. Because of that, he wants some say in how it comes about."

"You can't have any real control over that," Austin said, looking uncertain.

"Well, he figures he can control it to a point. After all, he owns the land he intends for the railroad to build on and where the spur will end. Of course, it crosses Atherton land, too, but they are supportive of the cause."

"Doesn't it seem kinda unnecessary to bring in the railroad? I mean, it isn't that far to drive the cattle over to Cedar Springs."

"It takes more time and manpower than you'd think. It's also getting harder to do, what with everyone fencing off. Pa thinks this is a good solution for several reasons. He wants to be able to get supplies quickly. If a store or two and maybe a bank could be situated in the new town, it would really benefit the community. Not to mention the idea of having a church and a school for the area people. It'd be real nice not to have to drive all the way into Cedar Springs for Sunday service."

"Won't it still take quite a bit of time for other folks anyway? After all, your pa owns a lot of acreage."

"Yes, but he's willing to allow others to cross his property. Not only that, but his plans for the town are on the main road, where his property abuts that of others. It'll be a good place for a town. There's water, the most important thing, and if the railroad will agree to Pa's terms, that will be the second most important accomplishment."

"I'm still not sure I'd like to see that happen. Towns always mean drinking and gambling. Pretty soon you have brothels and opium dens and folks getting killed or killing for what they want."

"That's why Pa wants to keep a tight rein on things. He wants to approve the businesses that go in. He doesn't intend for there to be any kind of opportunity for riffraff."

"It's been my experience," Austin mused, "that riffraff makes its own kind of opportunity."

Robert nodded. "I know you're right, but I also know my father's concept for this. He's always been a man of vision, and I think we can trust him to know best on this."

For a moment Austin said nothing, and Robert wondered if he'd pushed too hard. "Also, my mother wants you to know that there's no need to wait for an invitation to share our meals. You're always welcome, so don't go hungry."

Still Austin didn't reply. He stared out at the horizon as if contemplating what he would say. After another minute he turned back to Robert. "I like the solitude here. It's one of the reasons I bought the place. It's peaceful."

"Well, maybe it seems that way even more, given you're a lawman." Robert couldn't help but grin. "I have to say it's been a real comfort to Pa and me to know there's law close by."

Austin shrugged. "I'm a cattle inspector, not really a law officer. Not in the sense you mean."

"You're a Texas Ranger, and that makes you qualified in my eyes."

"Well, maybe that's why this whole thing bothers me. I know how it is when folks get together. There's always someone who wants to take what someone else has. I'm tellin' you from experience that it opens a whole new box of troubles."

"I understand your concerns. Have you always been a lawman?"

Austin gave a curt nod. "It's pretty much all I've ever known. Even before moving to Texas I was involved in . . . law enforcement."

"So what brought you to Texas?" Robert asked. "Where'd you come from?"

He saw Austin stiffen. "Not important. Heard this was a good place to live, so I came." He picked up the ax. "Tell your ma I said thanks for the invite. I'm sure to take her up on the offer, especially when it gets colder."

Robert thought it strange the way Austin had become almost uncomfortable. His stance suggested that he was keeping something hidden, but the rancher couldn't imagine what that would be or why Austin might feel the need.

Making his way back to the sorrel, Robert started to mount, then remembered the cookies. He pulled the bundle from his saddlebag and glanced back to where Austin was already hard at work swinging the ax.

"I almost forgot. Ma sent you some cookies." He held up the bundle as Austin took note. The latter crossed the yard to take the offering with a smile.

"Tell your mother I said thanks."

"I'll do that, but seems you could tell her yourself if you'd join us for dinner now and then. I know it would please her — she likes motherin' folks. Especially those who don't have any family around." Robert mounted his horse and could see that once again Austin had grown rather sullen. It seemed there was a lot about this man he didn't know. Maybe no one knew his secrets.

"A gathering for what purpose?" Jessica asked her parents over dinner.

"William Barnett and your father have been working with some of the other ranchers to bring in the railroad. Now that they have an idea of this happening, they want to discuss what is needed and how to go about setting up a community," Mother replied. She passed Jessica a bowl of ham and cabbage.

Taking a portion of the food, Jessica handed the bowl to her father before asking, "Why do I have to be there?"

"It's for the entire community," he said in a rather stern voice. "You're a part of that."

"But no one really cares what I think about the idea." Jessica picked up a cornmeal muffin and broke off a piece. "I'm not married, I don't own any land, and I'm a woman. So I have no say over what happens."

"Your father and Mr. Barnett are good to listen to the hearts of everyone — especially the womenfolk of this area. One of your father's thoughts is to get a doctor in this new community and pay him a regular stipend."

"How could they ever afford that? I know the world of finance has bettered itself, according to what I read in the papers, but we're still suffering the effects of a depression."

Tyler Atherton's expression softened, and Jessica saw a hint of amusement in his gaze.

"You always were the smart one. I appreciate you bein' up-to-date on current events. And you're right. We are still sufferin', but less so than other folks. Like your brothers said in their last letter, a lot of folk don't even have a house to call home.

"Will and I figure if we kick in enough money to keep the doctor satisfied with or without patients, sick folks will come around in time. After all, in this forty-mile radius there are over a hundred people. That doesn't include the folks who live in Cedar Springs, where there's several hundred. And when the railroad is established, more people will arrive to set up businesses. I figure we won't have to pay the doc forever — just long enough to get him on his feet."

"Your father and Mr. Barnett figure they can set the man up with a little house of his own, from which he can work and live," Mother said before sipping her tea.

"That's right," Father said. "If he lives rent free and we provide him with beef and canned goods from our gardens, then he'll have only a few expenses to meet. We'll probably look to get a preacher the same way. Of course, he'll have the tithes to help him out."

Jessica nodded and popped another piece of muffin into her mouth. She supposed they had reasoned out all the possibilities and problems.

"So the gathering is to be a picnic — a barbecue," her mother said, smiling. "Most everyone will be in attendance, so I would hate for people to say that our daughter didn't care enough to join her neighbors in discussion and celebration."

"Folks around here will look for any reason to have a party," Jessica said, toying with the cabbage and ham. "You hardly need my stamp of approval to draw in the crowds."

Her mother frowned. "Jessica, this really isn't like you. What's going on?"

Her accusing tone caused Jessica to sit up a little straighter. "Nothing. I just don't know that I want to be around a lot of people. We just had the cattle women here. It's not like I have no chance to socialize."

Her mother eyed her with suspicion. "You've never shied away from parties in the past. What is this really about?"

"Maybe I'm changing," Jessica replied with a frown. "Maybe I was too focused on parties before. Doesn't a person have a right to change?"

"Well, you don't need to go changing, darlin'," her father threw out. "You're practically perfect the way you are, just like your mama."

Her mother blushed, and Jessica bit her lip to keep from blurting out that she was nothing of the kind. But if she said anything

39

at all, her mother would want to know more, and Jessica wasn't done wrestling with her conscience. She had no answers that would satisfy her mother's curiosity.

CHAPTER 3

It was a typical Barnett party with glowing lanterns hanging from lower tree branches and on well-positioned poles. Multitudes of quickly built tables and benches were set up for people to relax and enjoy the meal. Other food-laden tables were arranged in such a manner as to allow people to serve themselves from both sides. Jessica and her mother had helped to supply some of the meal, but most of it had come from Mrs. Barnett's kitchen.

Once everyone was filled up on smoked ham, green beans, potatoes, corn bread, cheesy grits, and baked beans, not to mention an array of desserts, Mr. Barnett began to discuss the plan he and others had been working on.

"Each of you men should have received a drawing of what we have in mind. My wife and daughter-in-law drew those up so you wouldn't have to suffer through my attempts to make sense." A chuckle ran through the gathering, and most of the men held up their maps as if in answer.

Mr. Barnett nodded his approval. "Now, if you'll look at the drawing, you'll see that we've tentatively called the town Terryton. This is in honor of Ted and Marietta Terry. Ted often joked that he'd been in Texas longer than mesquite, so we figured he deserved a town named for him." Again the crowd chuckled.

"I know everyone misses 'em, but bein' the godly folk they were, I know we'll see 'em again in heaven." A murmuring of "amen" went up throughout the crowd.

Everyone seemed to be in such a good mood. To Jessica's way of thinking, there was no reason for them to be anything else. They were full and safe and, for the most part, healthy. Indian problems were no longer an issue. There'd been no epidemics or storms of late to wreak havoc upon the people or the land. God was in His heaven, and all was right with the world. What better time to create an entirely new community?

"Tyler Atherton and I have talked with a lawyer. He plans to join us sometime in the near future. His name is Harrison Gable. He's from Dallas but will relocate if we all come together to set this thing in motion."

"What's required of us?" Mr. Palmer asked.

William Barnett smiled. "Patience, support — both financially and intellectually — and faith that together we can accomplish this."

"Pardon me for sayin' so," Mr. Harper, another area rancher, piped up, "but it seems to me we are still facin' perilous times. It's only been three years since this country fell flat on its face. I think we might be rushin' things a bit."

"But if I might interject," Jessica's uncle Brandon Reid said, moving closer to the front of the gathering, "three years has also seen us regain considerable ground. Industry is back on its feet, the solvent banks have rebounded, and the railroad has gone through rebuilding and in some cases a change of ownership. I think this is the perfect time for us to consider such an endeavor."

Jessica listened, only mildly interested, as the conversation continued. Most of the people seemed excited about the potential for a church and a school, not to mention an easier way to get to Dallas. She couldn't help but wonder what the changes might mean for her. She'd grown up with all of her needs met, but many of these folks had struggled. Some families had even sold out and moved away because they'd been unable to make a living in the intolerable conditions.

She toyed with a piece of pecan pie and continued to listen half-heartedly. She heard a man question something about law enforcement and wondered if it might be the Texas cattle inspector she'd heard her father talk about. Glancing around, she tried to see who was speaking but couldn't.

"Having law and order is always uppermost on the minds of the people," Mr. Barnett declared. "We have solid plans drawn up for a town marshal to be in place before the first locomotive arrives in Terryton."

"Will he be elected?" Mr. Harper questioned. "I don't want any appointed man."

"Yes, there will be an election," Barnett assured him, "but only of those who sign on to assist with this project. You see, until there's a true town and population to make decisions, we will need some sort of board or co-op to see to the running of this town. That will include the position of a mayor. This board will act as the counsel for the mayor and the marshal."

Jessica tired of the talk and her pie and

got up from the table on the pretense of needing to refill her glass of lemonade. She made her way to the table where several pitchers of liquid stood waiting. The lemonade and iced sweet tea had been kept chilled in their springhouse, but having been out for several hours now, Jessica knew neither would be cold. Nevertheless she poured herself a glass of lemonade and began to slowly walk around the edge of the party.

Watching from a distance gave her more clarity. She studied with different eyes these people she'd known all her life. She could understand their fears of change. Change suggested a loss of control of the familiar. It could be a terrifying situation. But change could also be new and invigorating. Jessica had always relished change in that respect. Now, though, with everything going on in her life, she wasn't finding herself keen on the idea.

What's wrong with me? Is this what growing up is all about? Am I suddenly to become a fearful woman — afraid of my own shadow — unwilling to risk something different?

Jessica could see the hopeful expressions on the faces of mothers as Mr. Barnett spoke of a school and a church being their first building priorities. Such things equaled stability in the eyes of the gentler sex. But didn't they already have stability in the community? The area ranchers were good to help one another in times of need. The children already had a school and the people had a church to attend, although both were far enough away to discourage attendance. Why pull out of one town just to create another?

Without looking where she was going, Jessica backed away from the gathering. She turned abruptly and found herself face-to-face with a stranger. "Oh, excuse me." The glass of lemonade fell to the grass and spilled out across the man's boots.

"It was my fault," the man declared. "If I hadn't been hiding out over here, you wouldn't have had any trouble." He wiped his boot tops on the backs of his denim pants. "There. Now they're clean."

She smiled at the dark-eyed man and forgot about the glass. "I'm Jessica Atherton."

"Austin Todd," he replied. "I'm new to the area. I bought a small piece of land from Mr. Barnett."

"Oh, I know all about you. You've been the topic of conversation at many a meal or gathering."

He chuckled at this. "Really? And what are people saying about me?"

"That you're a cattle inspector who likes privacy."

"Is that all?"

"Well, no, but are you certain you want to know the truth?"

He frowned. "Is it that bad?"

Laughing, Jessica shook her head. "Not at all. Most of the women with single daughters are wondering if you're a good catch. Of course, for some of them, the only qualification a man need have is that he be breathing. And those single daughters are murmuring about you under their breath. They want to know what kind of provider you might be or how attentive you are to their gender. They have assessed you from head to toe and found you to be mysterious, handsome, and definitely of interest." She paused for a moment before adding, "Oh, and the men seem to admire you greatly. Probably because my father and Mr. Barnett have told everyone how you saved the day in Fort Worth when you shot down three bank robbers."

She looked at him with a raised brow. "I think that's about all."

"It's more than enough," he replied. "I appreciate the honesty. However, I had no idea I was being discussed in such detail."

Jessica shrugged. "I tend to speak my

47

mind and that of other folks, as well. It's sort of a problem of mine."

"I don't see honesty as a problem."

She leaned back against an oak tree. "Neither do I, but I have learned that most people aren't that interested in the truth."

"Seriously?"

She shrugged again. "Well, it sure seems that way. Most people avoid hearing the truth — at least the way I see it. Sick folks don't want to know that they're dying. Spurned lovers don't want to know that it really was their own fault the relationship couldn't work out. Women don't want to know that their new dress is the most atrocious thing you've ever seen."

Austin let out a roar, and Jessica was glad the gathering had grown noisy, with numerous people all speaking at once. She pulled Austin back into the shadows. "You're going to have everyone wanting in on the joke."

"Sorry. I was just remembering a few atrocious dresses my mother owned. She was always asking my father how she looked, and of course, you are right. He couldn't really tell her."

Jessica nodded, imagining the situation. "It's really a kindness in some ways. Mother says it's still a lie and therefore a sin, but I

48

know it's more often done out of good intentions than bad. Still, I prefer the truth."

"Always?"

She fixed him with a gaze. "Always."

"You're different from most women, then."

"I am. I make no claim to be otherwise. It's probably why I'm still unmarried and living with my parents. No one wants a blunt wife. Now, if you'll excuse me, I need to see if my mother wants help with the dishes."

"It was nice to make your acquaintance," Austin said. "And I *honestly* hope we can speak again sometime."

"I'm sure we will. After all, this town idea isn't going to just go away." Smiling, Jessica couldn't help but tease him. "I hope you won't worry overmuch about what people are saying about you."

"I make it a habit not to care what anyone thinks."

Jessica sobered. "I used to feel that way, but I've found it hasn't served me exactly as I'd hoped."

Austin thought about Jessica Atherton for a long time after she'd gone. He found her a refreshing change of pace, but at the same time her last comment confused him. Then he remembered the glass she'd dropped and moved back to retrieve it. Luckily, it hadn't shattered. Making his way to where folks had been instructed to leave their dishes, Austin placed the glass on a tray alongside others.

"I hope you got enough to eat, Mr. Todd," Mrs. Barnett said, coming beside him with several more glasses.

"Yes, ma'am. I got plenty, and please call me Austin."

"I'd like that very much, and you can call me Hannah." She placed the glasses on the tray, then started to lift it.

Austin reached out to stop her. "Allow me." He picked up the tray and looked at her for further instruction.

"I was going to take them over to where we're washing dishes. It's that table just over there." She pointed to where several women, including Jessica Atherton, were working to clean up the numerous dishes and cups.

"Looks like folks are still grazin'," he said, glancing over his shoulder.

Hannah laughed. "They will be until they load up for home. Even so, it's best to keep on top of the dishes. Someone might need a clean plate, and I've exhausted all of mine."

"I thought most of them brought their own table settings. Robert said something about that earlier. I felt rather remiss, but in all honesty I don't have anything all that fine."

She leaned closer as if to tell him a secret. "Well, I've never yet expected a single man to show up with his dinnerware or food to contribute. Usually when we get together around these parts, we do it potluck style, and everyone brings food to eat and their own dishes to eat it on. This was just a little bit different because Will wanted to provide for everyone. I think it was his way of winning them over to agree to the building of Terryton."

"Well, you know, they say that the way to a man's heart is through his stomach."

"Yes, I know that full well. I also know you can get right through to his head with a piece of Rosita's Mexican chocolate cake."

"I'm not sure I had any of that."

She took the tray from him and motioned with her head. "Then you'd better try it. It's chocolaty and moist with a hint of cinnamon, and her buttercream frosting tops it off perfectly."

Austin nodded. "I think you've convinced me. I hope there's some left."

"Oh, there is," Mrs. Barnett assured him. "She made twelve of them."

Making his way to the dessert table, Austin spied the chocolate cake. He hurried to take up a dessert plate and sample the treat. It was just as Mrs. Barnett had said. It'd been a long time since Austin had enjoyed anything nearly as much.

"I see you found Rosita's prize-winning cake," Mr. Barnett said, joining him at the dessert table. "It's pretty amazing. I'm here for a second piece, but don't tell my wife. She thinks I'm getting pudgy in my old age."

"Your secret is safe with me."

Mr. Barnett secured his cake, then suggested Austin join him at an empty table. "So what did you think of our talk tonight?" He waited until Austin was seated before adding, "I want your honest opinion."

The comment reminded Austin of his earlier conversation with Jessica and made him smile. "Well, Mr. Barnett —"

"Call me Will," the older man interjected.

Austin nodded. "It sounds to me you've thought of everything. I couldn't really find fault with any of it, even if I do wish things could remain quiet and simple around here."

"I know. A lot of folks are against change, but I believe it's the way of the future. It's hard to imagine, but the way Dallas is growing, I expect one day all of this land will be a part of that city."

"Surely not," Austin countered. "That's a long way to come. Besides, I thought building up was the new style. What is it they call 'em — skyscrapers? There are a lot of them back east."

Chuckling, William cut into his cake. "Yeah, I read about some buildings going up in London, England. It said that Queen Victoria put a limit on how high they can build. I figure we're still a rebellious country, however, and we won't have any restrictions put on ours."

"So maybe Dallas can just build up and not out."

"I doubt it. Texas has a lot going for itself with all its resources. We've had to tighten our belts during this financial upheaval, but we definitely have known harder times. During the War Between the States, it was mighty difficult. Still, I think this state is probably one of the healthier ones."

"Or maybe it's just that you know how to get through a bad situation and still find the good," Austin suggested.

"Maybe."

Will turned his attention back to his cake, and for a moment nothing more was said. Austin wasn't sure if he'd offended the man or not, but it certainly hadn't been his desire. He wondered if he should apologize, but just then Barnett began talking.

"The way I see it, this is all gonna be prime real estate. Not that it isn't already a good investment, but I figure now's the time to build and invest in the property."

"What about the ranches? Do you think folks will just up and sell?" Austin asked.

The older man rubbed his chin. William Barnett was a man known for his thoughtful consideration, something Austin had witnessed many times.

"I reckon they'll have to," he finally replied. "I'm not a real visionary, but even I know that as the cities expand, there's gonna be less and less room for ranches and farms in this area."

"People are still going to need food," Austin said. "What then?"

"They'll move farther from the cities, I suppose. There's still good homesteading ground to be had. Folks will move and start over."

"And will you?"

Barnett shook his head. "I doubt I'll be around when it gets that far along." He refocused on the cake. "That's something for my children's children to figure out. For now, I was kind of hoping you might consider taking on the job of lawman for our town. It's not something we'll need for a while. There's a lot to put in motion before we need to worry about that."

Austin was surprised by Barnett's news. "I hadn't really thought about quitting what I'm doing."

"Well, like I said, there's no rush. Just keep it in mind and think on it a while. You can always get back to me." Will finished off his cake and got to his feet. "Guess I'd better see to my guests. It looks like several families are leavin'. Safety in numbers, you know."

Austin sat at the table for several minutes more. He'd long since finished his cake and was actually thinking of having a second piece. He was thinking about Jessica Atherton, too. She had been easy to talk to, and he missed the company of women.

A frown came to his lips. That was a dangerous thought to have. Hadn't he worked hard to keep himself from entanglements of the heart? After Grace died, he had determined never to love again.

Grace.

Just the thought of her troubled Austin's conscience in a way he prayed to forget. She had been so young, and she had loved him so completely. But just as he'd killed his brother, Austin had killed her, too.

CHAPTER 4

Having accompanied her mother to Cedar Springs on this fine September morning, Jessica found herself caught up in making the rounds. They generally started at the post office. After picking up the mail, they would go to the bank. Next they headed for the feedstore and put in any orders sent by Jessica's father. Then it was off to the general store for most of their shopping. When everything was complete, Jessica and her mother would usually have a bite to eat and then call on friends in the afternoon before heading home.

This morning, however, her mother had added an unscheduled visit to the pastor's wife, Mrs. Baker. Jessica sat with the two older women for as long as she could. She felt like a fidgety child, unable to focus on the conversation or find pleasure in the visit. Mostly the women talked about church affairs and the upcoming October harvest party, neither of which overly interested Jessica. Finally, she asked to be excused, commenting that she needed a bit of exercise. Mother had given her an odd look but nevertheless dismissed her. Now Jessica was free to wander.

Perhaps I'll see what's new at the jewelry store. Jessica headed in that direction, careful not to snag the hem of her gown on the boardwalk. She had almost reached the shop when she saw Marty Wythe coming her way.

Great, now I will have to visit with her. The idea didn't set well. No doubt she would want to talk about Robert and Alice and their baby.

"Why, good morning, Jessica. Are you here alone?" Marty asked.

"No. Mother is visiting Mrs. Baker, and I needed some air." She gave Marty a smile. "How about you?"

"I'm here with my sister. Hannah decided we needed more fabric. We've been sewing like crazy for the children. With the three boys we adopted and Johanna and the baby, I find my time quite valuable. Johanna is two now and seems to be everywhere at once. She grows almost faster than I can make clothes. Little John Jacob is in need of more diapers, and the older boys need clothes let out or down almost every other week."

Jessica nodded. "Did you bring the children with you?"

"Goodness, no. Alice is keeping the youngest two. She can nurse John Jacob, along with little Wills. I'm sure Rosita is also helping, as Johanna will be quite the handful. The boys are with Jake. He's teaching them about running the ranch. They love life in Texas."

"I suppose they feel safe and loved now," Jessica said, trying to speak as her mother might. "And what do you think of your brother-in-law's plans for a new town?"

Marty tucked an errant strand of hair back into her bonnet. "I think growth is inevitable, and since it can't be stopped, it should be managed. I think the idea is a good one. I know I much prefer sending my children only six or seven miles away to school rather than twenty-five and have them board with other folks. I was teaching the boys at home because of the distance. If we get things up and running, a school will be established, and I can take them in the carriage, or Jacob says they could ride together on one of the horses." She shrugged. "I think they're too young for that, but he swears they aren't. What about you? Are you excited about the new town?"

"I really haven't given it all that much consideration," Jessica replied honestly. "I don't intend to stay around, so it doesn't matter to me."

"Oh? And where are you planning on going?"

Jessica met Marty's quizzical gaze. "I'm not sure. I guess . . . anywhere but here."

Marty smiled. "I used to feel that way myself, and you can see where it took me."

"Yes. You met a wonderful man and lived an opulent life in Denver. That sounds perfect to me. Well, maybe minus the wonderful man."

"You mean you don't intend to marry?" Marty asked.

Jessica looked away momentarily. She didn't really want to share her heart with Marty. Word might get back to Robert and Alice, and she didn't want pity from either one. On the other hand, refusing to answer would look just as odd.

"I don't. Not now, anyway. When I realized that I didn't love Robert, yet had long planned a future with him, it caused me to think. I was comfortable with the plans everyone had for us, but I was foolish. Not only that, I was wronging us both by hanging on to those plans. Now I think that leaving this place and venturing out sounds more beneficial."

"Well, just be careful. As I said, I used to have that same attitude." Marty shook her head. "I set out to answer a mail-order bride request. You never know what desperation will make you do. Looking back, I see how tragic it might have been."

"I don't intend to let desperation make my decisions for me," Jessica replied, knowing her answer sounded rather clipped.

Marty looked away from her and frowned. Jessica worried that she'd offended the woman and started to offer an apology, but just then Marty's brows knit together, and her expression suggested she was perplexed.

"That man looked so familiar," Marty said, finally looking back at Jessica.

"What man?" Jessica turned to look behind her but saw no one.

"A tall, bearded man just turned down the alleyway. He looked familiar but disappeared too quickly." She shook her head. "I can't place him."

"If you'd like, we could go after him," Jessica suggested.

"No." Marty continued to ponder the matter for a moment. After several seconds of silence, she shrugged. "I'm probably mistaken. Given all the new people coming into this area, there are bound to be folks who remind me of others I know." But even as Marty stated this, Jessica could hear the wariness in her voice.

Just then Hannah Barnett came from a shop down the street. Spying the two women, she waved and made her way to join them. "Jessica, how nice to see you again. Is your mother with you?"

"Yes, ma'am. She should be finished visiting Mrs. Baker most any time."

"I don't know about you two, but I'm ready for something to eat. Do you suppose your mother would find that appealing?"

Jessica cast a quick glance toward the parsonage and was happy to see her mother leaving the Bakers' house. "I think she probably would, but you can ask her yourself. She's coming just now."

"Hannah. Marty," Mother declared as she joined them. The women embraced briefly. "Isn't it a pretty day?"

"Yes, and the temperatures are so much more tolerable than they were just a month ago. Although it's still plenty warm," Hannah replied. "I was just telling Jessica and Marty that I am ready for something to eat. How about you?"

"I'm famished," Jessica's mother admitted. "I planned to suggest the same thing to Jess."

"Good. Why don't we adjourn to the new café on Broadway Street and enjoy a meal together?"

"That sounds wonderful," Mother said, looking to Jessica. "Don't you agree?"

"Delightful," Jessica lied, knowing that no one really cared how she felt.

She followed the women to the café and took her appointed seat at the table. Blue-and-white checkered tablecloths adorned each table and a white linen napkin was set at each place. A small bouquet of flowers in an amber-colored fruit jar added a homey atmosphere.

"Ladies," the proprietor, Sylvia Baldwin, announced in greeting, "you are my very first customers of the day." She beamed them a smile. "Let me tell you what's available."

Jessica settled back as the woman recited the menu. "Today I have a wonderful vegetable and beef casserole, served with bread and butter. For dessert, the most delicious apple nut cake just came out of the oven, and it is drizzled with fresh cream. If the casserole doesn't appeal, I can fry you up a steak — ham or beef."

"I think the casserole sounds wonderful,"

Mrs. Barnett declared.

"It does," Mother agreed and looked to Jessica. "Don't you think?"

Jessica nodded and Marty did likewise. "It's agreed, then," Mrs. Barnett said. "Please bring four orders and some tea." The woman nodded and hurried from the room as Hannah Barnett unfolded her napkin and placed it on her lap.

It wasn't long before Sylvia returned with a full tea service on a cart. She poured tea for each woman, offered them lemon, sugar, or cream, then exited with the cart as quickly as she'd come. Jessica sipped the hot liquid, not really in the mood for tea. She would have much rather had something cold, but unless the café made its own ice or had refrigeration, it wasn't a possibility.

As if reading her mind, Marty sighed. "I wish this tea were iced."

"That would be nice," Mother agreed. She started to take a taste of her own tea when she seemed to remember something. "Tyler told me the other day that several homes in California now have air-cooled rooms."

"Air-cooled?" Mrs. Barnett asked.

"Yes, but I haven't any idea how it works. It's something based on the way commercial refrigerators work, I believe Tyler said. That and fans. Apparently they can cool an entire

63

floor if the house isn't too big."

"That would certainly be welcome in the summertime," Marty said, pulling a fan from her reticule. She opened the lacy blue slats and began to wave it back and forth. "I know the weather is much cooler than last month, but I look forward to it cooling even more."

"You got used to snow in Colorado," her sister chided. "You know better than to expect such cold down here, although we have had our times, to be sure, and will again. In fact, William said it might be a cold winter."

"I would love a cold winter," Marty said with a sigh.

Jessica had very little to say during their luncheon. The food arrived and she immediately dug in, lest she be expected to talk. She had nothing to say that anyone would want to hear, and she feared these women might have questions for her that she didn't want to answer.

She had grown up knowing and loving these women as family — at least as much as she loved anyone — but she knew their penchant for wheedling information from unwilling victims. She frowned at this uncharitable thought.

How much of my life have I spent thinking

unkind thoughts of others? I don't know their hearts and have never endeavored to do so.

That feeling of dread came once again and washed over Jessica like a wave. In her previous conversation with Marty she'd spoken of her desire to leave Texas. Such a plan would break her mother's heart — her father's, too.

It wasn't long before other folks arrived at the café. Jessica nodded at some of her friends as they took seats across the room. Mother spoke to several people, as did Mrs. Barnett and Marty, but Jessica felt void of words. She had no desire to make pleasantries when her heart was in such a state of confusion. Would the answer ever come?

Austin arrived at the Barnett Ranch a little after noon. On his way to Dallas he figured to stop by and see if the ladies needed anything from the big city. To his surprise, however, the womenfolk were gone or, in Alice Barnett's case, busy caring for two infants and a two-year-old.

Robert greeted him at the door. He seemed genuinely happy to usher Austin inside and immediately invited him to share their meal.

"I have beans and bacon, corn bread, and

some of my mom's delicious cinnamon rolls."

"How could I refuse?" Austin said with a grin. "I have to admit I was hoping to make it in time for lunch."

Robert laughed. "As we've said on more than one occasion — you are always welcome to break bread with us." He led the way to the dining room. "Let me grab you some dishes and silver. Would you like a cup of coffee, too?"

Austin sank onto one of the chairs. "Sure. I make it a habit to never turn down a good cup of coffee."

It was only a matter of minutes before both men settled in to eat. Robert offered grace first. The prayer was simple, but it painfully reminded Austin of his upbringing. The family had always prayed over each meal. Mother prayed with them at bedtime, and Father had devotions and prayer in the morning. Austin had taken some of those practices into his adult life, but after losing Grace, he'd fallen away. It wasn't that he didn't believe in God or know what it said about Him in the Bible. It was more a sense that while God did exist, He really didn't care.

"So why are you headed to Dallas?" Robert asked.

"I have a meeting tomorrow related to cattle inspections."

"Are there problems?"

Austin savored a large spoonful of beans before answering. "Rustling is on the increase. There've been some cases where thieves have cut big sections of fence and run out quite a few head."

Robert's expression changed to one of concern. "Around here?"

"I'm not sure. That's part of what the meeting is for. I think they also have plans to give out the latest brand books. It's important for us to memorize the brands and be able to identify each ranch's animals."

"That can't be an easy task. There are hundreds of ranches just in the Dallas area."

Austin nodded and continued to eat. He knew the task would be laborious, but that was what he'd signed on for. Besides, he'd been working at this for quite a while now and had most of the established ranch brands memorized.

"It's hard to believe we're this close to the twentieth century and folks are still stealin' cattle. You'd like to figure folks would just find an honest way to make a livin'."

"That'd be nice. But so long as there's something of value that someone wants, you're gonna have thieves and rustlers."

Robert pulled apart a piece of corn bread and buttered it. "I'll talk to Pa. It probably wouldn't hurt to ride the fence line and see for ourselves if there are any breaks. We are due to make that ride anyway." He smiled. "I'm glad you stopped by, though. We haven't seen you for a while."

"Hasn't been that long." Austin crumpled his corn bread and stirred it into the beans. "I thought I'd stop here on the way to Dallas and see if you folks need anything."

"Can't say that we do. My ma and Marty are over in Cedar Springs today, so I imagine they'll be able to get most anything we need. Alice is here. I could ask her. She's takin' care of Marty's two youngest, along with our son."

"She's a good woman," Austin replied, uncertain what else to say.

Robert smiled. "She is that. And to think I almost settled for second best."

"What do you mean?"

"Well, it's just that for the longest time folks expected me to marry Jessica Atherton."

"Really?" Austin questioned. "Why?"

Robert finished his corn bread before answering. "Our mothers kind of figured for us to marry. Mostly 'cause Jess followed

68

me around like a puppy. Her brothers were too busy to give her much attention, and I made the mistake of feelin' sorry for her." He chuckled and pushed back his empty bowl. "I used to do rope tricks for her and make her little trinkets. I have to say I loved her like a little sister. I still do. But where marrying was concerned, she wasn't for me."

Austin wanted to know more but knew it wasn't smart to look too eager. He didn't want to give Robert Barnett the wrong idea. "So you married Alice instead."

"From the first moment I met her, I knew Alice was the one for me. Jessica couldn't understand it, even though I knew she didn't love me — not the way she needed to in order to marry. Jessica took it as somewhat of a personal blow, especially given that Alice has that scar on her face. I hardly even see the thing, but Jess seemed to think my choice was some sort of put-down on her. Like she was so bad that I'd choose anyone, even a scarred woman, rather than choose her. Nothin' could've been further from the truth."

"What do you mean?" Austin tried to sound only casually interested, but he couldn't hide his desire to know. He hadn't been able to put Jessica Atherton out of his mind since first meeting her at the Barnetts'.

"Well, Jessica is a beautiful woman — there's no denying that. She'll never suffer for beaus. But it wasn't mere physical beauty that drew me to Alice. She's like the other half of my soul. We see things pretty much eye to eye. I've never felt that kind of kindred spirit with anyone else, and now I know I never will."

Austin thought of his relationship with Grace. That was exactly how he'd felt about her. He knew he'd never again find a woman to love — one who would love him as Grace had. And that was all right by him. Austin had no intention of ever loving another woman. He might be fascinated with Jessica Atherton's boldness. He might even appreciate her fine form and pretty face, but that was it. He wasn't going to give his heart to anyone.

But still, there was that nagging vision of Jessica and her blatant honesty. Austin smiled. "I met Miss Atherton at your town planning party. She was full of information about the area."

"She can be very friendly," Robert said, getting to his feet. "But she can also be manipulative and selfish. She's been spoiled most of her life, and while she's got a good heart, Jessica is often only interested in what benefits Jessica." He moved toward the kitchen. "Now I'm gonna bring you some of my mother's cinnamon rolls. These rolls are famous around here. She even used them to appease the Comanche long ago."

Austin chuckled. "Then they must really be something."

CHAPTER 5

Jessica gave her hair a final touch before dabbing her earlobes with a tiny bit of perfume. She loved the flowery scent, so light and sweet, but she was going to the church social with Daniel Harper, so she used it sparingly. There was no sense in overdoing it. She liked Daniel well enough, but he wasn't exactly her ideal man. The son of one of the local ranchers, Daniel was handsome and could sing like nobody else, but he intended to remain a rancher, and that had never appealed to Jessica. Of course, right now, Jessica wasn't at all sure what appealed to her.

She made her way downstairs and paused momentarily at the drawing room door. She smoothed down the lace on her bodice and swept down the skirt of her gown to make sure everything was in place. The door was ajar, and Jessica could hear her father and Daniel talking inside the room.

"Well, you know our Jess," her father was saying. "If you're looking to win her heart, then you need to shower her with plenty of attention and an occasional bauble or two. She likes pretty things."

"Yes, sir. I know that's true."

Jessica frowned as the conversation continued. She knew she shouldn't be eavesdropping, but it was as if her feet were nailed to the floor.

"Jessica's always been different from her sister. She likes the best things in life. She's like a princess in a castle — spoiled, pampered, and beautiful."

"She's surely beautiful," Daniel declared. "She's the prettiest girl in the county, and I'd be proud to be her husband. With my inheritance, I could keep her in nice things."

"She'll want to take trips, as well. I've heard her say it many times. She has done a fair piece of traveling with her grandparents, but now they're gone and she has no one to take her abroad." Her father chuckled. "I swear that girl has covered more miles than my horse."

The men laughed and Jessica began to feel sick. *Is that all I am to Father? Ornamental and demanding?*

Tears came unbidden and she frowned. The painful words cut to the core of her being. She'd never thought her parents believed her so shallow and selfish. She backed away from the door and headed back upstairs. Her mind echoed with the reverberation of her father's comments.

"She's like a princess in a castle — spoiled, pampered, and beautiful."

What a horrible thing to say about her. Jessica plopped down on the bed and let the tears flow. It was horrible because it was true. She was spoiled and pampered. She'd never known real want. Oh, there had been lean years, but her father and Robert's father had wisely invested and were good to help others when times of trouble came.

"Jessica, Daniel is waiting for you," her mother called from the hallway. She tapped on the door, then opened it to find Jessica in distress. "What's wrong, darling?"

Unwilling to admit to her eavesdropping, Jessica went with the only thing she could think of. "I'm not feeling well. My stomach and head hurt something fierce." At least that wasn't a lie. "Please tell Daniel I can't attend the social with him. I'm sorry."

Mother came and felt her forehead. "Hmm, you seem warm but not feverish. I'll go tell your father and Daniel that you're indisposed. Oh, and I'll get some tea and crackers for you. That might help. Meanwhile, why don't you take your hair down and start undressing. I'll help you with the back buttons when I return."

Jess nodded and reached up to pull several pins from her hair as Mother disappeared from the room. She hated disappointing Daniel, but he would be seeking to get her to marry him, and she had no intention of doing so. Perhaps it was better this way. Was it wrong to step out with someone just for the fun of stepping out?

Pulling off her kid boots, Jessica continued to ponder the things she'd done when it came to beaus. She had never allowed for hand-holding or kissing, but she did flirt unmercifully. Was that a sin? Was it wrong to give false hope of marriage to a gentleman?

"I never meant it for harm," she murmured. "I only thought . . . of myself and having a wonderful time." Her conscience burned, and she knew in that moment that her intentions had been wrong, even if her actions could be excused.

Mother was gone for only minutes before she returned with a tray. On it was a cup of weak tea and a plate with several crackers. She placed the tray on the dresser and came to help Jessica with the buttons of her high-collared lacy bodice.

"I know you were looking forward to this social, but there will be others, and you certainly wouldn't want to go if you were coming down with something contagious."

Jessica sat at her dressing table and watched Mother's expression from the mirror's image. She was so kind and calm. She had no way of knowing the turmoil in Jessica's heart. Being freed from the gown and corset, Jessica rid herself of the petticoat and shift before donning a lightweight cotton nightgown.

Mother had her sit once again while she gently brushed Jessica's hair. "I remember doing this for you when you were little. Once you could braid your own hair, you didn't need me anymore."

Jessica frowned. "I'll always need you, Mother."

Her mother gave a light laugh. "Oh, my sweet girl, one day a young man will steal all of your interest. And that's the way it should be. But do know this: I will miss you."

Jessica turned abruptly. Her earlier thoughts haunted her. "Mother, do you think I'm a good person?"

"What?"

She sighed and tried again. "Do you think I have a good heart — that I'm a good person?"

"Of course." Her mother looked at her oddly. "Why would you ask a question like that?"

Jessica shrugged. "I don't know. I suppose I've just been thinking about too many things."

"Such as?"

"That I haven't always been kind to people or considerate of their desires and needs. I've been selfish at times and probably too concerned about things that don't really matter. I feel like I'm a rotten friend and daughter."

"Oh, sweetheart, just the fact that it bothers you proves that you're a good person. A bad person wouldn't care. If you were truly as awful as you seem to think, well, none of this would matter."

But it hasn't mattered . . . until now.

"I don't mean to be self-focused. I never meant to hurt anyone."

"Who have you hurt? Why all this remorse just now?" Mother tied a ribbon to Jessica's braid and stepped back. "Come on, let's get you lying down."

Jessica allowed Mother to lead her to bed. Once tucked in, Jessica posed another question. "Can a person truly change her ways?"

Mother brought the tray over to the bed.

"The Bible says that with God all things are possible. I believe people can change." Jessica sat up halfway as Mother handed her the cup. The weak tea sounded more inviting than Jessica had originally thought. She sipped it carefully, mindful of the heat. It was perfect.

"However," Mother continued, putting the cup back on the saucer, "they have to want to change. My first husband wasn't of a mind to change. He didn't believe that his cruelty and ugliness were a problem. He thought he was doing a good thing overall."

"But how? How could a man who was trying to sabotage the Union soldiers as they slept consider that a good thing?"

"Because, despite the war being over, the Union was making the South feel abominable. Malcolm thought that since they felt the need to put soldiers of color in charge of Corpus Christi, it was his right to put an end to it. He wasn't doing it because he thought it was evil or wrong. He felt vindicated in his choices."

Jessica considered that for a moment. Hadn't she always felt justified about her choices? She was always quick with an answer when her conscience prodded her with guilt for something she'd said or done. She'd fought against that prodding voice in her heart, convincing herself that she was innocent of wrongdoing.

Biting her lip, Jessica wondered if there was any hope for her at all. She had said things to hurt people. She had done things to satisfy her desires, no matter the cost to others. Maybe worst of all, she had thought nothing of using people to her benefit.

"What's going on, Jessica?" Mother sat on the edge of the bed and studied her with a questioning expression. "This isn't like you."

"I know," Jessica replied sadly. "But it should be. I should care more about other people. I've been horrible about such things. I don't know what's going on in the lives of my old friends, or even if we are still friends. I'm ashamed of myself and frustrated by the turn my life has taken."

"But, Jessica, you aren't the only one to have ever felt that way, and you aren't entirely to blame for any distance you feel with your friends. After all, most have married and have or are about to have children. That takes them away from society for a time. They change with that, as well. No one is the same after marrying and having children. You take on new priorities."

"Yes, but I have neither husband nor child. I should be able to pay visits and see to the friendships. I should have gone calling and checked to see if my friends needed anything. I didn't. I didn't even think of it — I didn't care."

Mother shook her head. "I find that hard to believe. Folks show their concern in different ways. Now, drink some more tea. I put some headache powders in it. Nibble on the crackers, but don't overstress your stomach. I'm sure you'll feel better by morning."

Jessica took the tea and sipped the warm liquid. Mother nodded in approval, then got up and walked to the lamp by the door. "I'll come and check on you a little later and put this out for the night." She turned back toward Jessica. "Just pray about it, darling. God has a plan in all of this. He will show you the truth." She left then, pulling the door shut behind her.

"That's what I'm afraid of," Jessica whispered to no one. "That's what I fear the most — the truth."

Days after his trip to Dallas, Austin Todd sat trying his best to read a book on memory and determine whether it pertained to the spirit or to the brain. There was quite a wide field of thought on the subject. The book told of the powerful effect memories had on people — a topic that immediately drew his attention.

Memories had a debilitating effect on him. They haunted and tormented him daily. He had hoped the book might provide some guidance for putting painful memories away from the mind or spirit. Wherever they existed, Austin wished to exile them to some faraway place where they couldn't hurt him anymore.

He closed the book and gave a heavy sigh. Without meaning to, he thought of his brother Houston. His younger brother would no doubt make fun of the book and tease Austin about being too intellectual. The thought made Austin smile, just for a moment. He and Houston had always been so close. They liked many of the same activities, foods, clothes, and even careers.

Both had signed up to work for the Treasury Department and, after proving themselves worthy, had been promoted to the Secret Service as field agents. They were responsible for tracking down counterfeiters and those who committed fraud against the government. And the brothers were good at what they did.

Austin and Houston made the perfect team. They were able to complete more cases than some of their fellow agents had simply because they knew each other so well and could anticipate what the other would do.

Until the night Houston took a bullet that was never intended for him. Austin replayed the scene once again.

It was the middle of the night, but both Austin and Houston were enthusiastic about their situation. For months they had worked to break a conspiratorial ring of stamp counterfeiters. However, the deeper the brothers dug, the more people it exposed, and some were highly placed in society.

Their investigation had taken them to a warehouse on the outskirts of the capital. It was here that Austin's world began to collapse. He could still remember the stench of old fish. He could still see Houston leaping in front of him to save his life. . . .

"Hey, Austin, you home?"

Austin roused from the memory, set the book aside, and opened the door. Much to his surprise he found Tyler Atherton and William Barnett waiting.

"Come in," Austin said, motioning to the men. Both did and Austin could see they were glancing around as if to inspect his living conditions. "I've tried to make the place as homey as possible, but I'm often gone."

It sounded like an apology.

"It looks just right," Barnett said, smiling. Tyler nodded in agreement.

"It's kinda damp and chilly out there tonight. Would you like a cup of coffee?" Austin asked, heading to the stove in anticipation.

"No, we just wanted to talk to you for a little bit. We're on our way back from business in Cedar Springs. Talked with the lawyer who's helping us with the plans for Terryton."

"Well, I don't know what I can do for you, but have a seat at the table. It's really all I can offer." He looked to the two benches.

The two men settled themselves on one side, while Austin took a seat opposite them. He waited for someone to say something.

"You know we asked you to consider heading up law and order for us," Barnett began. Austin nodded. "Well, in our discussions with the railroad, they've made it clear that they would like to have the law in place prior to the railroad setting up a tent city for their workers. With that, it puts us in sort of a spot to get an answer from you."

Austin drew a deep breath and considered the situation. With his Ranger work he was often away from home, traveling from one place to another. Taking on the town marshal job would put him in one area and al-low him to sleep in a bed every night. At least until some trouble broke out and he was needed.

"When would they want me to start? I don't want to leave the Rangers without some warning."

"I would expect nothing less from you," Barnett said. "The railroad won't begin building until January. And only then if we can get all the legal work taken care of. A lot of contract work goes into even the smallest spur line."

"January would work well," Austin said. That was little more than three months away. It would give the Rangers plenty of time to replace him. "I'll do it."

Mr. Atherton laughed. "Just like that? You didn't even ask what the salary was."

Austin shrugged. "I remember you talking about a few of those things at the meeting. I know you can't afford to pay much at the beginning. I figure as long as I have a roof over my head and food on the table, I won't have big expenses."

"Well, just the same, we will take good care of you. Rest assured." Barnett looked to his friend. "I don't know about you, Ty-ler, but I need to get on home. Hannah is going to start worrying if I don't show up soon. And knowing her, she'll set up a search party."

Barnett and Atherton got to their feet. Austin shook their hands and escorted them to the door. "I appreciate the confidence you have in me. You don't really know what kind of lawman I'll make, but you're taking a chance on me anyway."

Mr. Barnett turned and shook his head. "We aren't takin' a chance. I've seen you in action. I know everything I need to know. If you're good enough for the Rangers, you're good enough for me."

Austin closed the door once the men had remounted their horses. He felt almost deceptive. They didn't know everything about him. Maybe if they did, they wouldn't want him around at all, much less heading up the law for their new town.

Jessica appeared at the breakfast table prepared to take on the world. She was determined to make a change in her life and do something kind for someone. She had dressed neatly in a crisp white blouse and blue serge skirt. She had a little jacket that matched the material of the skirt and planned to wear that, too, but for now it hung on a peg by the front door.

"What has you up so early?" her father asked.

Jessica tried not to take offense at the comment. It was true she'd been lax in rising early. "I want to make some calls. I was hoping I could borrow the buggy."

"It's fine with me. You'll need to clear it with your ma."

"Clear what?" Mother asked, bringing in a platter stacked with griddle cakes.

"I want to make a couple of calls today. I asked if I could borrow the buggy. Osage said he could drive me."

"Well, that's fine with me, as well. I have plenty to keep me busy and won't be needing it. Just be home before it gets very late. Osage can't see all that well after dark. I don't want to be worrying about you."

Father smiled and put his hand to his face, as if to shield his words. "She'll worry about you anyway," he said in a low voice.

Jessica laughed and helped herself to a piece of bacon from the plate her mother passed. "Well, I don't want anyone fretting over me. I'm not waiting until regular calling hours, so I should be home by afternoon."

"Where are you headed?" her mother asked.

Jessica bit her lower lip and hesitated a

moment. Finally she drew a deep breath. "To the Barnetts'. I want to speak with Alice."

Her mother exchanged a look with Father, then turned back to Jessica as if to question her with a gaze. Jessica had seen her mother act in this manner before. Her expression spoke volumes.

"I owe her an apology. I haven't been very nice to her since . . . well, since she got here. I want to set things straight."

Mother smiled. "I think that's admirable."

Jessica nodded and refocused on the food. *I think it's much overdue.*

Once breakfast concluded, Jessica arranged for the buggy. She had decided the night before that she hadn't shown Alice Barnett much charity or kindness. It was a hard pill to take, but Jessica felt she needed to set things right with Alice before attempting to address any of her other shortcomings. Of course, Alice might be unwilling to receive Jessica. She might have no desire to forgive. But from what Jessica had observed, Robert's wife was probably one of the sweetest people in the county and would no doubt be gracious and forgiving.

"You ready, Miss Jessica?" Osage asked, putting a hat atop his balding head.

"I am. I see we have some clouds overhead. I hope we won't have rain to worry about."

"No. These are fair weather clouds. They're movin' east and won't bring us a drop."

Osage held fast to her arm as Jessica climbed into the buggy. He wasn't too strong anymore, but she would never have suggested he not do as he had always done. Father had told her that Osage was a very proud man.

He seated himself and picked up the reins before asking, "Where to?"

"I want to start by going to the Barnetts'."

Osage smiled. "I'm mighty happy to do that. This is Mrs. Barnett's day to bake cinnamon rolls."

Jessica laughed and smoothed her skirt with her gloved hands. "Then we'd better hurry."

It was a pleasant ride to the Barnett Ranch. The sun wasn't nearly as fierce as it had been in the summer months, and there was a slight breeze blowing in from the west. The weather was nearly perfect.

Jessica watched as Osage handled the single horse with ease. She was quite comfortable driving her own conveyance — it gave her a sense of control and freedom — but her parents seldom allowed her to go alone. Yet even with Osage at her side, Jessica felt very much alone.

Maybe I'm destined to spend my life like this. Maybe being in charge of myself will be more fulfilling than tying myself to a husband and children. Maybe I'll live at home for the rest of my life and care for Mother and Father as they age.

But as she considered the possibilities, Jessica felt the same sense of loneliness that had tormented her before. She was so lost in her thoughts that she didn't hear the rider approaching until he was nearly even with the buggy.

Osage slowed the wagon and put his finger to the rim of his hat. "Mornin', Austin."

Austin gave his hat a slight tip. "Good morning, Mr. McElroy. Miss Atherton."

"Good morning, Mr. Todd. What are you about this fine day?"

"Headin' to the Barnetts', and you?"

"We're headed there, as well."

"Mind if I ride alongside?" Austin's horse gave a bit of a whinny, as though adding his thoughts on the question.

"I don't mind at all. It will give us a chance to get better acquainted."

She wasn't sure, but she thought Mr. Todd actually frowned. He turned away quickly. However, when he looked back, he offered

her a pleasant smile. Jessica decided she'd
been mistaken. It was probably nothing
more than a trick of the sun.

Osage hummed softly to himself as he
usually did when family members were having a conversation. It endeared him to both
Jessica and her mother. They knew Osage
could still hear every word, but also knew
he would never dream of sharing that
information elsewhere.

"From where do you hale, Mr. Todd?" she
asked.

"Virginia, but my mother was born and
raised in Texas. I suppose that's why I
thought to come here."

"Was Virginia not to your liking?"

He hesitated. "Well . . . uh . . . it was just
time for a change."

"I see." Jessica thought he sounded
guarded and decided to change the subject.
"I was born and raised here, but I've done
quite a bit of traveling. My grandparents
were good to take me along on many of
their trips. I've been to Europe several
times, as well as to England and Scotland
and to several of the Caribbean islands.
Grandfather had business down there, so
we combined it with a pleasurable time, as
well. How about you, Mr. Todd?"

He shrugged. "Well, I've been all over the

eastern part of the country and up to Canada, but never abroad."

"Would you like to go one day?"

Austin shook his head. "I can't say that I've ever really considered it one way or the other. Though it could be exciting. When I was attending the university, I read about the Greeks and Romans. I thought it would be marvelous to journey to Italy and Greece someday."

"I think so, too," Jessica admitted. "We had plans to make a trip to that area when my grandfather fell ill. After he died, it wasn't long before Grandmother took a bad fall. She never recovered, and we lost her, as well."

"I'm sorry. Loss is never easy, even when it comes to those who are older."

Jessica arched a brow. "You speak as one who knows. Have you suffered much loss in your life?"

By this time they had arrived at the Barnetts'. Jessica awaited Mr. Todd's answer, but when he slid off his horse and thanked her for the company before walking toward the barn, she knew he wasn't going to give her one.

He is such a mysterious man. Sad too. It shows in his eyes. I'm sure he must know full well what it feels like to lose someone.

"I'm gonna go around back, Miss Jessica," Osage said with a wink. "I'll see if I can't sweet-talk a roll or two from Missus Barnett."

"I suppose I can take time for at least two rolls and a cup of coffee," Jessica said, amused by Osage's delight. She made her way to the front door and knocked. Her nerves returned, and for just a moment she thought of coming up with some other excuse for her appearance. But by the time Rosita answered the door, Jessica had regained her courage.

I'm more than ornamental and self-centered. I need to make a fresh start, and this is where I need to begin.

"I was hoping Alice might be here. I've come to call on her."

"Sí, she is here. You come in and sit. I will tell her you have come," Rosita replied. The small Mexican woman disappeared down the hall, and Jessica took a chair in the front room, where she knew the Barnetts usually received company. This was such a welcoming room. She studied the beautiful draperies and rugs. A fireplace adorned the middle of one wall. It was built from native rock and made a perfect contrast to the pine walls. Fancy work was displayed here and there. Someone had crocheted armrest covers for each of the chairs, as well as headrest guards. One could never tell when a visiting young man might have an overabundance of oil in his hair.

"Rosita said you'd come to see me," Alice said from the entryway. She held her small son and smiled. "Would you like some tea and rolls?"

Even though the aroma was tempting, Jessica declined. "No, I'd better not. It might distract me from my purpose in coming." Alice looked at her with a perplexed expression, and Jessica lost no time in adding, "I thought it was high time I apologized."

Alice looked at her strangely. "Apologize? To me?"

"Yes. I haven't been very kind to you. I was horrible to you, in fact."

Alice came and sat across from Jessica. She shifted the baby in her arms. "I'm not sure I understand."

"Well, when Robert chose you over me, I felt slighted. I wasn't in love with him, but it bothered me all the same. I know I said some things that weren't very nice." She bowed her head. "I made comments about your scar that I shouldn't have."

"Saying nothing about it wouldn't make it any less evident," Alice said with a smile. "I'm sorry that you felt slighted. I never intended to fall in love with Robert. I never planned for any of this life. I never figured I deserved anything more than servitude."

Jessica met her eyes. "But you do. You are the perfect example of a kind and gentle woman. You deserve to be happy, and I'm glad you have a wonderful man like Robert to see that you are. Robert was always good to me. He showed attention to me and made me feel special when I was a little girl."

"He certainly knows how to do that," Alice said, not sounding the least bit jealous.

Jessica was almost certain if the roles were reversed, she would be most unhappy. It only served to remind her of her failings. She sighed. "I hope you can forgive me, Alice. I'd like for us to be friends."

Alice's face seemed to light up. "But of course we're friends. As for forgiving you, well, I hold nothing against you. In my eyes there's no reason for forgiveness, but you have it just the same."

Jessica felt as if a small weight had been taken from her shoulders. "Thank you."

"Are you sure you wouldn't like some tea?"

Jessica shook her head. "No. I've already imposed long enough. One day soon, I will come to visit and spend more time." She looked at the baby in Alice's arms. "He's beautiful. I don't think I ever told you . . . congratulations."

Alice blushed and extended the sleeping child. "Would you like to hold him?"

Before Jessica realized it, Alice had placed the baby in her arms. She stared down at the infant and imagined he might have been her own. Hers and Robert's. The thought just wouldn't take shape, however. That was never meant to be.

She pressed the baby back toward Alice. The new mother quickly reclaimed her son. "Thank you," Jessica said. "He's quite a wonder."

"I think so, too. Sometimes I can scarcely believe I'm a mother."

Jessica didn't know what to say, so she said nothing for a moment. When she felt enough silence had passed between them, she began again for the door.

"Thank you for hearing me out." She stopped long enough to glance over her shoulder. "And for being so gracious in your forgiveness. Robert told me several times how wonderful you were. I guess I always knew that he was right."

"I'm glad you think so, but believe me, I have my moments, like everyone else." The baby stirred but didn't wake, and Alice continued in a softer voice. "I'm so glad you came today. I want very much for us to be the best of friends."

Her words drove away some of Jessica's sadness. "I know we will be."

CHAPTER 6

To further her plan for improving herself, Jessica arranged for Osage to drive her into Cedar Springs. This time they took the buckboard so that Osage could pick up supplies at the feedstore while Jessica attended to her plan.

The plan was simple. She wanted to check in with an old friend, Victoria Welch, now Victoria Branson. Victoria had married Marcus Branson, a man nearly twice her age, some three months earlier. Jessica hadn't approved the match and told her friend as much. She had begged Victoria to forget the man, but she'd insisted that she loved him. Jessica thought to put her foot down and prove just how disturbed she was by threatening not to attend the wedding. Then, before she knew it, Victoria had told her not to come. It had hurt Jessica deeply, but she'd never let on.

Around town, it was much talked about,

since it had been thought that Jessica would be Victoria's maid of honor. Jessica cried on her mother's shoulder and was only comforted when her mother promised they would go spend a few days in Dallas. Particularly on the day of the wedding.

How could I have been so judgmental? Jessica felt consumed with guilt. It was as if the scales had fallen from her eyes, and now she could see the ugly truth about her soul. Was there even hope for her?

Jessica hoped to make amends. She wanted to see Victoria face-to-face and tell her how sorry she was. Not only that, but she wanted to honor the new bride and show her support. On her lap, Jessica held a belated wedding gift — a beautiful, expensive tablecloth of Brussels lace. She hoped the gift might smooth the way to her apology for missing the wedding.

"I have some calls to make while you attend to business for Father," Jessica told Osage as he helped her from the buggy. "Why don't you pick me up around three-thirty. That way we can get home before it's dark."

"Sounds good to me. I won't need any more time than that." He threw her a wink. " 'Course it's been a lotta years since I had me a moonlight ride with a beautiful young lady."

Jessica laughed. "Why can't you be younger, Osage? I think you'd make a wonderful beau." The old man flushed red. She'd caused him to go speechless.

Smiling, Jessica patted his arm. "We can pick up the discussion on the way home."

His face remained red. "I think it might be better to find a new topic, Miss Jessica. I don't think your pa would approve of you and me sweet-talkin' our way home." He smiled and pointed toward the feedstore. "If you need me sooner, I'll be there playin' checkers with Charlie."

"Tell Charlie I said hello," Jessica replied. "Tell him I still remember coming to his feedstore with Papa when I was just a little girl." She hadn't thought about that in years. It had been a simple pleasure that she'd shared with her father and brothers. She paused and glanced toward Victoria's house. "Three-thirty, then. I'll be at Pritchard's store." Osage nodded and snapped the reins.

Jessica took the tablecloth and made her way up the path to Victoria's front door and knocked. Through the screened door she heard the sound of laughter. It would seem Victoria had guests. Jessica thought to leave, but it was too late. An older woman, wearing a starched white apron, approached the door.

"Welcome. The other ladies are in the parlor to the left. Would you like for me to take the gift?"

Jessica shook her head, uncertain what was happening. Apparently there was some sort of gathering that she had imposed herself upon. "I didn't know she had company," Jessica whispered. "I only thought to see Victoria and give her a wedding gift."

The older woman seemed to consider this for a moment. "Well, she has some of the local ladies here for their regular sewing circle. However, the gals planned a surprise birthday party for her. Victoria had no idea and is now enjoying that celebration. I'm sure she wouldn't mind."

"Well, I wouldn't want to interfere."

"Who is it, Mrs. Humphrey?" Victoria asked, opening the parlor's pocket doors. She looked surprised to see her guest. "Jessica. It's . . . been . . . well, a long time."

Jessica nodded. "I know and I'm sorry. I came to apologize and bring you a belated wedding gift, but I see I've come at a bad time."

"No, no. That's all right," Victoria said, glancing hesitantly over her shoulder. "Some mutual friends decided to throw me a birthday party. I'd like for you to stay."

"Perhaps for a short time," Jessica agreed. She extended the tablecloth. "This is for you — that and a long overdue apology. I'm sorry for the things I said about your marriage. You were right to react as you did. I was thoughtless and judgmental. I never should have tried to stand between you and Marcus. I hope you'll forgive me." She prayed Victoria would hear the sincerity in her statement.

Victoria didn't acknowledge the request but took the tablecloth and ran her hand over the delicate piece. "This is beautiful. Thank you." She gave Jessica a wary smile. "Come inside and see the others."

Jessica followed Victoria into the room as Mrs. Humphrey pulled the doors shut behind them. Many of Jessica's former schoolmates and friends were gathered in the parlor for the party. She had obviously not been invited to attend, and it caused Jessica both pain and embarrassment to have invaded their celebration.

"Look, Jessica Atherton has come with a wedding gift. Isn't it beautiful?" Victoria asked, unfolding part of the tablecloth. "I've never seen anything quite so fine."

"Would have been nice if she'd given it to

you at the wedding," someone behind Victoria murmured. Jessica couldn't tell for sure who had made the statement.

Beth Pritchard Englewood, daughter of the local mercantile owners Nelson and Dorothy Pritchard, got up and offered Jessica her chair. "Come sit, and I'll get you some cake and tea."

Jessica could see that the other women were just as surprised by her arrival as Victoria. They offered muffled greetings and then looked away, as if desperate to put some distance between them.

"How have you been, Jessica?" Karin Williams asked. Karin was married to one of her father's ranch hands and was just starting to show her pregnancy. "I saw you at church last week, but I didn't have a chance to speak with you."

I'm sure she didn't really want to speak to me. I spoke out against her marrying her father's hired man. The memory shamed Jessica. It was just one more example of her judgmental attitude.

"I'm sorry I missed you. I'm doing very well, thank you. How about you? Are you and Zeb settling into your new home?"

Karin gave her an enthusiastic nod. "We love our little house. Father says he'll help us add on to it later, when . . . we have more children." She blushed and lowered her head. "For now, it's big enough."

"I'm glad that you're happy," Jessica said. She looked around the room at the other women. "I'm sorry I've been so out of touch. I hope you'll forgive me for my lack of consideration. I haven't been a very good friend to any of you."

"Well, you're here now," Victoria said, rather uncomfortably. She smiled and looked to Beth. "You were just telling us about little Anna's teething troubles."

Beth handed Jessica a plate with a piece of cake and a cup of tea, which clattered a bit on the saucer as she handed it over. The tea sloshed, but Jessica said nothing. It wouldn't have been heard anyway as Beth began speaking of the woes her one-year-old daughter experienced as her teeth came in. Jessica listened, trying her best to be interested in the topic. As the other women commented and offered suggestions, Jessica felt more and more out of place. Everyone here was married.

"And Rusty is so very concerned about his little sister," Beth continued. "I told him she was getting new teeth, and he seemed completely in awe. Then he asked me why God hadn't given her any teeth before now."

The other ladies laughed and Jessica forced a smile.

"Oh, did I tell you that Jason is now fully in charge of my parents' store?" Beth asked. "Father is also making him a full partner."

"That's wonderful news," Victoria said, clapping her hands. "I know you've wanted that for so long."

"We got word that Ollie's mother isn't doing well," Millie Stapleton piped up. Millie was a year older than the rest and as such was the unofficial head matron of their society. "Since his father passed on, his mother has been gradually declining. I fear we may have to bring her here to live with us."

"Oh, I'm sorry, Millie," Beth said, shaking her head. "I'm sure that would be difficult."

"Yes, with the children so young, it would be hard to care for a sickly old woman. But what can I do? She is family and is our obligation. Ollie would never forsake her." She glanced Jessica's way. "We simply do not forsake the ones we love." Jessica knew the comment was directed at her failure to have supported Victoria's choice of husband.

I don't fit in here. I don't belong. I really don't even know these women anymore.

Jessica thought back to their childhood

days in school. They had all been quite close then. What had happened? Why had Jessica allowed them to slip away?

Because I was too worried about what I wanted for myself. I was too busy arranging my next grand affair, my next gown, my next trip.

Guilt washed over her. She took a bite of cake and felt it stick in her throat. Taking a quick sip of her tea, Jessica was able to avoid making a scene. She suddenly felt desperate to take her leave. That feeling grew stronger at the next question posed.

"So, Jessica, are you seeing anyone special?" one of the women asked.

Before she could answer, Millie spoke. "Jess is seeing a great many special people. I hear she goes out every week with a new beau." She looked at Jessica, as if daring her to refute the statement.

Jessica was floored by the comment, as well as the ensuing debate about her love life. She was mortified to find herself the center of this kind of attention.

"I think it positively risqué," Karin said. "A young lady ought to court only one man."

Jessica didn't think before answering. "If I were courting, then I would agree with you. I haven't chosen any one fellow, so I feel free to get to know each of them a little better. In this day and age a woman needn't feel it necessary to accept the first man who asks for her hand. I believe in taking my time and getting to know a fellow, learn what he stands for, what kind of husband and companion he'll make."

"But that's hardly a proper way to handle things!" Millie exclaimed. "It makes you seem . . . well . . . too forward."

The other ladies nodded. "You wouldn't want to get a bad reputation," one of them added, while another said, "It would shame your parents," making her angry.

"And how is it I would get a bad reputation and shame my mother and father?" Jessica asked, feeling defensive. "You all know my values and beliefs. You know I would never conduct myself in any way other than what was expected. Surely you would never speak out against me — slandering or gossiping about things that weren't true." The latter was issued as a challenge.

Her words hit the mark, and the women fell silent. Jessica sipped her tea and waited for their further attack. While it surprised her they would so openly show their disapproval, she was glad for it. It made her feel less guilty for having avoided them, and for a moment she forgot all about her campaign to make amends.

"Well, I believe a young lady of values should see only one man at a time, rather than stringing along several. It seems only proper," Millie finally said. "When I was courting Ollie, I never would have looked at another man. In fact, even before we were officially courting, I had eyes only for him. My heart knew from the time we were young that we were meant for each other."

"I envy you." Jessica drew in a calming breath. "I haven't had that experience."

"Well, you had Robert but then lost him to that woman from Colorado."

Jessica squared her shoulders. "I never really had Robert. We were good friends, and folks just assumed we would end up together."

"But you assumed it, too," Beth threw in. "I remember our discussions about how you would one day be Mrs. Robert Barnett. Of course, no one knew what was yet to come."

Jessica wanted to end the conversation but knew it was her own fault for allowing it to begin in the first place. "Robert and Alice are perfect for each other. They are well suited and love each other very much. I can't say that I ever felt that way about Robert. Frankly, I don't feel that way about anyone. Therefore, I believe I have the right to explore the possibilities of each single man."

"That sounds like a very modern way of thinking," Victoria murmured, sounding rather embarrassed. "Some of this new philosophy seems a bit scandalous to me." The other ladies nodded.

"Why, I was just reading the other day that in some places it's perfectly acceptable for women to go unescorted to dances and such. Can you imagine the commotion that must cause?"

To Jessica's relief, the woman began discussing social mores, leaving Jessica free to calm down. She knew if she didn't leave, she might very well say something she would regret. She supposed her old nature wasn't completely set aside.

Just then the clock chimed three. "Oh goodness. I didn't realize it was getting so late," she announced. "I have to meet my driver soon, and I still need to pick up some things." She put her teacup aside. "I do hope you'll excuse me." She turned to Victoria. "I wish you the best of birthdays and a very happy marriage. I wish all of you ladies well and hope you will come visiting soon."

The women seemed surprised by her sudden need to depart, but no one tried to stop her. Jessica knew they were just as glad to get rid of her as she was to go. No doubt they would spend the rest of the afternoon discussing her shortcomings.

She left Victoria's and made her way down to Main Street, where Pritchard's and other stores could be found. Jessica tried not to be bothered by the things the women had said, but she couldn't help it. Their comments had angered her. Did they truly believe her to be so scandalous? Was her love life really such a fascinating topic that they had nothing better on which to focus? Who were they to establish rules for her?

Glancing into the shop windows, Jessica tried to clear her mind. Changing her outlook on life and the driving forces of her internal nature was harder than Jessica had originally thought. There was so much to overcome — so much she hadn't even realized was at issue. Who knew that the women of Cedar Springs and the surrounding area were keeping track of how many different men with whom she stepped out?

Still, they were right. Reputations once lost were not easily regained. Jessica didn't want to cause her parents pain or disgrace. Perhaps she should find some charity and spend her time and efforts there. She thought of her sister, Gloria, and her generous nature and penchant for hard work. She was in Montana teaching Indian children to read and write English while her soldier husband worked to keep the area safe. Jessica's brothers, Isaac and Howard, were busy helping a local church join with other churches in building houses for the destitute in and around Corpus Christi. Her siblings were well known for their giving nature, their compassion for the less fortunate.

"What am I known for?" Jessica pondered. Sadly, she knew the answer. She was known for loving herself — for spending all of her time looking for ways to make herself happy.

For all my desire to do better, I find there are many hurdles to overcome. I wonder if I will ever be able to remake myself into a better person.

She browsed the aisles at Pritchard's. In days gone by she would have consoled herself with a new shawl or a pair of embroidered stockings, but now she had no interest. She knew they wouldn't help to ease her misery — they never really had. Jessica made her way outside to wait for Osage. She felt a sense of relief when she saw the heavily loaded buckboard pull up. All she really wanted was to go home — to get away from people and their condemning thoughts.

Thoughts that I no doubt deserve, Jessica realized. Again, she couldn't help but wonder if there was any hope for her to change. Transformations came with a price, she realized. Would she be able to afford the cost?

CHAPTER 7

"I'm certainly glad to see you," Jessica said as Osage pulled up alongside her.

He jumped down and helped Jessica. "Hee-hee! A fella likes to hear that a gal is anxious to be in his company."

Jessica shook her head and forgot her frustrations with the ladies. Osage never failed to improve her spirits. She folded her gloved hands and waited for him to climb into the driver's seat. After he settled in and snapped the reins, she jumped right into conversation.

"Did you get all the feed and supplies Pa needed?"

"Got 'em. I noticed the horse was walking funny, and when I took a look, I found he was about to throw a shoe. I went to the smithy."

"Good thing you caught it. Pa won't be happy that it happened. I suppose Manuel will get in trouble."

"Oh, your pa won't go too hard on him," Osage said.

For several minutes neither one spoke. Then, to her surprise, Jessica found herself asking Osage a rather personal question.

"Osage, did you get what you wanted out of life?"

"I did, for the most part. I found me a good job with your pa's pa, and then I found me a sweet gal to marry. We were happy and had a couple of boys. Had a good life those first few years. Then my wife died, and the boys were taken by their grandparents because I was about half outta my mind. When things settled down, I knew it was for the best. I couldn't have taken care of them. I would've liked my family to have stayed together, but otherwise, life has been good." He turned to look at her for a moment. "So, Miss Jessica, what is it you want out of life?"

Jessica searched her heart to give him an answer but couldn't find one. A month ago, she might have said she wanted travel and wealth and all manner of importance, even fame. Now, knowing how she'd presented herself throughout her life, Jessica was no longer sure what she wanted. Perhaps to clear her reputation and mend fences would be a good place to start. But she couldn't say that to Osage.

"I guess I'm still trying to figure that out."

Hours later at home, Jessica heard Osage's question posed again. This time it came from Lee Skelly. It was worded a little differently, but nevertheless pressed her for answers she didn't have.

Lee had ridden up while she was walking around the pasture just behind the house. Reining his horse to a stop, he'd looked at her in curiosity. "What are you lookin' for, Miss Jessica?"

She looked up to see Lee watching her closely. "I don't know. I'm just walking and thinking."

"Thinkin' about life and what you want out of it?" He didn't give her time to answer. "What do you want, Miss Jessica?"

"I want to be left to my thinking," she replied, irritated at the interruption.

"Thinkin' about me? About how you'd like to marry me?" He gave her a lopsided grin.

"To be quite honest, I don't know what I want."

"So then, you could be wantin' me and just not know it, right?" He jumped down from the back of his horse.

His determination fascinated her. Was he really that much in love with her? Did he

114

actually pine for her? She had to ask. "Lee, are you in love with me?"

The question caused the young man to cough and then clear his throat rather noisily. "Miss Jessica, that's a silly question to ask. You know I worship the ground you walk on."

"But that's not the same." She looked out across the pasture-land. She knew it as well as she knew the back of her hand. What she didn't know was her own heart.

"You speak of marriage and a future with me, but you don't talk about the important things."

"Like love? Well, of course I love you, Miss Jessica. I've been sweet on you since you were fourteen."

Jessica looked at Lee and shook her head. "I didn't know that."

"Well, why would you? We don't exactly socialize in the same circles." He laughed. "I'm just the boss's hired hand. Still, I would feel mighty proud to capture the heart of the boss's daughter. I can just imagine how the other fellas would react. They'd see me in a whole new light."

"And that would be important to you?"

"Yes, ma'am," he said enthusiastically.

"But why?"

Lee's expression suggested she ought to

know the answer. "Because it would prove my worth. I ain't never had nothing of value belong to me. If I was to marry you, it would show everyone that I was important, that I mattered."

"And you don't feel you matter otherwise?" Jessica hadn't expected this turn of conversation, but it fascinated her at the same time.

He shrugged. "I know I matter to me, but I want to matter to others. I want to be somebody. If I married the boss's daughter, that would make me special. The other fellas would look at me with respect. And more than a little envy," he added, laughing. "I guess I'd just like some say in my life, some control."

"I can tell you from my own experience that taking control of a situation isn't all it's thought to be. It requires a great deal of attention and work."

"Well, all I know is that you took control of my heart."

"Oh, stop it, Lee. I know what you want from me, but I can't give it. I don't love you."

He frowned. "I know that, but I'm willin' to take a chance on you learnin' to love me."

Jessica felt sorry for the man, but she couldn't give in. She shook her head. "Well,

I'm not."

Austin thought long and hard about his decision to leave the Rangers as he rode home from Dallas. He'd told his superior of his plan, and the man hadn't tried to stop him. Instead, he'd congratulated Austin and said he thought he would make a fine town marshal. Some of the other men standing nearby had agreed.

The sun was near to setting, and it left a cold, empty feeling to the clouded sky. Twilight was not his favorite time. It always made him feel lonely. He couldn't help but think of Grace. They had married with only one thought — to spend the rest of their lives loving each other. They had planned for many children and a large house in which to put them. Austin smiled and then felt a sense of wonder. Thinking about Grace didn't seem to hurt like it had before. In fact, it was almost like a faint dream.

He allowed himself the memory of their wedding. She had been so radiant in her wedding silk. Her parents had died when she was little, and her grandmother had raised her. Having lived the life of a privileged only child, Grace's desires were surprisingly modest and simple. She had attracted Austin's attention from the first day he'd seen her walking along the street in Washington, D.C. Just a few short months later, she walked down the aisle to him.

Remembering her smile as he lifted the veil to kiss her, Austin had thought his life perfect. If he'd died in that moment, he would have died the happiest man in the world. Instead, she had died and he had killed her. Killed her by his absence. When she went into labor, no one had been there to help her, and both she and the baby had died.

He bore the responsibility like a heavy mantle. Austin was the one who had made her move to the country — away from her beloved grandmother and the city she so enjoyed. He had worried about her living in the city and being alone when he had to be gone on special assignments. Oh, certainly she had her grandmother, at least at first. They were still living in town when the old woman had taken ill and died only six days later. Even so, Grace loved to visit the cemetery, as if she could see her grandmother face-to-face. She loved to take flowers to the grave and spend time in reflection. She told Austin that she knew her grandmother was in heaven, safe and happy, but she felt certain God gave Grandmother the messages from Grace. And Austin had taken that away by insisting on the move.

Three months after her grandmother's death, Austin had found a place away from the city. He told Grace about it and about his desire to move. He could see the disappointment in her expression and knew she didn't approve.

"But she never complained," he murmured. He shook his head and gazed up at the darkening sky. It was starting to look like rain. "You never did complain."

When she'd told him they were going to have a baby, Austin had nearly fainted. It was the only time he'd felt so consumed by fear that he'd thought he might pass out. Even in all the close calls he'd had with his work, nothing had prepared him for the daunting task of fatherhood.

The thought of raising a child in a city the size of Washington gave Austin some concerns. It was a beautiful place, to be sure, and had much to recommend it. However, he had made enemies, and he knew there could be great danger for his family. He worried that even living ten miles away wouldn't be far enough. What if his enemies followed him and found Grace?

By August of 1890 they had settled into their country home. Grace was due to deliver in March, and despite her growing

119

size, she'd made them a lovely home. Grace longed for the hustle and bustle of the city, but she assured Austin that she was happy. And he believed her. They truly had been happy there — at least for a short while.

When winter arrived travel became more difficult, and Austin insisted Grace do nothing to put herself in danger. He often had to leave her alone, and it worried him greatly. He managed to scrape together enough money to pay a housekeeper for the winter. The case Austin and Houston had worked for the past year was about to break wide open. They had been following stamp counterfeiters and felt certain they would have the entire ring rounded up by February.

Austin had figured after it was over, he would request cases that would keep him close to home. Close to Grace and his unborn child. It seemed so reasonable that when everything fell apart, Austin only knew a deep and painful shock.

January 31 of 1891 had started out routine, but by the next day, Houston Todd was dead and Austin was explaining to his parents what had happened. The grief was overwhelming, but the blame was even worse. His parents had nothing kind to say about Austin's participation in the event.

He closed his eyes and saw their accusing faces. He felt betrayed and abandoned. He was grieving the loss of his brother, as well, and already felt so much guilt that it threatened to swallow him whole.

"It's your fault! You killed your brother!" His mother pointed her finger at Austin.

A rider approached from the north, and Austin quickly forced his thoughts from the past as Robert Barnett drew up and stopped his sorrel.

"I've been out checking the fence," Robert explained. "I'm headed home for supper. Why don't you join us?"

Austin felt half starved, but he was in no mood to be around people. "I'm tired and just gonna head home."

"You have to eat," Robert pressed. "Besides, my place is closer, and it looks like it might start raining any minute. I believe I'll have more light to see by, and it'll only get darker as you make your way home."

"I'll be fine. I'm not that far, and I have some of the food your mother sent over a couple of days ago."

Robert looked at him for a moment and then nodded. "I guess you do look worn down. I'll give Ma your regrets."

"Thanks." Austin turned his mount away from Robert.

"Hey, Austin — is there anything I can do?"

He glanced over his shoulder in the dimming light. "No. There's nothing anyone can do."

The skies were dark by the time Jessica and her family sat down to dinner. Father had been busy with one of his new foals and was late getting back to the house for supper. When he finally bounded through the door, he was ready to eat immediately.

Mother lit extra lamps and placed them around the house, but it didn't seem to dispel the gloom. Rain threatened at any moment, and flashes of lightning could be seen in the distance.

Father led them in grace, then dug into a bowl of jalapeños and corn. "Looks like we might actually get a good rain."

Mother nodded from her side of the table and extended a different bowl to Jessica. She took one of the smaller potatoes and passed the bowl to her father. While he continued to comment on the coming storm, Jessica mashed the potato on her plate and added butter, salt, and pepper. She couldn't help returning her thoughts to the events of her day and the way the women had treated her at Victoria's. It wasn't unkindness, she told herself, but rather disapproval. She realized that she cared quite deeply what those women thought, and it troubled her.

"Well, I have to say I'm surprised," Father said, turning to Jessica.

She startled and shook her head. "Why? What are you surprised about?"

"I went to help Osage with the feed, and when we finished I asked him where your parcels were. He told me you hadn't bought anything. I have to say, Jess, this is the first time you've come back from town without havin' a wagonful of purchases. I figured you'd be bringing home some new doodad or fancy dress."

Jessica frowned. "You know, there really is more to me than clothes and pretty things."

Father's expression turned troubled. "I know there's more to you, Jess. I didn't mean to hurt your feelings. I always kinda got a kick out of seeing how those things made you happy. It pleased me to give 'em to you."

Jessica knew that her tension from the day threatened to ruin the meal. "I'm sorry. I'm just feeling out of sorts."

Father laughed. "You got no need to be. The world is at your fingertips, and life is good." He put his fork down and smiled.

"Tomorrow you'll be all sunshine and smiles. Just wait and see."

Her father's words seemed shallow and offered no comfort. Nevertheless, Jessica drew a deep breath and let it out slowly to calm her anger. "I'm sure you're right, Papa. Things are bound to be better tomorrow."

With that matter resolved in her parents' minds, they went back to discussing the ranch while Jessica ate in silence. Would things truly be better tomorrow?

CHAPTER 8

Austin pored over the new brand book provided to him by the Cattle Raisers Association of Texas. He was already familiar with a good many local brands, such as those that belonged to the Barnett, Wythe, Reid, and Atherton ranches. Those families represented a good portion of the area to the north and west of Dallas, but they were a small fraction of all the ranches he'd cover.

Thumbing through the book, Austin wasn't surprised to see that there were hundreds of brands listed. People took great pride in their own unique brands. It seemed a pity that others couldn't respect the marks as a "hands off" sign. Rustling was up from earlier in the decade, but the meeting with his fellow Rangers suggested that there were signs of it waning. He hoped that was true. It was one thing when people stole because their children were starving, and quite another when they stole just for the extra cash they could get. At least that was Austin's way of looking at it. Neither way was right, but it had more to do with a matter of heart. He found himself more forgiving of the man who stole out of desperation. Even so, he couldn't turn a blind eye.

Putting the book aside, Austin got up and poured himself a glass of buttermilk. Tyler Atherton had just brought it over an hour earlier, and it was still chilled from his springhouse. He let the tangy liquid slide down his throat and thought it about the best he'd ever had. He quickly finished off one glass and then poured another. At this rate the buttermilk would be gone by morning.

He marveled at the way these neighbors took care of one another. Everybody seemed to have one talent or another and shared the benefits of those talents. He'd seen Mrs. Barnett load him up with food, while Mrs. Atherton was quick to give him bedding and linens. Mrs. Reid had stopped by with her sister, Mrs. Atherton, and both women had brought him a whole carriage full of food, candles, and lamps and oil, not to mention several books. He was mighty grateful for their kindness, but it also made him feel uneasy. He'd never intended to get close to anyone ever again.

After losing his brother in January of 1891, he'd lost Grace and the baby the following month. By May his father had suffered a heart attack and passed, leaving only Austin and his mother to carry the grief. Mother wasn't able to bear up under the load, however, and she fell ill and died in June. Within less than six months, Austin had lost everyone he'd ever loved. It was a pain he never intended to repeat.

Still, visions of Jessica Atherton came to mind. She was feisty and high-spirited. Nothing like Grace had been. In fact, Miss Atherton might very well be the extreme opposite. While Grace hadn't quite come up to his shoulder, Jessica was taller. And while Grace probably weighed no more than ninety pounds, Jessica had a little more meat on her bones, and it curved in all the right places.

The real differences, however, were in their personalities and desires. He wasn't at all sure what Miss Atherton wanted out of life. It seemed the few times they had shared each other's company, she had been outspoken and independent. Grace had always been quiet and relied on him for everything.

He didn't know why he was comparing the two women. There was really no comparison. Grace had touched his heart and soul in a way that no other woman could. His biggest sorrow had been in losing her and the baby — a son.

Austin paced the small cabin, wishing he could drive Jessica's image from his thoughts. He wasn't about to let his heart get involved again. He'd made himself a pledge, and he would stick to it.

Miss Atherton probably has no idea that I'm even thinking of her, so it's best I not. Besides, I have plenty of other things to put my mind on.

He drew a deep breath and went back to the kitchen area, where a small wood-burning stove sat. He used it for cooking as well as for heating the cabin. He put a pot of coffee on to heat. It was left over from earlier and just needed some warming. Checking the stove's fuel, Austin added a few sticks of wood and let the fire build a little. After a few quick pokes with the wood tongs, the flames flared nicely.

It proved a good way to regroup his thoughts and put aside his sorrows. There was work to be done, and he couldn't waste time with memories.

Suppressing a yawn, Austin returned to the table and took a seat. He picked up the brand book and returned to memorizing.

■ ■ ■ ■

The next morning Austin made his way into Cedar Springs. He wanted to make sure the local law understood what he had planned.

Greeting the town marshal, Austin showed him his brand book. "Marshal, I just wanted to tell you that I'll be traveling around to the various ranches to check brands against what's registered. I want to look over the cattle as best I can and hear any complaints the ranchers might have. I wanted you to know, so if anyone asked, you'd already have knowledge of my plans."

"I appreciate that, Austin. You're a good man."

The marshal's words made Austin wince. "I don't know about that, but it is a job."

"Rustlin' doesn't seem quite as bad as it did last spring. Still, I'm glad the Rangers are takin' this seriously." The older man smoothed back his graying hair. "Why don't you take a walk with me? I was just about to make my rounds. We could have a bite of something to eat before you head out."

"Sounds good," Austin admitted. He had already decided to make a visit to one of the cafés in town.

The marshal pulled on his Stetson. It was

a "boss of the plains" style, with a flat brim and straight four-inch crown. The top was rounded, and it was unadorned except for a hatband that had been added. Austin knew the hat had cost him a pretty penny.

"I see you're admirin' my hat. My wife bought this for me as an anniversary present. Saved up her egg and sewin' money. Ain't it a dandy?"

"It is indeed." Austin's own hat had seen better days.

The two men left the jail and walked out into the late morning air. The temperature had risen considerably since Austin's morning ride into town. "Looks like it may be a hot one today."

"Yeah, I was thinkin' the same," the marshal answered. "Seems like it never can make up its mind this time of year." The marshal paused to tip his hat to a couple of ladies exiting one of the dry goods stores. Austin did the same.

"As a town marshal you have to get used to being the face of law and order, as well as a comfort to those in need," the marshal said.

Austin looked at him and shook his head. "What are you talking about?"

"Well, I heard about the plans for Terry-ton. I heard, too, that you'd been asked to

130

take on the responsibility of law and order."

"That's true." Austin had no idea who had explained all of this to the marshal, but no doubt he needed to be told. "But it won't be for a while yet."

The marshal nodded, then gave a wave to a man sweeping his portion of the board-walk across the street. "Matt, you're gonna wear that broom out."

The man laughed, waving the broom. "Already did. This is my third one in a month's time." The men shared a laugh.

Austin felt a little out of place. He didn't know many of the people in town. He seldom came to Cedar Springs unless it was to catch the train to Dallas or to pick up canned goods. The way the nearby families had taken care of him, he hadn't needed to do that very often.

"It's not always peaceful around these parts. We've had killers and thieves just like in the big city."

"I'm sure you speak the truth. Criminals scarcely stay within boundaries."

"That's true. If they did, they'd be a whole lot easier to catch," the marshal said.

They came to the bank and the marshal peeked inside. "Things runnin' okay today?" he called out.

Austin heard someone answer, "We're doing quite well. Off to a good start."

"Glad to hear it." He closed the door and motioned for Austin to follow him. "Got to make sure the Bisby Mercantile is locked up tight. They had to go east for the burial of her mother. Didn't know enough about the folks here to get someone to cover the store." They crossed the dirt street and made their way to the building. After a quick check of the front door, the marshal went around back. Satisfied that all was well, he nodded to Austin. "Now we can go have that bite to eat. I'll check the other half of town afterward."

"How many times a day do you do this?" Austin asked.

"Well, it depends. If we have a bunch of rowdy cowboys in town, I check a lot more often. And, of course, we check more at night than durin' the daylight hours."

"Makes sense."

The marshal kept glancing around as they walked. Austin could tell that he wasn't missing much. The man seemed concise and to the point in his conversation and attentive to everything that went on around him. Austin liked that about him.

"I do the town walk during the day. My deputies do the night hours unless they're sick or otherwise occupied. I usually walk the town first thing in the morning when the stores are opening. Then I check again around the noon hour and again at closin' time. During the evening the checks run every hour or two. It's a good way to make your presence known. But don't go at the same time each night and don't go exactly on the hour. You don't want folks ever believin' you have a set pattern. It'll get you in trouble every time."

Austin already knew that was true. He'd been warned of that on many of his Secret Service cases. Diversity was a good way to stay alive.

"Keep track of the troublemakers," the marshal offered. "Just because they aren't doing anything in particular doesn't mean they aren't up to somethin'."

With a smile, Austin turned toward the man. "You've no doubt seen it all."

"That I have. I used to be a deputy and then a marshal up north. I've seen men run stark naked down the middle of the street in winter because they were too intoxicated to know better. I've seen women, young and old, create scenes that would curl your hair. One woman was so angry about her husband spending all his pay each week at the saloon that she came to town with her double-barreled shotgun and blew a hole in the wall above her husband's head. He and his cronies looked pert near scared to death. When she told him to git . . . well . . . he got, and quick. You never know what you'll get yourself into."

"Maybe I should stick to inspecting cattle," Austin said, still smiling.

"Nah," the man replied. "What fun would that be?"

They shared a pleasant lunch together and then made the rounds for the rest of the small town. There was a busyness to the town, with folks making their way from business to business. Yet, even amongst the chaos there was a kind of order to everything.

"At night we check all the doors and windows. We look for any sign of forced entry. We check the water troughs to make sure nobody drowned themselves." He stopped and looked at Austin. "Had that happen to a drunk once, up north. Don't wanna ever see it happen again."

Austin nodded. "I wouldn't want to see such a thing, either." They were nearly back to the jail when Austin asked, "What else do you do?"

"Well, come with me and I'll show you. There's some paper work I sometimes have to see to. I keep track of the hours my deputies work and their pay. I sometimes have to go to the town council and ask for things we need at the jail. Then, of course, there are the wanted posters that I receive and the folks who amble in off the street for one reason or another. Some just wanna ask questions about the law, and other times they use me as a deterrent. Had a mother a couple of weeks ago come here with her eight-year-old son. Apparently he'd been stealin' from her milk money. She wanted him to know what it was like to sit in jail. So we put him in a cell while she went off shoppin'. The boy was mighty glad when she returned. I doubt she'll have too much trouble with him in the future."

They reentered the jail and the marshal was just showing Austin a logbook when a stranger entered.

"Good afternoon, Marshal. I wonder if you might lend me some assistance."

The man was well dressed in a brown suit, complete with a crisp white shirt, vest, and tie. He was older — probably in his fifties or sixties, Austin guessed. At least his well-trimmed beard and hair showed signs of graying.

"Could be, stranger. Why don't you tell me what you're needin'," the marshal replied.

"Thank you. I'm looking for the Wythes' ranch. I thought perhaps you could direct me."

At the mention of the name, Austin took more interest.

"Well, that depends." The marshal eyed him carefully. "Who are you and what do you want with the Wythes?"

The man smiled. "I do apologize. I'm Randolph Cuker. I was a good friend of the Wythes in Denver, when Jacob worked for one of the banks. They encouraged me to stop by their ranch anytime I was in the area. They assured me that just about anyone in town could direct me, but they particularly mentioned you. I had business that brought me to Dallas and thought I would pay them a visit."

"I see. Well, I suppose that's a good enough reason," the marshal declared. "There's a main road north of here that heads out and turns to the west. You follow that about twenty miles. You'll pass several farms and a couple of small ranches. Then you'll come up on a long stretch of land that belongs to the Athertons. The road will curve again and take you past the Barnett place. They have a big spread and the main entry to the property has a sign bearing their brand — looks like this." The marshal drew a line and put the letters NT beneath. "Just keep goin' another five miles or so to the Wythe place. Marty Wythe is sister to Mrs. Barnett and has the property that adjoins theirs. The Wythe place sits back off the road a ways, so just take the turnoff on the road to the right, and you'll find your way."

"Thank you. That was most thorough. I'm sure to find them." The man stretched out his hand. The marshal took hold and shook it. "I am very much in your debt, Marshal."

"Are you stayin' in town, Mr. Cuker?" Austin asked. He leaned casually back against the wall, as if only mildly interested.

"I have taken a room at the hotel. I'm not here for long, but it seemed prudent." The man pulled a watch from his vest pocket. "Now, if you'll excuse me, I must see about renting a horse and buggy."

He left without further comment, but Austin felt an uneasiness that made him want to follow the man. He went to the window and watched him cross the street.

"I'm not sure about him," Austin finally said.

"He seemed likable enough. He didn't shy away from coming in here. Most men who are trouble would avoid the jail like a dull knife."

Austin didn't want to stir up trouble. He gave the marshal a nod. "I'm sure you're right. Now, I better head out to start inspecting brands. Thanks for the company and the lessons in marshaling."

The older man gave a chuckle and took a seat behind his desk. "I was happy to help. Come back anytime."

"Manuel brought us the mail from town," Hannah declared as she joined Alice in the front room. "There's a letter here for you."

Alice frowned. "Who would write to me? I don't have any family or friends except those who live right here, and I just had a letter from Mother."

Hannah smiled. "Maybe it's from an old friend."

"I don't have any," Alice replied. She took the letter and studied the script. It was flowery and full of loops. The kind of writing a woman might make.

"Well, I don't suppose you'll know unless you open it," Hannah said, thumbing through the rest of the mail. "Mostly payments due. I had hoped Eleanor would write. I'm afraid my daughter is rather caught up in the women's movement for the right to vote. Writing to her mother to let her know how she's doing might delay

138

the cause."

Alice smiled at her mother-in-law. She liked Hannah Barnett very much. The older woman was motherly and attentive — more so than Marty had been — although she never tried to impose herself on Alice.

Alice gave a brief nod, then carefully opened the letter. A single piece of paper was inside. Unfolding it, Alice read the brief message. She gasped before she could hide her fear.

"What is it?" Hannah asked and then apologized. "If you don't mind telling me."

Alice shook her head slowly and held the letter up to her mother-in-law. Hannah took it and read it aloud.

"Congratulations on your new baby. There are just some things money can't buy."

She looked back to Alice with a puzzled expression. "What an interesting message, but it's not signed."

"I don't have anyone who would write to me here. At least no one that I would *want* writing to me." Alice turned the envelope over. "It has a back stamp marked Dallas. I don't know anyone in Dallas except my mother, and this isn't her handwriting." She gave a shiver, but the older woman was already looking again at the letter.

"It's not really bad tidings," Hannah said, shaking her head. "But it *is* a mystery."

"A mystery I could do without," Alice said, afraid of what the letter might well mean to her family's safety.

CHAPTER 9

The skies opened up and poured rain just as church services began that September morning. Jessica tried to focus on the words of the hymn, rather than the sound of rain on the roof, but at one point she worried that the gully washer might cause damage. The land was still pretty dry, and if the rain came too suddenly, there would be flooding.

The congregation was just starting the second hymn when Jessica heard a disturbance at the back of the church. Apparently some poor soul had come into the service late. She didn't bother to look around from her family's pew in the front.

The congregation continued singing, drowning out the rain somewhat. Jessica had never been much for singing. She didn't find it all that appealing and had difficulty carrying a tune. For all her talents, singing wasn't one of them. Even so, she mouthed the words and tried to look involved.

There was a rustling sound to her right, and without so much as a whispered hello, Austin Todd slipped into the row right beside her. He was dripping wet and held his hat in his hands. Jessica knew she looked at him in surprise, but she couldn't help herself. When the song concluded, she took her seat and threw Austin a quick smile. His presence, even though he was dripping water everywhere, was pleasing to her.

The service lasted another hour, with the preacher teaching on the story of Daniel in the lions' den.

"Daniel's faith, much like that of Abraham and Joseph, whom we studied in the weeks past, saw him through much adversity — even in a dark lonely pit with man-eating lions."

Jessica was familiar with the story. She rather enjoyed all of the Bible stories she'd been taught in her youth. They spoke of great adventures and of people who left all they knew and traveled to make a new start for themselves in unknown lands. Such ideas had always appealed to her. Perhaps that was why she'd enjoyed traveling with her grandparents, while her siblings preferred to remain at home.

Maybe that's what I need to do.

Here in Cedar Springs, Jessica knew her reputation was that of a spoiled little girl. Maybe a new start in a city far away would suit her.

I could start over somewhere else. I could be my own woman, just as the women's movement encourages. Who knows, I could even join Eleanor Barnett in her cause. Jessica almost giggled aloud at the thought.

It might suit me, but Mama and Papa would have kittens.

She continued smiling at the thought only to find that Austin was watching her. He seemed neither disturbed by her amusement nor supportive. She felt her cheeks grow hot and lowered her head. It was then that she noticed Austin was dripping water onto the skirt of her gown. She frowned, then chided herself mentally. *It's only a dress and it will dry out.*

Lifting her head to look to the front of the church, Jessica tried to focus on the lesson. She stared at the pulpit with its handmade wooden cross nailed to the front while the pastor continued his sermon.

"When morning came and they opened that pit up, the king was mighty worried about his friend Daniel. You see, he hadn't wanted to put Daniel to death — not really. But sometimes folks in authority don't lead properly. They get impressed by the folks around them, and they're afraid to make the right decision. The king knew what was right but didn't choose to follow through, because the law at that time didn't leave room for changing.

"Now, you can find yourself relating to Daniel or to the king, but the important thing is this: God was faithful and trust-worthy. The king halfway believed that Daniel's God would save him. But Daniel knew that his God was the true God, and He would take care of the details, whether Daniel lived or died. We must all strive for faith like that."

But how does one get faith like that? It's hard enough to trust the people you spend every day with. It's much harder to trust God, whom you can't see.

Jessica pondered the subject even while the pastor began to pray. She'd attended church all of her life. She'd accepted that she was a sinner and without Jesus she would be forever separated from God. When her Sunday school teacher had told her class that it wasn't hard to get saved, Jessica had listened closely. She could still hear old Mrs. Rogers explaining salvation. She had stretched out her arms and demonstrated that in this position her body formed a cross. She then said that Jesus had died on the cross to take away our sins. The cross was a bridge that allowed us to get to God.

"Anyone who would like to get saved has only to ask God to forgive their sins through the blood of Jesus, and then they need to walk in repentance and stop doing the bad things they did before."

Those words had greatly affected Jessica. And she had prayed silently as the teacher led the children in prayer. Jessica's parents had instilled in her respect for God and for her teachers, but this experience seemed different . . . more personal. When she told her mother about it later that evening, Mama had wept with joy and told Jessica they would arrange for her to be baptized. She was proud that her little daughter had made such a grown-up decision.

The congregation now rose to sing a final hymn, and Jessica got to her feet, as well. She put aside thoughts of her childhood and considered instead the man beside her. She'd never before encountered Austin at church and wondered if he was a new convert. He was certainly handsome, and his hands bore the rugged, tanned look of one who was used to working hard.

He extended the hymnal to share with her. She took hold of the book, but neither of them sang. The moment seemed to connect them in a way that startled Jessica. She couldn't help finding Austin fascinating. She'd heard so much about him from others, yet now that she had met him face-to-face, none of those assessments seemed complete.

To Jessica's disappointment the song ended, and with one final prayer, the service was over. Austin took the hymnal and put it back while Jessica glanced around at various people shaking hands and greeting one another. The sanctuary hummed with voices. Jessica had started to follow her mother and father from the pew when she felt a slight touch on her arm. Turning back, she found Austin looking at her with an apologetic expression.

"I'm sorry for getting your skirt wet," he said, nodding to the damp spot. "Guess I pretty well washed my portion of the pew, as well." They looked in unison at the pew.

"It's wood," Jessica replied. "So as long as we dry it off, it won't suffer much." She took the dry edge of her skirt and gave the seat a quick wipe. She knew her action was rather scandalous, but it happened so quickly she didn't think to stop herself.

"That won't help your skirt any," Austin murmured, seeming just as surprised by Jessica as she felt.

"My skirt will dry and be just fine. It's only water." She met his eyes and fell silent. For a moment they stood staring at each other, neither one seeming to know what to say.

"Jessica, I want to introduce you to someone," her mother said from behind. "This is Harrison Gable."

She reluctantly turned. To her surprise she found a handsome man, probably in his midthirties, staring with a grin. Jessica smiled. "I'm pleased to meet you."

"The pleasure is definitely mine, Miss Atherton," Mr. Gable replied. "I've had the privilege of working with your father and Mr. Barnett on the plans for Terryton."

Jessica nodded. "You must be the lawyer from Dallas."

"Not anymore. I just moved here," he told her, looking quite pleased. "And I must say I'm not disappointed with the . . . area."

He looked her over from head to toe, making Jessica feel self-conscious. This man's confidence suggested he was someone used to getting what he wanted. She did her best to appear unaffected.

"This is a wonderful area," she countered with a coy smile. "We have many beauties."

"I noticed only one," he said, glancing

147

over his shoulder.

He was flirting with her, but Jessica found that she enjoyed the attention. Still, she couldn't help worrying what Mother might think. Jessica's concern was for naught, as she found her mother was already busy speaking with Hannah Barnett. For a moment there was an awkward silence between Jessica and Mr. Gable. She wasn't at all sure what to say. Just then she remembered Austin and turned to introduce him. He was gone.

Jessica frowned and looked back to Harrison Gable. "I had thought to introduce you to Austin Todd, but it seems he has already departed. Mr. Todd works with the Texas Rangers to inspect cattle."

"Mr. Gable," Mother interrupted, "I understand you plan to have a late afternoon meeting with Mr. Barnett and my husband. I wonder if you might like to join us for the noon meal. Our place is right on the way to the Barnetts'. This way you can eat and rest before you and Tyler head over to your meeting."

Mr. Gable smiled, and for a moment Jessica felt her breath catch. "I would love to," he said.

Jittery and rather weak in the knees, Jessica tried to appear unmoved. She didn't know why she was acting like a silly school-girl with a crush.

"Wonderful. You can follow us home if you'd like, or we've plenty of room in the carriage. You could ride up front with Tyler as he drives. I'll ride in the second seat with Jessica."

"Oh no. I can't take your place beside your husband," he said, shocking Jessica by throwing her a quick wink.

Mother didn't seem to notice and continued. "It will be quite all right. That will give you two an opportunity to discuss any business that hasn't yet been tended. Come along. We're nearly ready to depart."

"I have my horse," Harrison Gable said, as if only then remembering.

"That's not a problem," Mother replied. "You can tie him to the back of our carriage." She left to join Father, who was already near the back of the church.

To her surprise, Harrison Gable leaned closer. "I would much rather sit beside you for the journey." His warm breath on her ear caused Jessica to jump back. Her eyes widened momentarily, but she straightened and feigned a reserve she didn't feel. Mr. Gable gave a low, almost inaudible chuckle.

Harrison Gable enjoyed the meal offered

him by Carissa Atherton. She was a beautiful woman with impeccable manners, as was her daughter Jessica. He found he rather enjoyed the effect he seemed to have on the young woman. She'd been watching him with furtive glances from her seat across the table. Her interest pleased him, and he was equally attracted to her.

They settled in the drawing room after lunch, and Tyler asked him a few personal questions.

"You have family in the area, Mr. Gable?"

Harrison shook his head. "My kin are all in Alabama. I came west to explore the possibilities. I have to say, I'm truly more of a big city man. I prefer legal cases and the complicated practice of government law. In fact, I would like to one day work in Washington, D.C., or New York City."

He saw the way Jessica seemed to take note. Perhaps city life appealed to her, too. Before he could comment, however, Tyler Atherton asked yet another question.

"What about a wife and children?"

"Neither one," Harrison admitted. "Never seemed to have the time while studying to become a lawyer, and then I focused on actually practicing law. It's been an uphill battle, but I finally feel ready to consider marriage." He glanced at Jessica and added,

"It would seem the possibilities are quite promising."

Tyler laughed, but it was Mrs. Atherton who commented. "I think you'll find some very nice young ladies in this area of Texas."

Harrison nodded, most serious. "I'm sure I will."

The conversation carried on in a casual, slow manner that put Gable at ease. He'd always had difficulty relaxing and enjoying people. Trained to listen to the details of client conversation and actions, Harrison usually found himself playing the lawyer even in his private life. Today, however, he felt as though he'd been accepted into a close group of people.

I think I'm going to enjoy this job. Maybe living out here in the sticks won't be so bad after all.

"I'm glad we can ride to the Barnetts' together," Tyler told him. "It's not hard to find, but we can discuss some of the other area ranches and farms on the way."

"I'm going to need to speak with all of the families," he replied. "Perhaps someone could accompany me as I make my rounds."

Jessica seemed to perk up at this. He watched as she leaned forward and opened her mouth to speak. Harrison smiled, sure that she would volunteer for the job, as he had hoped. Instead, Tyler spoke up.

"I'd be happy to show you around and introduce you. Why don't you plan to stop by here tomorrow?"

"Oh, I wasn't trying to impose myself upon you. I know you're a busy man."

"Bah," Tyler said, shaking his head. "I can take the time. This is important — not just to me, but to everyone in the area."

Jessica eased back against the chair and folded her hands. She looked disappointed but bowed her head. Harrison felt a sense of pleasure at her response, because he felt the same regret. It would have been wonderful to get to know her better. Especially away from others who might interrupt or interfere.

He scowled, thinking of the rain-soaked cowboy sitting beside Miss Atherton in church. He didn't know who the fella was, but he could very well be a rival.

"Well, I've stayed long enough," Austin declared, getting to his feet. He'd enjoyed a wonderful Sunday meal with the Barnetts and Wythes.

"I'm sorry you have to leave," William said, also standing. "Come back as soon as you can. You're always welcome here."

Austin nodded and looked to where the

three ladies sat. "Thank you again, Mrs. Barnett."

"Please call me Hannah," she said, for what Austin figured was about the tenth time.

"I'll try, ma'am, but I wasn't raised to speak so casually to a lady."

William and Jake walked out with him, but Robert remained inside, seeming enamored with his young son and wife. A twinge of regret ran through Austin's heart, but again it didn't hurt nearly as bad as it once had. Maybe time was truly easing his misery.

"I'm meeting with Tyler and our lawyer here in a couple of hours," Will said as they walked to where Austin's horse had been tied to graze.

"I hope everything goes well."

"I plan to tell him that you've agreed to be our lawman in Terryton. That way he can get back to the railroad authorities and assure them that we have law and order in place."

"It's going to be interestin' to watch all of this fall in place," Jake interjected. "With the way Dallas is spreadin' out, I can't help but think our little town will suit the needs of folks who'd rather live in a smaller place."

"And it seems there are plenty of new folks," William added.

"Speaking of new folks," Austin said, turning to Jake, "did your friend find the place all right?"

"What friend?" Jake asked.

Austin looked from the younger man to the older. Returning his gaze to Jake, he spoke. "While I was visiting with the marshal in Cedar Springs, a fella stopped by the jail asking how to find your place. Said he was a friend from your banking days in Denver. He said you'd told him to stop by if he was in the area. Marshal told him how to find you."

"I don't have anyone from Denver who knows about me livin' here." His brow knit as he narrowed his eyes.

Just then Jake and Marty's three oldest boys came flying out the front door and disappeared in a flash around the house. That seemed to give Jake an idea. "There was the orphanage director. Maybe it was him bringin' more children to the ranch. You know he had the Barnetts take some older boys for local ranch help."

"He didn't appear to have anyone with him," Austin replied. "Said his name was Cuker. Randolph Cuker."

"I don't know any Cuker. What'd he look like?"

Austin could easily remember the man.

"He was tall, lean, and had brown hair and a beard, although both were graying. He was well dressed and probably somewhere in his fifties, as far as age goes."

"I don't know anyone like that," Jake said with a frown.

"That's mighty strange," William said, his voice edged with concern.

"Seems to me," Jake began, "there have been a lot of strange things happening around here. Marty felt certain someone was watching her hang clothes the other day. Said she felt it more than saw anything, but it made her uncomfortable just the same. And then there's that note Alice received."

"What note?" Austin asked.

"It was one congratulating her on the baby, but it wasn't signed, and given her past, that doesn't bode well."

Austin felt perplexed. "What past?"

Jake looked to Will and received a nod before continuing. "In Denver some men killed Alice's father over some forged gold certificates. That's how Alice got the scar on her face. They held a knife to her and cut her when her father wouldn't give them what they wanted. He tried to interfere and they pushed him away. He fell and hit his head and died almost instantly. Alice passed out. Some folks found her and hauled her off to the hospital. After she recovered, one of the men followed her around and tried to bully her into finding the missing certificates. Then he started threatening her and Marty. When it got to be really bad, Marty and Alice decided it was time to join me here in Texas."

"I've worked around counterfeiters before," Austin admitted, without thinking. "I worked in the Secret Service for the Treasury Department. Counterfeit and fraud were my areas of work."

"Then maybe you'll have some insight to offer us. If this stranger is someone from Alice's past who's come to seek those certificates, we may all need to lend a hand," Barnett said. "All I know for certain is the letter scared my daughter-in-law to such a state that she's scarcely slept or eaten since it came."

"I can well imagine," Austin said, remembering the way the man at the jail had seemed most eager to find the Wythes. "I'll keep an ear out. If I hear anything, I'll let you know. I've got friends back in Washington. I can let them know about the situation."

William nodded. "Maybe you should. If you want, you can come by tomorrow for breakfast, and I'll fill you in on more details. I'll let you know what we figure out tonight, too."

Austin agreed, but there was a heightened sense of concern that he'd not felt since working for the Secret Service. Counterfeiters could be quite ruthless, as those men in Denver had proven to Alice and her father. They would stop at nothing until they got what they wanted, and Austin had no plans to see these people hurt.

CHAPTER 10

With the harvest party only a week away, Jessica began to worry that she'd made a mistake in turning down the beaus who'd asked her to accompany them. She had hoped that perhaps Harrison Gable or Austin Todd might ask her, so she had refused the others. Now, with the festival nearly upon them, Jessica wasn't sure what to do. She supposed she could just attend with her parents. Or perhaps on her own.

She'd helped her mother can pumpkin all day. It was a tedious job, and it heated the house something awful. Mother had planned to do all of the cooking and canning outside, but then changed her mind. Now Jessica longed for cooler air. She was grateful the kitchen help had already cleaned out the insides of the pumpkins and had cut the edible parts from the thick orange skin. This shortened their work considerably. After that, it was easy enough to cook the pumpkin and jar it up. It was just far too hot.

"You certainly seem quiet today," Mother said, handing Jessica a cooled jar to label.

"I suppose I'm just thinking about things."

"Things?"

Jessica grimaced. She didn't want to admit her worry to Mother. "Just life, Mother. I'm just thinking about my life."

"And did you come to any conclusions?"

A loud knock sounded at the front of the house. "Who could that be?" Mother wore a puzzled look. "It never fails that when we get caught up in something like this, someone shows up to visit." She laughed and quickly washed up, dried her hands on a towel, and pulled off her apron. "I'll see who it is. You get the rest of these sealed jars off the stove. Let them cool before you try to label them."

Jessica nodded and lifted the heavy kettle off the stove. She'd barely made it to the wooden table before the weight and steam threatened her hold.

Her mother appeared at the door. "Jess, take off your apron and come. Mr. Gable is here."

Excitement flooded Jessica. She dabbed her forehead with a towel, then tossed her apron aside. Hurrying down the hall, she touched a hand to her hair, hoping she didn't look a fright. Everything felt in place, however, so she entered the front room with a smile.

Harrison Gable gave her a look that Jessica found almost invasive. He seemed to study her with great interest. "Miss Atherton, what a pleasure to see you again." Gable took hold of her hand and pressed a light kiss on the back.

Jessica trembled and pulled her hand away more quickly than she'd intended. "It's nice to see you again." Why did this man affect her so?

"Since it is Saturday, I thought I might have better luck seeing some of the local ranchers in the area. Your father suggested Saturday afternoon and evening might be best."

"I'm sure he's right," Mother said before Jessica could respond. "Most will be at home getting ready for the Sabbath. Tyler is out in the barn. I'll go ask him to join us."

"Thank you, Mrs. Atherton," Harrison said with a slight bow.

Once Jessica's mother left the room, Harrison moved closer. "I was hoping I might see you today. And here you are."

Jessica worried about her appearance and felt an explanation was in order. "I've been helping my mother to can pumpkin. I'm afraid I didn't have time to arrange myself."

"You look lovely." His gaze swept over her again. "Quite lovely."

"Thank you." She couldn't help but feel the intensity of his compliment.

For a moment neither said a word. When Jessica heard voices coming from the kitchen, she knew her time alone with Harrison was over.

Father bounded into the room with his hand extended. "Good to see you again, Harrison. I hope you'll stay till supper."

"I can't. I need to speak with some of the ranchers who border your property and Mr. Barnett on the north. I know there's just a couple, but it is important I get their signatures."

"Of course. That would be the Harper and Watson places. Let me get my coat, and I'll go with you."

"Thank you. I'd be much obliged." Tyler started to go, but Gable cleared his throat. "I wondered, too, if I might ask permission to escort your daughter to the upcoming harvest party."

Tyler smiled. "Well, it's good with me if Jessica gives her approval. I can have Osage bring her to town, and the two of you can meet up there."

Everyone looked to Jessica. Without hesitation she said, "Of course. I would like that very much."

Gable grinned. "Then this has been a most productive day. Shall we meet around ten that morning? I understand there is to be a bountiful noon meal and thought we might partake of that, not to mention the other activities."

"Of course. There's a dance later in the evening," Jessica offered.

"We plan to attend, as well," Mother said. "So it's no trouble for us to stick around for the dance. That way Osage won't have to wait in town until late."

Harrison looked to Mother. "Thank you, ma'am. That is quite considerate. I'd very much enjoy sharing a dance or two with Miss Atherton."

Jessica enjoyed his charm. There was something engaging about the man. She tried not to show her delight in his asking her to the party, for she didn't want to appear too eager, and she certainly didn't want him to know how he made her feel. That might truly cause embarrassment, since she didn't really know him.

"Well, if you're ready," Tyler said, "we might as well head out."

"Don't you want to eat something first?"

Mother asked. "You might be gone a good while."

"No. I'll just see Harrison to the Harpers' and eat when I get back. I'm sure Hank Harper will show him how to get to the Watsons'. They'll probably offer you a room for the night," he said, looking to Harrison.

"Folks around here are certainly accommodating," Gable commented.

"Not like folks in the city, eh?" Father questioned.

"Indeed, they are nothing like the guarded and cautious folks who cross your path there. However, they guard themselves with good reason. Life in the larger cities can be quite difficult and even dangerous."

"Well, I wouldn't want it," Father said. He leaned over and kissed Mother. "I'll be back soon."

"We'll wait dinner for you, sweetheart," Mother said, embracing Jessica's father.

Jessica watched her father gave Mother another quick kiss, then he slapped Harrison's back and guided him to the door.

"That was quite exciting, don't you think?" Mother asked.

Smiling, Jessica didn't even try to feign confusion at her question. "I'm so happy I could fly."

"Don't do that," Mother chided playfully.

"Flying is for birds and angels — not for people."

"I was afraid he might not ask."

"You two make a beautiful couple," Mother replied, leading the way back to the kitchen. "I can see your being attracted to him. He has a profession and plans for the future that would suit you well."

Jessica took up her apron but didn't put it on. Mother's words troubled her. "What do you mean?"

Mother was already donning her apron. "Well, it seems to me that Mr. Gable already does well for himself. He's been impeccably dressed each time I've seen him. He carries himself as a man of quality, and I believe he could provide the things in life that you love."

"Why does everyone think I'm interested only in *things*?" Jessica said, throwing down the apron. "I'm tired of people looking at me that way. I might have been spoiled and useless in the past, but I'm trying to change."

"No one said you were useless," Mother countered. "But you've always preferred nice things and expensive clothes. You've often said how much you enjoyed traveling with your grandparents and how much you love city life. It seems to me that Harrison

Gable shares your interests."

Jessica knew her mother was right, but she still felt insulted. "Those aren't the only things that are important to me. I would never marry a man just because he had money. I would only marry if I loved him."

"I'm glad to hear it," Mother replied. "I know it was difficult for you to adjust after Robert married Alice. I have been more than a little worried that you would take up the first marriage proposal offered."

"I've been asked to marry several times," Jessica said, hands on hips. "You should give me more credit than that. I'm not a silly simpering girl. I know what's valuable in life, and I'm sick and tired of people suggesting otherwise!"

Harrison Gable enjoyed the ride north. There was still plenty of light, and Atherton had chosen to cut across his land rather than go all the way back to the road. It would shorten their trip by at least fifteen or twenty minutes, the older man had told him.

"I don't suppose you ride a lot back in Dallas," Atherton began. "Hope you won't be too saddle sore after all these visits."

"Surprisingly enough, I do ride quite often. I love it. I have, ever since I was a small boy."

"Me too," the older man admitted. "There's something peaceful about being out here in the fields — cattle grazin', clear skies, sun slowly settin'. If not for the fences, it might seem like old times."

Harrison glanced at the man. "You don't approve of fencing?"

Atherton shook his head and didn't look Harrison's way. "I can't say I'm very fond of it. I know it's helped cut down on damage done to some of the farms. I even understand it comes with the settlin' of a place. I just don't happen to like it.

"I suppose that might sound strange to you." He paused for a moment and seemed to be lost in thought as he studied the landscape. "When everything was open, it was like the entire state was yours to be had. You could ride from one area to another and never worry much about somebody takin' offense at you for crossin' their land. Seems like the fences have popped into place almost overnight. Feels kind of like a noose being tightened."

"But fencing helps in keeping your herds together," Harrison offered.

"Yup. I can agree with that. It's not nearly so difficult to round them up, and you don't have nearly the trouble with strays. In the past Will and I have run our cattle together with the Watsons' and Harpers'. And the Wythes', too, of course. Now with the town being platted, the Watsons and Harpers are putting in fence, and Will and I have set ours in place, as well. It's the end of an era, to be sure."

As they approached the northwest edge of Atherton's property, Harrison spied a gate leading out of the pasture and onto the road. Tyler managed the gate, never leaving the back of his mount. Harrison could see this was second nature to the man. Once they were on the road, he couldn't help but regard Tyler Atherton.

"You have the bearing of a man who's worked hard and accomplished much," he told Atherton. "Have you always lived here?"

"Pretty much. There were times when I had to be away. Before the railroad came to Cedar Springs, we had to drive the cattle north to Kansas each year. Then I was gone quite a time during the war."

"Were you in many battles?" Gable asked.

Atherton considered the question for a moment. "Enough to make me know I never wanna see another war."

Harrison nodded. "That's exactly what my father said. I was born during the conflict, and my mother was terrified we would be killed in the midst of it."

"A lot of innocent folk died. Those were sad times."

"Did you have to fight the Indians out here, or was the area already civilized?"

Atherton frowned at this. Obviously this wasn't a pleasant topic. He was silent so long, in fact, that Harrison feared he'd offended his host. Harrison didn't know what to say, so he said nothing at all.

Soon Atherton picked up the conversation again. "There were always Indians around when I was young. They would raid and threaten death. My people would rally and fight back. Eventually the Comanche managed to get the upper hand. They killed my father and several of his men. It wasn't easy to have much grace for them after that."

"I can imagine. If they'd killed my father, I'd feel the same way."

Atherton gave a heavy sigh. "It didn't serve me well to bear a grudge. I learned that revenge couldn't satisfy the void. I had to forgive and move on. I knew it was what God would have me do."

Harrison wasn't sure how to respond. It was clear the man didn't enjoy the subject. Who could blame him? Still, with his years of training to understand people by their actions and words, Harrison was certain there truly was a peace about Mr. Atherton.

"Looks like Austin Todd is headin' our way."

Gable looked down the road to see the same rain-drenched cowboy he'd seen sitting beside Jessica Atherton in church. Only this time he was dry.

"Afternoon, Austin," Mr. Atherton called out as they came together.

"Near to evening," Todd replied.

"Do you know Mr. Harrison Gable?" the older man asked.

"Only by reputation." He gave a nod and smiled at Harrison. "Mr. Barnett speaks highly of you."

"I'm glad to hear it. I have enjoyed doing business with both Mr. Barnett and Mr. Atherton."

Atherton chuckled. "He's only enjoyed doin' business with me because it got him a date to take Jessica to the harvest celebration next Saturday."

"That right? Well, I hope you have a good time."

Harrison wasn't sure, but Todd didn't sound any too sincere. Perhaps he'd better watch himself. This man might also be after the lady's affection.

"I intend to," Harrison said. "Thank you."

"I'm glad we ran into you, Austin. I have some things to discuss with you." Atherton looked to Harrison. "If you don't mind, I'll let you go on ahead by yourself. Just follow this trail north, and you'll come to the river, where there's a bridge that will bring you pert near to Harper's drive. Just cross the bridge, angle to the right, and you can't miss it."

"Thanks, Mr. Atherton. I'm obliged." He tipped his hat at the older man, then again toward Austin Todd. "It was a pleasure to meet you, Mr. Todd. I'll look forward to seeing you in the future."

But hopefully not sitting in church beside the woman I intend to marry.

CHAPTER 11

Jessica placed a china plate on the dining room table, then went to the silverware drawer. The day's work had left her feeling sluggish. She moved in slow, purposeful steps, as if each one needed to be thought out. Reaching the sideboard, she took up place settings for herself, Mother, and Father and put them around the table beside the plates.

"Jess, you'd better set another place. I see your father has brought Austin Todd back with him."

Her heart fluttered a little bit, and Jessica felt a burst of energy. She rushed to the mirror that graced the dining room wall above the sideboard and frowned. She looked so worn — tired, really. There were dark circles under her eyes, and her head was starting to hurt. She glanced down at her dress. It bore spots of pumpkin and flour.

Maybe I should go change my clothes. I

don't want to appear shabby and unkempt when Austin sees me.

Immediately, Jessica stopped fussing and frowned. *Why am I so concerned about my appearance?* It was just one more reminder of her self-centered ways. It was painful to remember the many times when looking beautiful to impress someone had been her only thought. The guilt made her feel ill.

As penance, Jessica decided to remain as she was. She had spent most of her life primping and making certain that she wore the perfect outfit. It needed to stop. It was one thing to be concerned with looking presentable and dressing appropriately for the occasion, and quite another to do so for the sake of impressing others or, worse yet, making others feel inferior.

She lifted her chin and reached down to the sideboard to take up more silver and china. By the time her father entered the house with Austin, food graced the table and everything was ready.

Austin offered Jessica a smile when he and Father entered the dining room. "Your pa thought I needed a meal," he said and shrugged. "Who was I to turn down good food?"

"How do you know it's good?" Jessica teased.

Her father laughed and spoke before Austin could recover from his surprise. "Anything your mother makes turns out perfect. The fact that she still likes to have a hand in the kitchen, though she has hired help, always amazes me." He looked to Austin. "When I first met Mrs. Atherton, she was not as accomplished as she is now. She was rather spoiled and selective in what she would and wouldn't do. Her sister took her in hand, however, and taught her how to cook and clean."

"I can do more than that," Mother announced, bringing in the bread plate. She placed it on the table to reveal pumpkin bread.

"That she can." Father took hold of Mother and kissed her soundly. He held her for a few moments after the kiss ended. They were still very much in love. Jessica watched as her father helped Mother into her chair, then took his own place. He was a true gentleman.

To her surprise, Austin pulled Jessica's chair out for her and waited to seat her before taking his place. Jessica thanked him, barely able to say another word. Father offered a prayer and then began to help himself to the fried ham steaks. The other dishes were passed, and the men seemed in particular awe of the pumpkin bread.

"I don't think I've ever had anything like this before," Austin commented, taking another piece only after Jessica's father did. He slathered it with freshly churned butter and bit into it with a look of pleasure on his face.

Jessica found she wasn't all that hungry. She tried to keep up with the conversation, but she felt so tired and her head throbbed. They had worked hard that day, canning pumpkin and pressing clothes for Sunday. Then too, it had been very hot. Apparently it had taken more of a toll than Jessica realized. She poked at her food and hoped no one would see that she wasn't actually eating.

Father and Austin discussed the new town and their ideas for bringing in businesses. Even Mother added her thoughts regarding the church and school. She mentioned that Jake Wythe had a friend named Rob Vandermark who was a pastor looking for a church. His wife was an accomplished teacher. Mother thought they should write to him right away. If they could secure a schoolteacher and a preacher in one letter, they would be well ahead of the game. Father agreed and promised to speak with Jake.

"Are you planning to attend the party on Saturday?" Mother asked, perking Jessica's attention.

"I doubt it. When folks set to partying, that's usually the time rustlers get busy. I'll just keep an eye out, and you folks can have yourselves a nice time," Austin replied.

"I think Will wants you to be there. He's going to say a few words about the new town and the rail line, and he wants to introduce you as the new law for the town. I wouldn't be surprised, too, if folks will want to talk to you about the rustling."

"Well," Austin said thoughtfully, "I could probably come by for a little while and then head out to look for rustlers."

Mother offered him more coffee as he downed the first cup. He gave her a quick nod and waited while she poured it from a silver pot. Jessica felt as if her body were leaden. She was clearly coming down with something. A wave of dizziness caused her to drop her fork and take hold of the table. Mother immediately noticed her condition.

"Jess? Don't you feel well?" Mother reached out to touch her head. "You have a fever." She got to her feet and helped Jessica to hers. "If you'll excuse us, I'm going to put Jessica to bed. I think she's managed to catch something."

Austin was on his feet. "Is there anything I can do to help? I could carry her."

Jessica closed her eyes even as Mother assured him she could manage. Feeling as she did, Jessica almost wished her mother would have let him assist. She wasn't at all sure she could make it to her bedroom upstairs.

"I'm so sorry, Mother. I haven't felt like myself all day. I thought I was just tired."

"Well, it's clear that you've taken sick. I'm not at all sure what the problem might be, but we'll get you to bed and then see what you feel like tomorrow."

Letting her mother take charge, Jessica was relieved when Mother finally managed to get her upstairs and settled on the bed.

"Let me undo the buttons on your dress," Mother said, reaching out to Jessica's collar. She unfastened the bodice and pushed it down to the waist. Careful to keep Jessica from collapsing, Mother managed to pull her to her feet so the gown and petticoat could slip to the floor.

Jessica's head throbbed all the more, and she longed for the comfort of her bed. She turned to climb in, but Mother stopped her again. "Let me unlace your corset and get that off, as well. You can sleep in your shift, if you'd like, but you'd probably feel better in a nightgown." She made quick work of the corset and eased Jessica onto the bed.

"Thank you," Jessica whispered. "I'm sorry to be so much trouble."

"You aren't trouble. You're my daughter and I want to see you through this. Now stay here," she said, pulling the covers over Jessica's body. "I'll be right back with some medicine."

Jessica wasn't about to go anywhere. She could scarcely settle the covers comfortably around her. Every muscle, every fiber of her being longed to be still. She thought of Austin downstairs. So close but so distant. He was a strange man — mysterious, quiet. She couldn't help but wonder at his past. Maybe Father could tell her more.

Mother returned and helped Jessica sit up a bit to take a spoonful of a nasty tasting liquid. "This will help you sleep."

"I don't think that will be a problem," Jessica replied.

"It will help with the fever, as well." Mother eased her back onto the mattress, and Jessica closed her eyes. "I'll check on you in a little while."

The sickness didn't lose its grip on Jessica until sometime in the night on Wednesday of the following week. Her fever finally broke after her mother had tried both to sweat and freeze it out of Jessica. The illness left Jessica almost more tired than she'd felt when this had all started. She got her first restful sleep in the wee hours of the morning and slept through until late Thursday afternoon. When she awoke she found Mother by her side.

"Are you feeling better?" Mother asked. She touched Jessica's head ever so gently. "Your fever is gone. You should start to feel much better."

"What was wrong with me?" Jessica asked, her voice weak and throat dry.

"The grippe or ague I suppose — I'm really not completely certain. You were delirious for a time and shivering, so I thought for sure it was ague. But then you started heaving, and I thought perhaps it was grippe. Either way, your fever was high and I feared it might cause harm to your brain."

Jessica sighed and closed her eyes. "May I have some water?"

"Of course. I have a glass right here. I've been trying to keep liquids down you since you fell ill."

Taking Jessica in her arms, Mother helped her to sit up long enough to take a drink. Jessica shook her head as Mother helped her to lie back. "I don't remember hardly anything after you helped me to bed."

"I'm not surprised." Mother got to her feet. "You rest and I'll fix some chicken broth for you."

The rest of the day Jessica focused on taking in fluids as her mother insisted. By night she felt a little better, and by Friday morning Jessica was able to sit up and not feel as though she might break in half.

She'd had a long time to ponder her life while recovering. Images of the past came to life to remind Jessica that she had often handled people harshly, without care for their feelings. She didn't like the girl she'd been, yet back then Jessica had seen nothing wrong in her actions. When her mother came in to check on her, Jessica posed a question.

"Mother, do you think I'm selfish?"

Her mother looked at her as if she'd posed a difficult mathematics problem. "What is this all about?" Mother asked.

Jessica pressed the question again. "Do you think I'm selfish?" Jessica looked at her hands and smoothed the covers. She was almost afraid to meet her mother's gaze. "Have I always been self-centered and more concerned about myself than others?"

"I wouldn't exactly say that. You've had your moments, but everyone does."

"But people think me to be shallow. You and Father even think me that way."

Mother actually laughed at this. She came and sat down beside Jessica and took hold of her fidgeting hands. "Hardly that. You are anything but shallow. In fact, you are by far and away my most complex child."

"How so? Was I that difficult?"

"You misunderstand me. You are rather like an onion with many, many layers. Each time one layer is pulled away, another appears. I've seen layers of your heart and mind stripped away over the years, but always there's another layer, and no one has ever yet reached the core of who you really are."

"And how does that happen?" Jessica felt perplexed by her mother's statement. "Is there something I can do?"

Mother shook her head. "Not in total. It's partly a matter of what other people think, but mostly it's how you stand in the eyes of God."

"I didn't used to care what people thought," Jessica said. "At least I told myself that. In truth, I really cared too much. I wanted to be the prettiest and the most fashionable girl. I wanted others to envy me — to wish they were me. I only cared about me," she confessed. "And now . . ."

"And now?" Mother asked in a gentle manner.

Jessica shook her head and looked across the room at the armoire that was filled with beautiful clothes. "I'm ashamed. I want to change, but I fear people will always believe me to be that same selfish girl. Even you and Papa tease me about caring for new gowns and other beautiful things. I overheard Papa once telling one of my beaus that the way to win my heart was with pretty doodads and plenty of attention, or something like that. First it made me angry, and then it broke my heart."

Mother tenderly stroked Jessica's hand. "Darling, you can change your ways, but people who've been impressed by them or fallen victim to them will need time to believe the change is real. You can start living your life in a way that will prove your heart has changed, and soon folks will come around. Take it to God and He will direct you."

Jessica bowed her head. "I'm afraid I've not concerned myself much with God. I doubt He'd even listen to me."

"Well, that seems to be the crux of your problem. Without God you are stuck making decisions on your own. And, Jessica, that's a very lonely place to be — troublesome, too. You've put God off for a long while. Why not try turning this concern over to Him. I think you'll be surprised by His answers."

"Maybe," Jessica admitted. After all, she hadn't yet tried that.

Mother smiled. "Where's your Bible?"

Jessica pointed to the chest of drawers. "In the top drawer."

Crossing the room, her mother found the Bible and brought it back to Jessica. "You might want to read this and pray. I find that reading God's Word and praying always brings me understanding." Mother turned. "I'm going to go prepare something for you to eat. Oh, I forgot to tell you. Your father ran into Mr. Gable and told him you were recovering from illness and wouldn't be able to attend the harvest party."

"But I might be strong enough by then," Jessica argued. She didn't want to miss getting to know Harrison Gable better.

"No. That's too soon. You are in no condition to get out of bed, much less take a long ride into town and participate in a large outdoor event. Now, try reading, and I'll bring you a little broth and a few crackers."

Disappointment settled upon her, and Jessica could only sigh for what might have been. *I hope this doesn't cause Harrison —*

Mr. Gable — to lose interest in me. After all, he might fear me to be a weak and sickly woman. But even as she thought this, her gaze fell on the Bible. The book reminded her that once again she'd been thinking only of herself.

"I hope you have some answers here for me, God, because I sure don't have any for myself."

CHAPTER 12

Cedar Springs overflowed with visitors for the harvest party. Crystal blue skies and cooler temperatures made the affair too appealing to refuse. The streets flowed to capacity, and everywhere vendors were hawking their wares and enticing the people to buy. Jugglers and fire breathers came all the way from Dallas to entertain and impress. Children ran up and down the closed-off Main Street with squeals of delight. They seemed to think it novel to be allowed in the roadway when they'd so often been cautioned against it.

Austin had always avoided these kinds of things, but Will Barnett and Tyler Atherton had insisted he be there. They wanted to talk to him about Terryton and his agreement to be marshal. Sometimes Austin wondered if he'd made the right decision. With the Rangers he could move around all over the state. Being Terryton's marshal would keep him in one place for some time to come.

"I see you made it," Barnett said, coming up as Austin tied off his horse.

"I did, but I'm still not sure I should be here. Every rustler around these parts is gonna know we're celebrating up here today. It will be the perfect time to strike."

"Relax. You don't have to stay for long. I'm gonna make an announcement here in just a couple of minutes. We'll go over to the platform and speak from there." Austin noticed the makeshift structure and nodded. He looked around for Tyler but didn't see him anywhere. "What about Mr. Atherton?"

"Couldn't make it," Barnett replied. "Jessica was still pretty weak from her sickness, so they decided to stay home."

"But Miss Atherton is feeling better, isn't she?"

"That's what I hear." Barnett's expression changed. "The mayor is signaling for us to join him. Come. Just follow my lead. You know what's expected of a marshal, and the people who don't already know you, need to."

Barnett led the way to the dais. They shook hands with the mayor and awaited Will's introduction.

"I'm glad to have this opportunity to tell you about our progress in creating a new town about twenty-eight miles to the northwest. I donated land for the creation of Terryton to honor my old friends, Ted and Marietta Terry, who settled a good part of this county. Please understand this is in no way a decision made lightly. And we certainly do not anticipate harm to Cedar Springs."

Austin saw more and more people press in to hear what Mr. Barnett had to say. It made him nervous to be the focus of attention, but Barnett didn't seem concerned.

"As most of you already know, this area will no doubt be incorporated into Dallas as the city grows. Terryton will still be accessible if our plans go well. The railroad has agreed to our request for a spur line to Terryton, primarily for shipping cattle and goods. The only stipulation was that we have some form of legal authority in place prior to the ground breaking. For that purpose, we have hired Austin Todd." He motioned Austin to step forward.

Feeling all eyes on him, Austin did as instructed and tried not to concern himself with the crowd. He was glad when William continued.

"Austin, as most of you know, is currently

a cattle inspector. He has extensive experience with law enforcement and, I believe, will be a real asset to our little town. Eventually, once the town is formed and running well, we will hold elections for this position. For any of you interested, I'd urge you to keep in touch. We will be looking for various businesses to join us, and I'd be happy to talk to anyone who would like to know more."

"What about the problems with rustling?" someone called from the crowd.

"Yeah," another man piped up. "I lost two dozen of my prime beeves."

William looked to Austin. The crowd did likewise. Austin felt the weight of their stares and fought back discomfort in order to answer the questions.

"The Rangers are well advised of the situation and have men staked in various areas. I myself plan to head out after this announcement. We believe we're close to capturing the men who've been particularly active recently. But that's all I can say regarding those responsible. I can talk to you individually if you have questions." He stepped back and swallowed the lump in his throat. Public speaking was something he did not enjoy at all.

Barnett had a few more comments to

make, and then the two men descended the platform to find many people had additional questions. Austin found himself separated from Barnett as men and women pressed around the two for answers.

"Ranger Todd," one of the men began, "you boys gonna hang 'em when you catch 'em?"

Austin shook his head. "No. We'll see them brought to trial and let the courts deal with them. The days of lynching are a thing of the past. We're civilized now, and we'll abstain from taking the law into our own hands."

"Well, those rustlers sure don't care about the law," another man claimed.

"True enough," Austin said, feeling as if the pressing crowd would soon trample him into the dirt. "But we honest citizens do. Upholding the law is important — otherwise we're no better than the thieves stealing our cattle."

"If they show up on my land and I catch up to 'em, I'm puttin' a bullet in 'em," a stocky man declared. There were murmurs of approval, but Austin waited until the crowd quieted down before finally speaking.

"You can certainly handle things for yourself — protect what's yours — and most likely you won't run afoul of the law.

However, I know what it is to kill, and it's not a pleasant thing to live with. I doubt most of you have had to kill a man and watch the life go out of him." Austin looked around at the disgruntled men. "It's easy enough to talk about putting an end to a man's life and quite another thing to actually do it." This quieted any further comments about killing. It seemed his words had sobered even the angriest of men.

There was another round of rapid-fire questions, and Austin began to regret ever having agreed to come. Moments later, a rescuing angel came to his side.

"I'm sorry, but Austin is needed elsewhere," Marty Wythe declared. "You can speak with him later." She didn't wait for comment but pulled Austin by the sleeve, forcing him to follow.

Once they were well away from the crowd, Marty dropped her hold. "You looked like you were a drowning man going down for the third time."

"I felt like one," he admitted. "Folks definitely get themselves riled up over these things."

She shrugged. "Well, beef is their livelihood. Take that away, and we'll have another financial crisis on our hands."

"I'm sure that's true." He glanced around.

"You here with your family?"

"Of course. Robert and Alice are showing off their baby over there." She pointed and Austin easily spotted the couple. "And Jake is over there, where they're roasting pecans and handing out samples. The older boys wanted to watch and, of course, eat." She smiled.

"And what about the two little ones?" he asked to be polite.

"With Jake. The baby was sleeping, and Johanna was her busy self. I did promise Jake I wouldn't be gone for long."

Austin started to say something, but the stunned look on Marty's face stopped him. He turned to follow her gaze and found the same tall bearded stranger he'd met in the jail. "Mr. Cuker." He gave the man a nod.

"His name isn't Cuker," Marty declared. "It's Paul Morgan. He once employed my husband." She shook her head. "I knew there was something familiar about you when I saw you from afar a while back. Why are you trying to conceal your identity with the heavy beard and change of name?"

Morgan smiled. "The years have been good to you, Mrs. Wythe. You are even more beautiful than you were when you first married our Jacob."

Her eyes narrowed. "*Our* Jacob?"

He chuckled and looked to Austin. "I don't believe I know you."

"Austin Todd, cattle inspector with the Texas Rangers," Austin replied, trying to reassess the man. Usually if a man hid from his name, he was up to no good.

"Glad to meet you. Always appreciate a good lawman." He turned to Marty. "I suppose you deserve to know why I'm here."

"I'd definitely like to know how you even found us."

"It wasn't the easiest thing in the world, but I had my ways," he said, grinning as if he'd really managed something good.

Austin could see that Marty didn't think it was good. Her brows were knit and her lips formed a frown. Usually nothing disturbed this strong woman overmuch. He couldn't help wondering what was wrong.

"You said you were good friends with the Wythes." Austin eyed the man, determined to get some answers. "How is it you really know them?"

"My dear sir, the Wythes are good friends," Morgan protested. "I gave Jacob his first banking job in Denver."

"You took it away from him, as well," Marty added.

Morgan looked at her with great sympathy. "Now, Mrs. Wythe . . . Marty . . . the financial troubles this country suffered robbed your husband of his job. However, I'm here to offer it back to him. It's taken a good two years, but I've managed to get back on my feet. That's why I'm here."

"To ask Jake to come back to Denver and work for you?" Marty gave a bitter laugh. "That will never happen. He hated banking then, and he hates it even more now. He's doing what he loves to do — ranching — and you can't say anything that will convince him to return to Denver."

"Still, I'd like to ask him about it myself."

Austin could see her apprehension. For the little time he'd known her, Austin had never seen her look so afraid. He couldn't help but wonder what her worry might be. Was this man a threat to her or to Jake? Austin gave the man another close look. He was well groomed and nicely dressed. He seemed friendly enough. Maybe Marty was just afraid her husband would agree to go back in this man's employ.

"I'll take you to Jake. He's with the children right now."

"I had heard you had a family. Adopted some boys, didn't you?" Morgan asked.

"Yes." Marty seemed unwilling to offer any more information. "Come along, Mr. Morgan. I don't wish you to have to wait for your answer."

Austin smiled to himself as Marty made her way through the crowd. She was a strong woman and could no doubt handle the matter on her own. Making his way back to his horse, Austin gave the scene one final look. Folks were enjoying themselves with the revelry. Celebrating the harvest was something everyone could get behind. Barnett had told him that next month they would begin slaughtering hogs and a few steers. Putting up food for the winter wasn't nearly so critical in the southern part of the country, but Barnett had maintained that his wife was a stickler for planning ahead. With that in mind, they had already ordered a large shipment of ice from Dallas in order to preserve the meat they didn't smoke.

Austin had to admit he admired these people. They were good, God-fearing folks who had a penchant for reaching out to those in need — like him. Heading for his horse, Austin almost wished he could stay and share their company a little longer. But deep in his mind a warning sounded that he was getting too close, caring too much. It was time to put some distance between him and the others.

As the band struck up a rousing rendition of "The Yellow Rose of Texas," Austin felt someone touch his shoulder.

"Hey there, Austin. Why don't you come join us?" Robert Barnett was all smiles. "Alice brought some mighty fine pies, and the town fathers roasted three of the biggest hogs I've ever seen."

His stomach rumbled at the thought of such a delicious meal. "I suppose I could force myself to stay a little longer," Austin said with a grin.

Robert laughed and slapped Austin's back. "That's the spirit. I knew you were a smart man."

Marty wasn't at all happy to see Paul Morgan. The man had all but left them to die back in Denver. He'd stripped away Jake's job and their home. How could he possibly think Jake would want to work for him now?

"I must say I'm surprised you would even attempt this," Marty told the older man. "After all, you deserted us in Denver."

"Not by choice, I assure you."

"Oh, well that makes it all better." Her sarcasm was not lost on him.

"Mrs. Wythe, you must believe me. We were all suffering. I had no choice but to close the bank. I lost a great deal, too."

Marty tried to rein in her anger. "I'm sure you did. I have to warn you, however, Jake

194

is back to doing what he loves. He's not going to return to banking. I'd stake my life on that." She spotted Jake just where she'd left him and the children. "He's over there." She made her way to Jake. "Darling, look who's come to see you."

Jake was holding an exhausted Johanna. The two-year-old was sleeping peacefully in his arms and looked rather angelic, Marty thought. Jake glanced up and frowned in disapproval at the sight of the man standing beside Marty.

"Mr. Morgan? I hardly recognized you." He gently placed Johanna on their ground blanket, where the baby was sleeping, and got to his feet. "I have to say this is a bit of a surprise."

"Yes, isn't it," Marty declared. "I asked him how he found us, but he wasn't forthcoming with an answer. Perhaps you'll manage to get more out of him."

Morgan appeared to ignore her comment. Instead, he extended his arm to Jacob. "I'd like for you to join me for a little while. I have some things to discuss with you."

Jake shrugged. "I guess that's all right." He turned back to Marty. "The boys are gettin' some pecans. They're supposed to come right back."

"You could have your discussion here,"

Marty said, looking to Morgan.

"Nonsense. I wouldn't dream of imposing on your day of fun," the man replied.

But you already have. You have imposed and made me most uncomfortable.

The two men left her standing there, wondering what they would discuss and why Morgan had invaded their peaceful lives. She didn't trust him, especially now that he'd lied about his name and had worked to hide his face from recognition. He'd not done anything to help them when the economy went bad, yet here he was thinking Jake would just give up his dream and return to banking. Or was that not really what he had in mind?

"Wasn't that Mr. Morgan, the man Jake used to work for in Denver?" Alice Barnett questioned, coming alongside Marty.

"Yes. I'm afraid so. He thinks he's going to talk Jake into coming to work for him again."

Alice touched her arm. "How did he even find us?" There was real fear in her eyes.

Marty didn't wish to worry Alice, but she felt as fearful as the younger woman looked. "I don't know. He said it wasn't easy, but that's all he told me. He clearly had no desire to waste his time with me."

Alice glanced over her shoulder in a

nervous manner. "But if he could find us, others could, too. We haven't exactly been hiding out, but I was hoping we were safe . . . from the past."

"Don't let your imagination get the best of you," Marty cautioned, hoping she sounded reassuring. She certainly didn't feel it. "The economy isn't doing so well that folks can afford to throw their money around. No doubt the men who hired Smith will be just as strapped for cash as many others. They wouldn't have been so frantic for the gold certificates if not."

"Yes, but that's what worries me — they were frantic. I'd feel better if I knew what Mr. Morgan had done to locate us."

"Even if we knew, Alice, we couldn't prevent others from using the same avenue." Marty frowned and shook her head. "No, we'll just need to be on our guard and keep an eye out for strangers. If Mr. Smith shows up, we're bound to see him before he sees us." At least she hoped it would be so.

Jessica smiled, feeling rather shy at the appearance of Harrison Gable in her bedroom. Mother had escorted him in only moments before. She had taken a seat in the corner in order that propriety might be observed and pretended to read. At least Jessica presumed it was pretense.

"I brought you these," Gable said, pulling a bouquet of roses from behind his back.

Jessica gasped at the sight of a dozen pink roses. "They're beautiful. Oh, Mother, look."

Her mother glanced up from the book. "They are lovely. If you give them to me," she said, getting to her feet, "I'll have Lupe put them in water."

Mother took the roses and headed for the hallway. Leaving the door open, she turned from the hallway. "I'll only be a moment."

Jessica knew it was her mother's way of letting them know there would be no time for anything untoward. This seemed to amuse Mr. Gable, who gave a low chuckle.

"She must think me the worst of rogues."

Jessica shook her head. "It's not that. She just doesn't want my reputation ruined. I've never had a man — who wasn't a relative — in my bedroom."

"Well, I'm honored to be the first." He pulled up the chair Mother had used during Jessica's worst hours of sickness and sat beside the bed. "I must say, you are looking quite lovely."

Jessica laughed. "You are a sweet-talker. I know how ghastly I look, so you needn't try to persuade me to think otherwise. This sickness took its toll."

"I'm glad to see that you've recovered, but you're wrong. You are far from ghastly in appearance. There are roses in your cheeks and a warm glow of joy in your eyes. Dare I believe it's because of my arrival?"

Her cheeks flushed hot. "I am happy for the company," she admitted. "It's been rather dull. Did you manage to attend the harvest party? I'm sure they're still having a wonderful time, so you might not want to remain here for long."

"I did indeed walk through the crowd of festive folk, but without you to accompany me, it wasn't nearly so pleasant. That's when I got the idea to leave and ride out here to see you. I had to assure myself that you were past the worst of the illness."

Jessica believed him to be one of the most striking men she'd ever known. His perfectly sized nose and thin, well-formed lips gave his face a dashing appearance. And those eyes — those dark, dark eyes — suggested power and capability and also passion.

Mother slipped back into the room and retook her chair. Jessica ignored her, but she knew that Harrison had noted her return.

"I appreciate your concern. I am feeling much better now."

"Perhaps we'll have a chance to try again," he replied, lowering his voice.

Jessica nodded. "I'd like that."

"I'll be tied up most of next week, but I'll do my best to call again on the Sunday after next, if that would be acceptable?"

Feeling overwhelmed with happiness, Jessica could only nod and smile. She didn't trust herself to speak. Gazing into Harrison's eyes, she found herself feeling rather consumed. He seemed to look right through her, almost as though he could read her thoughts and feelings.

"I see you've been reading the Good Book," he said, noting the Bible beside her.

"Yes," Jessica said and picked up the book. "It's afforded me a great deal of comfort."

"I can well imagine. I'm particularly fond of the Psalms. How about you?"

"I do love the Psalms, but of late I've been reading the Gospels — particularly John."

"I can't say that I've read that one lately. I'll have to give it a go when I can find the time." He glanced at his pocket watch. "Speaking of which, I must go. I have to catch a train this evening, and I still haven't packed."

"Are you going far?" she asked, trying not to sound overly interested.

He smiled, as if knowing her concern.

"Not at all. I'm going to be in Dallas filing paper work and holding meetings with the railroad and with bank officials most of this next week."

He took hold of her hand and rubbed his thumb over the back of her knuckles. Jessica shivered from the sensation. The feel of his warm fingers upon her skin left her almost breathless. Looking into his eyes, she could see his desire. It both frightened and excited her. Jessica wasn't at all sure which emotion was stronger.

"I . . . uh . . . I'll look forward to your return," she finally managed to say.

Harrison lowered his lips to the back of her hand, and again Jessica shivered from the rush of emotions. He kissed her hand and stood. Looking not to Jessica but to her mother, he said, "I believe Miss Atherton is chilled. She seems to be shivering." He looked back at Jessica and winked.

She could see the amusement in his expression as her mother came forward with a shawl. "Here, this will help," she said, wrapping it around Jessica's shoulders. But Jessica knew from the look on Harrison's face that they both understood that it wouldn't help at all.

He took his leave, and Mother escorted him downstairs while Jessica threw off the shawl and leaned back against her pillows feeling rather breathless. How was it that this man should affect her so strongly? He was certainly handsome, but then, so was Austin Todd, and she hadn't gone all weak-kneed and silly over him.

At the thought of his name, though, Jessica found herself forgetting Harrison Gable. What was it about Austin that fascinated her? He clearly wasn't interested in her. Maybe that was the attraction.

Maybe I see him as a challenge.

She pondered that idea for a moment. Perhaps it was only because the man came across as aloof and disinterested that Jessica found herself wanting to know more about him.

"He's certainly a fine young man," Mother said, breaking Jessica's thought. "It was particularly thoughtful that he would come all this way to check on your health."

Jessica put aside her contemplations of Austin Todd and returned to the subject of Harrison Gable. "He was very thoughtful. I have to say I was surprised to see him."

"I don't think it was such a surprise to me. He seems quite smitten," Mother said, smiling. "I think the two of you make a handsome couple."

"Mother, please," Jessica protested but not

too sincerely.

Mother laughed. "I'm not so old that I can't remember how it was to have young men interested in me. I can see that Mr. Gable has a strong interest in you."

"He doesn't plan to stay around here for long," Jessica reminded her. "Don't go marrying me off just yet."

"Your father told me of Mr. Gable's plans to one day work in Washington, D.C., but that doesn't worry me. There are trains between here and the capital." She looked at Jessica and shrugged. "I rather enjoy train travel, and I've heard that Washington is a wonderful city, with all the amenities you love."

"There you go again," Jessica chided. "I've not even had a proper outing with Mr. Gable, and already you have us married and living in Washington. Really, Mother, you are quite the hopeless romantic."

Her mother laughed and headed for the door. "I suppose a lifetime with your father has done that to me. Now, if you'll excuse me, I'll have Lupe bring up your flowers and also something to eat. I'm sure you're going to need your strength for the days to come. After all, you don't want to still be weak when Sunday after next rolls around."

CHAPTER 13

"We should tell Robert what's happened," Alice said, still looking quite worried.

"We should," Marty agreed. "It's important that the menfolk know about the possibility of others finding us. I know William will want to know. He doesn't take chances when it comes to the safety of his family."

Alice wrung her hands together. "I can't help but worry that Mr. Morgan might have been watched. Someone could have easily followed him here, and he'd be no wiser for it." Alice's face paled, and her tone revealed her fear.

Marty patted her arm. "Don't fret, at least not until we're sure there's something to fret about. I don't know exactly how he found us. He wouldn't say."

"I'm so afraid," Alice said in a hushed tone. "We aren't safe anymore."

"Nonsense. No one is going to try to hurt us here. We've family and friends aplenty, and Texans don't take kindly to anyone who threatens the well-being of their women-folk." Marty shook her head and stared off into the crowd where she'd last seen her husband. "I know Jake will refuse the offer, and then Morgan will have no choice but to return to Colorado alone."

"I hope you're right, but I still can't help being afraid." Alice moved her hand upward to touch the fading scar on her right cheek. "After all this time, it seems strange that Mr. Morgan would show up now. I want my family to be safe. I had so hoped it was over."

"You're borrowing trouble. As I said," Marty said, softening her tone, "Mr. Morgan didn't come here to harm you or your family. He wants Jake to return to Colorado. He no doubt is getting back on his feet and wants Jake's help in recreating his empire. But Jake won't go."

"I understand that," Alice admitted, "but you know there are plenty who would harm us. All they'd have to do is get wind of Mr. Morgan's plans to find us and follow him. I'm going to tell Robert. He should know there's a chance of trouble."

"I agree that he should know, but, Alice, please try not to worry. We'll be fine."

"Alice!" a feminine voice called out.

Turning in the direction of the cry, Marty found Alice's mother, stepfather, and brother making their way to join Alice. Mother and daughter embraced, and the earlier fears seemed to give way to the joyous reunion.

"Mother, I'm so glad to see you." The relief in Alice's voice was apparent.

"Well, we knew this would be quite the affair, and it seemed reasonable to ride the train over. Roy gets some free passes from time to time for his work with the railroad and freight." She threw her husband an admiring smile.

Marty thought the man seemed quite happy, and the previously widowed Ravinia Chesterfield James looked positively aglow. Even Simon seemed to fit right in. The couple hadn't been married all that long, but already it was clear that they were a family.

"And look at you," Alice said to her young brother. "I think you've grown ten inches since I last saw you."

"I am getting taller," Simon replied. "Pa says he'll have to put a brick on my head to slow me down."

They laughed at this, and Marty was happy to hear that Simon was calling Mr. James *Pa*. The boy needed a father in his life, for his own had never been there for him.

"Pa, can we go watch the bronc riders?" Simon asked, quickly forgetting about his sister.

"Sure, son. We'll go in a minute. Just be patient." Simon clearly looked disappointed but said nothing.

Alice's mother looked to Marty. "I understand from Alice that you, too, have a new baby."

"Yes. John Jacob is just a little older than your grandson."

"John Jacob sounds like a fine name," Roy James interjected. "A strong name. That's always good for a boy."

Marty nodded. "We named him after my father and Jake . . . well, really after Jake's grandfather. The baby's sleeping just there on the blanket with his older sister."

Ravinia stepped aside to gaze upon the baby. "He's beautiful and so is she. What a joy they must be."

Marty laughed. "Johanna looks angelic when she sleeps, but when she's awake she is like a Texas twister, wreaking havoc wherever it sets down."

They all chuckled at this, causing Johanna to stir slightly. Marty couldn't imagine why their laughter would awaken the child when all the noise of the crowd hadn't. Perhaps she worried subconsciously that someone was having fun without her.

"And your older boys? The ones you adopted?" Ravinia asked.

"They are doing well. They're just over at the pecan vendor's stand. Jake sent them there with a little spending money. I'm sure they'll return stuffed to the brim with nuts."

"They could be interested in far worse things," Alice's mother said with a smile.

Johanna seemed to settle back to sleep, so Marty motioned them away from the blanket.

"It's so good to see you. Will you be staying in town?"

"No. We plan to take the early evening train back to Dallas. Roy is teaching Sunday school tomorrow."

Marty nodded. "Well, I know you're anxious to meet that new grandbaby of yours, so don't let me keep you. He's quite a handsome boy."

"Yes!" Ravinia said enthusiastically. "I can hardly wait to hold my grandson."

"That's all she's talked about since the babe was born," Roy declared. "I figured we had to get up here if I was gonna have any rest at all."

"It seemed that everything conspired

against me to get here. If it wasn't one problem, it was another. I'm still bound and determined to come stay for a few weeks. Maybe next summer."

"You will be welcome to stay with us as long as you'd like," Alice told her.

Marty added, "And if the Barnetts run out of room, you can come stay with us. Our household is a sight noisier, but you'd be welcome just the same."

"See there, Ravinia." Roy gave her a gentle elbow to the ribs. "I told you they would be happy to have you and Simon."

"Well, I do want to make certain I spend plenty of time getting to know my grandson," she said in a serious tone. "A few years back I never thought this day would come, and now that it has, I want to enjoy it to the fullest. Now, where's my grandson?"

Alice laughed. "Robert is watching over him just now, but I'm sure he will be happy to see you three. We were just talking of making a trip to Dallas so you could meet little Wills."

After they'd gone, Marty gazed around the crowd. Here and there she recognized old friends, but there was no sign of Jake or of Mr. Morgan. She was beginning to worry about what might have taken place during their meeting. It surely wouldn't take that long to hear Morgan's proposal and refuse it. She saw her boys returning just then and momentarily forgot about anything being amiss.

"Look, Mama, we got roasted pecans," ten-year-old Wyatt announced. His brothers — Sam, nine, and Ben, seven — followed close behind.

"These have sugar and cinnamon baked on 'em," Ben announced, holding up a small spiraled cone of newspaper. Inside were a handful of the sweet nuts. "Try 'em, Mama."

Marty smiled at the threesome and sampled their treats. "They are delicious."

"I think we should plant some pecan trees," Wyatt said. "Then we could have our own all the time."

"Nut trees can be a lot of hard work. When they bear, you have to pick up the nuts from the ground, then dry them, and sometimes even husk them before you can get to the shell. Remember the black walnut tree at Auntie Laura's house?"

The boys nodded. "But that was fun," Sam said. "I like stompin' on the green balls and seeing the black balls with the nuts come out."

"And it made our hands black," Ben added, as though that were a particularly good point.

"Yes, so while I agree that nuts are delicious, we might be better off to focus on raising cattle."

"Papa's gonna teach me to rope a steer," Ben told her. "He said we could do it when we get home."

"Well, roping takes a lot of practice, but I'm sure you'll master it quickly." Marty smiled at the boy. Johanna began to stir and then sat up, rubbing sleep from her eyes. The baby slept on even as Marty lifted him and put him in the perambulator. "Boys, fold up our blanket here and bring it along. We need to find your father."

Johanna was all smiles as Marty hoisted the girl onto her hip. "Just look at you, sleepyhead. Your hair is all mussed."

The little girl laughed and patted Marty's cheeks. "Mama go now."

"Yes, we're gonna go find Papa."

Marty turned to Wyatt and Sam, who had completed folding the blanket. "Just tuck it into that pack Papa affixed to the back of the baby buggy. Wyatt, will you please push the carriage for me? Sam can carry your pecans."

"So long as he doesn't eat 'em all," Wyatt said, handing his cone over.

"I won't eat 'em all," Sam assured him.

211

"Just a few."

"You got your own," Wyatt said, taking hold of the buggy's handle.

"Boys," Marty interjected, "no fighting."

"Yes, ma'am," Sam and Wyatt said in unison.

Marty didn't go far before running into Alice and her family once again. "I wonder if the children could stay here with you and your mother for a moment. I need to go see what's happened to Jake."

"Of course they can," Alice said. She looked to her mother. "You don't mind, do you?"

"Of course not," Ravinia James replied.

Alice frowned. "But maybe you shouldn't be the one to go. We can send Robert. Why don't you wait until he and Roy get back? They've just gone to fetch us some drinks."

"I don't want Robert to have to leave his family for this." Marty looked back in the direction Mr. Morgan and Jake had gone. Just then the baby began to fuss. No doubt he was hungry.

"Well, there's Austin. Why don't you ask him to go? Then you can tend to John Jacob, and I'll keep an eye on Johanna. The boys will be just fine." Alice smiled. "They are good boys, and look, they're already playing with Simon. It's been a long time since they've seen each other, so they'll keep occupied telling one another their adventures."

The boys were caught up in a game of marbles over to one side, where the dirt was level. They were carrying on a lively conversation as they knelt in the dust to eye their next move. *Oh, to be that innocent of trouble,* Marty thought.

She gave a sigh and made up her mind. It would be better for a man to go in search of Jake. Then, if there was to be any trouble, Jake wouldn't be distracted with worries about his wife. "I suppose I could ask Austin. He would obviously be the better one to intercede if something has gone wrong."

Alice waved Austin over. Marty could see that he was preparing to leave and hated to ask him for this favor if he planned to head out right away.

"Afternoon, ladies. I was just heading out to check some of the area ranches. I don't want the rustlers taking advantage of this gathering."

"That's a good idea," Marty said. "But before you leave, could you help me with something?"

He looked at her with a question-raising brow. "And what would that be?"

Marty hurriedly explained, then said, "They went in the direction of the train yard, but I can't be sure where they are now. I'm just worried that Mr. Morgan will try to bully Jake into something."

"I can't imagine your husband letting anyone bully him into anything, but if it makes you feel better, Mrs. Wythe, I'd be happy to help."

"Thank you. It would mean a lot to me."

"Then it means a lot to me, too. I'll go find him and tell him you're in need of his company."

Marty watched Austin disappear into the crowd. The band struck up a Sousa march just then. It almost seemed as if they were heralding Austin's search. Marty shivered for no reason. She knew she was being silly. There was no reason to worry about Morgan and the meeting. Jake was indeed as strong a man as Austin had implied. He would never let Morgan have the upper hand.

"Look, Marty," Alice said, holding up a large packet of letters tied together with a string. "Mother brought these. They were the final business correspondences of my father. They were in the box that was shipped to her from Colorado."

Looking at the letters, Marty couldn't help but wonder if they might provide any better understanding of what had gone on in the past. She knew Alice was still trying to fit the pieces together. Maybe the letters were the final element needed.

"Have you read them?" she asked, looking first to Ravinia and then to Alice. Both women shook their heads.

"I never saw a need, since they were marked as business correspondence," Ravinia answered. "I thought to throw them away and then decided I'd let Alice be the one to either keep them or discard them."

"Oh, I want to read them," Alice declared, adding, "as soon as we get home." She tucked the large stack of letters into her picnic basket. "Oh good, here come Robert and Roy."

Marty said nothing more, but she couldn't help wondering what the letters contained. She hoped Alice would be quick to let her know the contents. Maybe the letters would explain everything that had happened in Colorado.

Austin Todd waited until the older bearded man he'd known as Cuker departed. He could see Jake sitting on the edge of a stone bench. The look on his face suggested something bad had taken place during his encounter with Morgan.

"Mind if I join you?" Austin asked.

Jake shook his head. "I don't at all. In fact, I'm glad it's you."

"Why's that?"

"I want your advice on something, but first I need to explain my past to you."

Austin leaned back against some fencing. "Sure. What do you need me to know?"

"Well, you know Marty and I lived in Denver for a time. I worked at the bank for Paul Morgan. He was good to us — always giving me gifts. He arranged a house for me since I was marrying and gave me a really great deal on the mortgage and interest. He filled it with fine things and told me the contents of the house were his wedding gifts to me and Marty."

Jake fell silent for a moment, but Austin could see he had more to say. "Morgan advanced me in the bank very fast. I was branch manager in no time at all. I replaced Alice's father after he was killed couriering bank papers. That's when Alice was cut up."

"I remember you telling me about it, but why are you bringing that up now?"

Jake looked most uncomfortable. "A man named Smith was constantly following her after she healed from the attack and was released from the hospital. He pestered her at every chance and demanded she find those papers. She and Marty went to search for them but found nothing. They even went back to the house were Alice and her father had lived. A new tenant living there told Alice that the only things left in the house were her father's personal effects and correspondence. She had mailed everything to Alice's mother. Now keep in mind that Alice thought her mother was dead, because her father had told her so. It was quite a shock for her."

"I can imagine." Austin shook his head. "So this is far more complicated than you told me before."

"It is, and I'm sorry to have to fill you in on everything at once, but this entire matter has just taken a new turn."

"And that's why you wanted to speak to me?"

"Yes. Morgan is determined that he needs to find those certificates before his adversary does. He wants me to come back to Colorado and help him, since I worked with many of the banking customers and employees. He's quite adamant that I assist him."

"And if you don't?"

"There will be problems."

"And that's why you wanted to tell me all of this. Are you thinking I might have answers?"

"I'm hoping you'll have advice for me," Jake said with a heavy sigh.

"Advice on what exactly?"

Jake looked up with a forlorn expression. "On how to stay out of jail."

CHAPTER 14

Feeling nearly recovered from her bout of sickness, Jessica sat reading by the fireplace. The day was warm enough that a fire wasn't needed, but this chair was Jessica's favorite. Upholstered in a soft mauve color, the fan-backed chair was far and away the most comfortable. With an added ottoman, Jessica felt like a queen on her throne. Of course, she never told anyone that and would now have been quite embarrassed if she had. She'd given a lot of thought to how she might go about changing the way people saw her. Jessica wanted desperately to have people love her and respect her just as they did Mrs. Barnett or even Mother, and taking on queenly airs wasn't the way to accomplish that.

She was looking at the words of Matthew chapter five and pondering the meaning of the Sermon on the Mount when her mother ushered visitors into the front room.

"Look who I ran into, Jessica, as I was coming back from the springhouse."

It was Marty Wythe and her sister Hannah.

"Miss Hannah . . . Marty," Jessica greeted with a nod.

"How are you feeling, Jessica?" Hannah Barnett asked.

Jessica smiled. "Much better, thank you." She could see that the ladies clearly had something on their minds. "If you need, I can retire to my bedroom."

Hannah shook her head. "No. You can be of help in this matter. We are putting together a group of women to pray."

Jessica grimaced. For all that she had been doing to try to know God better, she wasn't at all sure her prayers would avail much. But already Hannah Barnett was looking to Mother.

"We have a problem, a family problem, and we need the Lord's counsel and protection."

"Why don't you sit down and tell me what's happened," Mother more insisted than questioned.

The two women took a seat on the sofa and began to share the story, first one explaining and then the other.

"We can't help but think that Mr. Morgan

means to see Jake put in jail unless he goes to Colorado and helps him," Hannah told them.

"But how can he possibly do such a thing?" Mother asked. "Surely no one would believe that Jake embezzled anything."

Marty spoke up. "Mr. Morgan gave us everything and made us feel that it was a perfectly normal procedure for him to follow with his employees. We had no way of knowing that the money, gifts, and even the lower interest rate on our home were part of his scheme to control Jake. Of course, Mr. Morgan had no idea the financial crash would come and close down many of the banks."

"But Jake no doubt worked hard for the man," Mother countered.

"He did. He did all that he was instructed to do. But that doesn't seem to matter," Marty replied. "Jake said there's no way to prove that those things were gifts or that the extra money was given and not taken from the bank. Mr. Morgan told Jake that he has plenty of friends who will help him doctor the books and make it apparent that Jake stole from Mr. Morgan. So if Jake doesn't help him, he'll end up in jail for something he didn't do."

Jessica listened in fascinated silence. Such intrigue was not the everyday topic around these parts. The thought that someone innocent might be jailed was abhorrent to her. Just as it obviously was to the others.

"We will pray, and we'll get others to pray, as well," Mother offered. "I won't say who the family is or offer details. I'll simply say that a family I know needs prayer for a private request."

Mrs. Barnett nodded. "I'd appreciate that, Carissa. If we get folks praying, I'll feel better. The Lord has something in mind for all of this, but I surely don't know what it is. Alice spends most of the day in tears. She's been so upset since finding out about Mr. Morgan's threat that she's hardly had any milk to feed the baby. Marty has had to help a time or two."

"And Jake feels to blame," Marty explained, "even though he had nothing to do with the gold certificates."

Mother considered this a moment. "I'm sure he feels responsible, but we can clearly see he's not. He's not the type of man to do such a horrible thing."

"No, he's not," Marty agreed. "Jake was always meticulous in his dealings with Mr. Morgan and the bank. To have Morgan tell him now that he'll see him jailed for embezzlement unless Jake helps him . . . well . . . it's deeply wounded Jake."

"So you can see our need for immediacy where prayer is concerned," Mrs. Barnett added.

"I do," Mother replied. She looked to Jessica. "We both do."

Jessica nodded in agreement but had serious doubts as to how her prayers might help. She hadn't exactly been close to the Lord. Would He still listen to such a backslider?

Hannah and Marty got to their feet, and Mother escorted them out the front door while Jessica continued to ponder the situation. When her mother returned, Jessica was ready with her question.

"Mother, will God listen to me if I pray? I mean, I haven't been a good person. I didn't read my Bible for a long time, and frankly, I'm not sure I even knew what I was doing when I prayed for Jesus to forgive me and come into my heart."

Instead of Mother looking shocked, as Jessica had feared, she only smiled. "Jess, God listens to the earnest prayers of sinners seeking forgiveness. You've had a reckoning of the heart, so perhaps now would be a good time to offer up an earnest prayer."

Her mother's words stayed with Jessica

throughout the day. By the time afternoon rolled around, Jessica was aggravated in even thinking about it, and the confines of the room only made matters worse. She was relieved when Mother shooed her from the house and suggested she sit on the porch or take a walk to get some air.

The day was warm but not unbearable. Jessica had only just settled herself on the porch when a horse and rider came loping up the long drive. It was Austin Todd. Jessica felt her stomach flip-flop. It wasn't the same as how Harrison Gable made her feel, but it was just as intense. There was something special about this man. It didn't hit her over the head like Harrison Gable's presence did, but rather it was like an all-consuming fire. The feelings had started small, but they were building with each encounter and now had become a threatening blaze.

"Miss Jessica," Austin called out as he dismounted. He left his horse to graze on the front lawn and joined Jessica on the porch. "I came by to see how you were feeling. It's been almost two weeks since you came down sick."

She smiled at his concern. "I'm doing much better. You were kind to concern yourself."

Austin looked almost embarrassed. "Well, since I was here the night you took ill, I've had it on my mind quite a bit."

"You have?" Jessica couldn't imagine that Austin Todd gave her a second thought, but she was delighted that he had.

"It seemed pretty bad. I wasn't sure if it was something contagious or serious, but it surely was a fearful thing to watch."

Jessica frowned. Had he only been worried about whether or not he might contract the same illness? Surely Austin wasn't that shallow. She glanced up to meet his concerned expression. He seemed sincerely worried for her sake.

"Mother said it was probably either a bout of the ague or the grippe. Could be contagious, I suppose, but I couldn't say. You might need to check in with Mother to be sure."

"Oh, that doesn't worry me," he replied. "I was just fearful for your sake. I figured you'd be pretty miserable in quarantine, and if it was life-threatening . . . I would truly regret that."

Jessica felt pleased at his response. "You needn't worry anymore. I'm recovered . . . well, very nearly in full. Mother wants me to continue to take it easy for at least another day."

"I'm sure that's wise." He seemed at a loss for words, and the conversation lagged. Tugging at his collar, Austin looked rather miserable. Jessica took pity on him.

"Father said there have been problems with cattle rustling."

"Yes, but the Rangers have caught up to most of them. The losses are way down."

"That's good news. I know there've been years when the rustlers were a worry to my father. Seems about six years ago we lost quite a few head."

Again strained silence surrounded them. Jessica was determined to keep Austin with her, so she hurried onto another line of questioning. "You once told me that you were from Virginia. Did you like it there?"

Austin looked at her for a moment, as if trying to figure out how to answer.

Jessica chuckled. "I apologize if I was too forward. You know that I speak my mind. It's just normal curiosity. Why don't you sit and we'll have a proper talk?"

He glanced at one of the nearby chairs and finally gave a nod. "All right. I liked Virginia for a great many reasons, but I also didn't like the area for other reasons. What else do you want to know?"

"I don't know." Jessica hadn't expected this at all. "I guess I would have to ask what some of those reasons were. For instance, what did you like best about Virginia?"

He looked away from her and gazed across the yard. She thought he looked almost sad. "The people. The people were good and kind. Not that they aren't here in Texas. Fact is, the people here remind me a good deal of the folks in Virginia."

"And what didn't you like?"

"The crowds. Too many people. For all the good ones, there were equal numbers of bad." He paused and looked back at her. "I told you that my mother was originally from Texas. She used to tell me stories about growing up here, and Texas sounded . . . well . . . peaceful and unpopulated."

"We're growing by leaps and bounds, my father says. Still, I can't imagine just up and moving because there were too many people."

He smiled and Jessica felt her stomach flip again. Goodness, but he was a handsome man. Not only that, she loved his rich baritone voice. Deep, but not too deep. And his eyes were just as enticing as Harrison Gable's, even if they were a lighter brown.

". . . because that kind of life wasn't what I wanted anymore."

She hadn't been listening and regretted it immediately. Jessica needed to know more

227

about this man. "I'm sorry, would you say that again?"

"I said Virginia has some peaceful, less populated parts, but I lived near Washington, D.C., where there was constant noise. I decided to come west because that kind of life wasn't what I wanted anymore."

Jessica tried to keep her mind on their discussion. "What kind of work did you do?"

"Much the same as I do now. Oh, I don't mean inspect cattle, but working for the law."

"And do you have family back there?"

She couldn't be sure, but Jessica thought he frowned. He lowered his head rather quickly and blocked his face from view. For a moment she thought he might not respond, but finally he looked up.

"I had family, but they died."

"How tragic. That must have been hard for you."

"It was. Sometimes it still is."

Austin wasn't at all sure why he was telling Jessica all of this. His life had been a very private one, even before the death of his family. Now, however, he felt compelled to tell this woman everything. He supposed it had to do with his attraction to her. There was just something that drew him back to

228

her no matter how hard he'd tried to ignore it.

"So you came west hoping for a new start and to escape memories?" she asked in a soft, gentle tone.

"I did." The admission wasn't as difficult as Austin had feared.

"And has it worked?"

He looked at the young woman with the beautiful dark brown eyes and smiled. "As well as anything has."

She pushed back reddish-brown bangs from her forehead and smiled back at him. "Hopefully time will help. Mother always says that time heals our wounds. Time and God."

"God?"

Jessica nodded. "Mother believes that God cares deeply for our every need."

"But you don't?"

She shrugged. "I'm not sure what I believe."

This was something Austin completely understood. It gave him a sense of relief to find someone who felt just as he did. "I know what you mean."

Cocking her head to one side, Jessica seemed surprised. "You understand?"

"I do. I feel about the same as you do. I'm not sure what I believe anymore. I was raised in a God-fearing home. I even attended church with my . . ." He fell silent. He'd very nearly told her about Grace.

"With my family," he added. "I read the Bible and prayed, but when I lost my family, I lost my connection to God. It felt as if He'd removed His presence along with my loved ones."

"How awful," Jessica said, looking thoughtful. "My distance grew out of pure disinterest and self-centered sin."

Austin didn't say so, but he admired her once again for her straightforward conversation.

She continued. "I suppose I found other things far too fascinating. There were parties to attend and new gowns to be purchased. I'm ashamed to say I lived a spoiled and pampered life."

"Why ashamed? If your parents chose to lavish you with attention and possessions, I don't see anything wrong with that."

"It wasn't wrong in and of itself," she said. "It was the way it stole my focus — my heart." She looked at him with an expression of regret. "I don't like the person I became. That's why I'm working to change."

He was completely captivated by this confession. He'd never in his life heard a woman speak in such a manner, especially one so young and beautiful. Ignoring the sound of an approaching carriage, Austin said, "I understand what you mean. I've been working to change myself, too. It's not easy."

"No," Jessica said, shaking her head. "It's probably the hardest thing I've ever done."

For a moment they just sat there looking deep into each other's eyes. It was a silent sort of bonding that drew them together in an inexplicable manner.

"Well, I must say I thought to hear at least a hello."

Austin bristled at the sound of Harrison Gable's voice. He turned to look at the man and gave a terse nod. "Mr. Gable."

"Mr. Todd. What a pleasant surprise."

"How so?" Austin asked. He thought the man looked insincere and figured to put him on the spot. Gable was too experienced to fall into that trap, however.

"I had hoped to discuss your duties as marshal to Terryton. You need to know what the railroad expects of you. I have just returned from meetings in Dallas and have much to share. Hence my surprise to find you here."

Austin refused to let him off the hook. "So what does the railroad expect?"

Gable smiled. "Let's not bore Miss Atherton with such talk. I can speak to you another time. I'm sure you have somewhere you need to be."

Austin leaned back in the chair and shook his head. "Nowhere in particular." He saw a quick flash of irritation in Gable's expression. But just as quickly as it came, it was gone, and he returned to his smooth-talking ways.

"I must say, Miss Jessica, you are looking quite well. I am glad to see you feeling better. Perhaps you'll be up to an outing soon?"

"Of course. Mother says I only need rest another day or so. Perhaps we could go riding. My horse, Peg, needs to stretch her legs. She hasn't had a good run in some time. We could get Osage to come along with us."

Austin hated to hear her respond so positively. He wanted to say something but knew anything he said would make him sound like a jealous beau.

"I'm afraid I'm rather saddle weary. I've been riding a great deal back and forth from Cedar Springs to the railroad site. Perhaps we might borrow your buggy and take a ride?" He motioned toward the small conveyance.

The momentary relief Austin felt at the news that Gable didn't wish to ride quickly

232

dissolved with his comment about the carriage.

No doubt you'd like to take her for a ride. That buggy is tight enough to keep you two snuggly fitted. You would just spend the time wooing her and trying to convince her of how dear she has become.

"I doubt that would meet with my father's approval," Jessica said with a smile. "He's very protective of my reputation — and of me."

Austin breathed a little easier at this. She was a woman of integrity. He realized in that moment how much he'd come to care for Jessica.

Don't let it happen, his heart warned. *Don't feel too much, or you'll just get hurt.*

In a most intimate fashion Gable reached out to Jessica and took hold of a loose curl. He let it wrap around his finger and then leaned down to whisper inappropriately in her ear. Austin noticed the way she shivered. It hit him hard.

She cares for him. She's enjoying his attention.

"I have the utmost regard for you and your reputation, Miss Atherton," Gable assured her.

Austin got to his feet. "I guess I need to

be going. I'm due for supper with the Barnetts."

"What a pity," Gable said, straightening. "Perhaps we can talk another time."

Austin met the man's gleaming eyes. "I think that would be wise." He hoped the tone inferred the seriousness he felt. He intended to find out what Gable's intentions toward Jessica might be.

Again his thoughts were of warnings to back off — to distance himself from feeling too much. The memory of losing his wife pierced him, and he forced a pleasant expression. "After all, if we don't discuss it, I won't know what the railroad needs me to do. Good talking with you, Miss Atherton. Gable."

Gable nodded in a knowing fashion, then turned back to Jessica, as if dismissing Austin altogether. "So as I was saying, my dear, we need to put a little color back in your cheeks, and I have just the plan."

Austin ignored the anger that was building. Instead of saying anything more, he mounted his horse and headed for the Barnetts'. He couldn't understand why Gable's interaction bothered him so much. He wasn't about to give in to feelings that could only result in pain. Not even for one as beautiful as Jessica Atherton.

CHAPTER 15

Two weeks after his visit with Jessica, Austin sat at the Barnett dining table and shared his news with William, Robert, and Jake. Having been tied up with arresting a rustling gang, this was the first chance Austin had to explain what he'd learned about their situation.

"I wrote to my former boss, Ellery Turner, regarding Morgan and the counterfeit gold certificates. He wired me that the department had some knowledge of gold certificate counterfeiting, but they'd hit a stone wall in their investigation. He was excited to learn this new information and arranged with the Texas Rangers for me to begin a further search for them."

"That's wonderful news," Will said, looking to Jake. "Hopefully Morgan will find himself too occupied by that to cause you any further trouble."

Jake shrugged and looked less than convinced. "Morgan still says that I embezzled from the bank. It's his hold over me to get what he wants."

"I figure to let it get around that I'm investigating bank fraud," Austin replied. "I might even pay Mr. Morgan a visit on such pretenses and ask him about his banking practices."

"To what end?" Jake asked.

"I'm hoping it will make him nervous — maybe even make him leave the area." With that matter resolved, Austin pushed back the empty coffee mug and took some papers from inside his coat. "I have a list of questions that I'll need to ask you, Jake. This will help me get a better feel for the situation."

"I'll do whatever I can."

"Okay. When does Morgan plan to get back in touch with you?"

Jake's face took on an expression of confusion. "I don't know. He just said he'd be in touch." With a look of concern Jake continued. "I don't even know where he's staying. He could be in Cedar Springs or he could be elsewhere. I just don't know."

"I'll figure it out. Did he mention being here with anyone else, perhaps a cohort?"

"No. I think Mr. Morgan is alone." Jake looked toward the ceiling and seemed to grow thoughtful. "I'm sure that if his money is back in place, he'll have no trouble getting help when he needs it. He's never been shy about paying for what he wants."

Austin considered the matter for a moment. He had been rather excited when Mr. Turner let him know that the agency needed him for this investigation. There was always that old nagging doubt about his capability for such work. Doubt that seemed to grow daily since watching his brother die.

"Austin?"

He looked up and realized the other men were watching him. "Sorry," he said sheepishly. "I was pondering our next move."

"And what did you decide?"

"That I need more information. Robert, you said that Alice had been followed and even approached by a Mr. Smith. But he wasn't with the men who attacked her and killed her father?"

"Right. Mr. Smith appeared after the attack. Alice said she was still in the hospital when one of the nurses told her that a man had come to see her. The doctor turned him away, explaining that Alice was enduring a bad infection and couldn't be disturbed. The man left but tried again to approach her at the house of friends where she was staying after her release from the hospital.

Finally, he took to followin' her, and any time he found her alone he would pester her about some missing papers that her father should have had on the night he was killed. Papers that we now realize were really gold certificates."

"And all of this took place in Denver?"

Jake piped up here. "Yes. We didn't know about it when Alice first came to work for us."

"I didn't realize she had worked for you," Austin said, writing this down for future reference.

"She came to us lookin' for a job. Her friends had left the area, and she was homeless, without hope for her future. Marty took to her right away and hired her as her lady's maid."

"Did the man who'd been following Alice approach her at your home?"

"He did," Jake said. "The man eventually started watching our house and following Alice to the shops whenever Marty sent her out for something. Eventually Mr. Smith got bold and showed up at the doorstep. Marty made his acquaintance with a shotgun in hand." He smiled. "She's quite a woman, my wife."

Will laughed. "You don't know the half of it, Jake. That girl used to keep us up nights just trying to stay ahead of her shenanigans."

"I learned some of my best orneriness from Aunt Marty," Robert admitted.

Austin immediately thought of Jessica Atherton. He imagined she had always been a feisty but ladylike worry to her parents.

"Do you suppose," Jake said, looking rather skeptical, "that Mr. Smith might know Mr. Morgan?"

Austin gave a slight nod. "Anything is possible. It would seem to fit, since Morgan has come here seeking help in getting those certificates back. On the other hand, it could be that he realizes others are looking for them and desperately hopes to find them first. There is a possibility that the man is completely on the up and up and has nothing to do with the counterfeiting."

"I suppose it's also possible that there is more to this than we realize," Jake muttered. "I, for one, am sorry I ever went to work for Morgan. I didn't wanna be a banker anyway, and I should have stuck with my resolve and told my father no."

"Actually, I can see the hand of God in all of this, Jake," Mr. Barnett declared. "If not for you going to work for Morgan, we might not be able to get to the bottom of this mess."

"He's right." Austin gave Jake a smile.

"You have insight to the man, and now a connection that might very well allow us to get to the truth."

Jake seemed to think about this for a moment. He scratched his head. "I'll do whatever it takes. I want Alice and my family to be free of these threats."

"Can you take some time to join me in Dallas?" Austin asked. "I'd like to sit down and discuss this with a couple of my superiors. I think they can give us some advice for how to go about things."

"I can get away," Jake said, looking to his brother-in-law for approval. Austin knew the man still assisted the Barnetts with their ranch work from time to time.

Will nodded. "I think that'd be a good idea."

"But I can't leave Marty and the children alone," Jake said, looking back to Austin. "It wouldn't be safe. Mr. Morgan knows where we live, and he's bound to know I've talked with Marty. He might decide to threaten her in order to push me to a decision."

"They can all stay here," Will said. "We've got enough room, and Hannah will love having Marty here."

"Marty will enjoy being with her sister and Alice, as well," Jake replied. "I think that's a good idea. I know they'll be safe here."

"Any intruders will have to get through us and a good number of our men before they can cause harm to any of the womenfolk," Robert added. He grinned. "And then, God help them, they'll have to deal with our gals."

Will laughed. "He's right. You know, Hannah can be pretty fierce when she feels her family is threatened."

Jake nodded. "Marty, too."

Austin felt a deep emptiness as the men talked about their wives. It wasn't really a pain these days, but more of a dark void that seemed to go on forever. He wondered if he'd ever know the peace of mind he sought. He was so weary — so burdened.

Come unto me, all ye that labour and are heavy laden, and I will give you rest.

The words came as a nearly audible voice. Austin looked at the men who sat opposite him, but no one seemed to notice him. They were all busy talking among themselves. None of them had spoken that Bible verse from Matthew.

For a moment Austin remembered a time when he had shared that verse with Grace during morning prayer time. She had told him that the verse had always been a comfort to her, especially when her workload was heavy.

"So when do you want to go?"

Austin barely heard Jake ask the question. He put aside his memories and answered. "The sooner the better. We need to put an end to this." He put his thoughts completely back on the case. "I'm figuring it might be possible that whoever is involved in this may be after more than the forged certificates. I think it's quite possible they might be looking for the actual plates themselves. After all, a few forged gold certificates won't get them far."

"I'm guessin' you're right," Robert replied. His expression grew a bit darker. "But no matter what, they have hurt my wife for the last time, and I intend to see this through to the end."

"Agreed," Austin said, knowing he had the full cooperation of the men before him. Again he thought of Jessica and how willing he would be to protect her from harm.

Then protect her from yourself, Austin's mind seemed to mock. *You're the only real danger to her.*

"You look beautiful," Mother told Jessica as she descended the stairs.

Jessica hoped so. She'd taken great care to dress for her outing with Harrison. Robert and Alice would ride with her into Cedar

Springs, and then Harrison would join them in attending a musical affair. Jessica was determined to look her best, as this was the first proper event she would attend with the handsome lawyer.

Mother motioned. "Turn for me."

Jessica did so indulgently. She knew her mother was anxious for everything to be perfect. The gown had a beautiful skirt of Muscovite velvet that had come all the way from Russia. The black velvet brocade set upon dark green corded silk gave the gown an opulent look. The high-necked silk bodice was a buttery cream color, trimmed with black and dark green bands, which served to enhance the beauty of the piece.

Mother plucked a piece of lint from one of the voluminous sleeves. "Harrison Gable will be completely captivated."

"So long as he's not too captivated," Jessica's father said with just a hint of disapproval. "I don't know that this is a good idea, but I won't take back my agreement to let you go."

Jessica stepped to where her father stood. Stretching up on tiptoes, she kissed his cheek. "You worry too much, Papa. Besides, I'll be with Robert and Alice."

"I know, but that's a long ride into town, and it will be an equally long ride home."

"But our house isn't nearly as far from town as the Barnett house, and besides, they've already arranged to have their baby cared for by Marty and Jake," Jessica argued. "Everyone thought this would be a good diversion for Alice."

"Tyler, you've already given your word," Mother declared.

He looked to the ceiling and shook his head. "I know. I know. I must have been crazy."

"Oh, Papa, don't fret." Jessica always called him Papa when she wanted to soothe him. "You needn't worry. We'll have supper and then attend the concert. I'll be staying in an adjoining room near Robert and Alice at the hotel. There will be locks on the doors. Mr. Gable won't even be at the hotel. He'll be in his own home. Tomorrow morning after breakfast and some shopping, Robert will bring me back safe and sound. You have no reason to doubt me."

Jessica knew her father thought highly of Robert. After all, he had hoped Jessica might marry the son of his best friend. And, while the current hotel arrangements had given Jessica a twinge of discomfort, she had been far more excited by the news that Harrison Gable would escort her that evening. It was worth it, even if she was being chaperoned by her friends.

"I wish you would have waited to dress at the hotel," Mother said, fussing with the velvet bands that encircled Jessica's waist. "You're going to be all dusty by the time you get there."

"Since Robert couldn't get away any earlier than this afternoon," Jessica reminded her mother, "we wouldn't have time for changing our clothes at the hotel. Besides, Robert has promised he'll bring Uncle Brandon's enclosed carriage. Alice and I will be quite comfortable."

The sound of an approaching carriage caused Jessica to rush to the window in a most unladylike fashion. "They're here. Where's my overnight bag?" She searched around the room and spied it by the front door. Excitement coursed through her like a steady electric current.

"Don't forget your wrap," Mother said and brought a long black cape to her. "It could be quite chilly by nightfall."

Jessica took the cloak and kissed her mother. "I'll be just fine."

She took up her bag, but her father reached out and claimed it. "I'll take this."

She followed him from the house. Robert had just brought the carriage to a stop near the house, and Jessica saw Alice give a wave through the window. It seemed strange that they should come together for this event. Alice had been her enemy at one time, but now Jessica only longed for a friend.

"I see you're ready to go," Robert said, jumping down from the driver's seat to retrieve the bag her father held.

"Robert, you take good care of my gal," Father told him and handed him the bag. He turned to Jessica. "And you, behave yourself. You know what I expect out of you." His voice was stern, but Jessica could hear the love in his voice.

"I promise, Papa. I will be a perfect lady, just as I've always been."

Her father gave her a skeptical look, then helped her up into the carriage. Jessica smiled at Alice as her father closed the door. Settling into the seat opposite Alice, she blew out her breath. "I wasn't at all sure he'd allow me to escape."

Alice grinned. "Well, I'm glad he did. I'm looking forward to spending time with you. Robert decided not to bring a driver. He said that way you and I could sit inside and talk up a storm and get to know each other. He thinks it will take my mind off of . . . everything."

Jessica noticed Alice's beautiful gown of turquoise. Lace edged the neckline, and the bodice was decorated with tiny silver beads. It wasn't anywhere near as fancy as her own, but in some ways, Jessica thought it lovelier. "Your gown is exquisite," she told Alice. "It complements your hair perfectly and gives you the tiniest waistline."

"Thank you. I was about to comment on *your* dress." Alice shook her head. "I haven't seen anything like it since Marty's clothes in Denver. They were all so beautiful and so delicate. I enjoyed helping her to dress just to feel the rich materials. I suppose you have a dozen such gowns?" The carriage lurched forward as they began to move out.

"I have my share, to be sure," Jessica said, feeling rather self-conscious. She gave her parents a wave and then turned back to Alice. "I used to worry about such things. I thought gowns and jewelry to be so important. Now I don't feel the same way."

Alice's expression grew thoughtful. "I suppose everyone comes to a place in life where they learn what truly matters most."

Jessica thought of how much she wanted to change. Life lessons had been slow in catching up with her, but now that they had, her reformation was all consuming.

"I like to think that I have changed for the better. Of course, I still have to prove

247

myself," Jessica replied. "That's the hard work ahead of me."

CHAPTER 16

Being inside a bank on a Saturday afternoon seemed a little strange to Austin. However, the second-floor office of the National Exchange Bank of Dallas was exactly where they'd come to meet with a federal court judge and two Secret Service agents. The walls were papered with green and gold stripes, and of course there was a great deal of mahogany. The table and chairs were mahogany, as were the room's trim, doors, and floor. And, despite the fact that someone had opened one of the two windows, musty warmth made the room most uncomfortable.

The bank manager sat at the head of the table and began the introductions. "Gentlemen, I'm happy to be able to meet with you here today. As many of you know, my name is Claude Reiman. I am employed by the bank and will act as their representative. Mr. Todd, I believe you already are acquainted with Judge Weimer?"

"Yes," Austin said, nodding toward the older man. He'd known Judge Weimer through business with the Texas Rangers when certain situations had led them to federal involvement.

"Judge Weimer, this is Jacob Wythe," Austin continued. "Mr. Wythe is the reason we are here today." He turned to the two agents. "These are agents Carson and Deeters." The men gave a slight nod in unison.

"I'm pleased to meet y'all. Happy to have the opportunity to assist you in any way I can," the judge answered. His thick southern accent suggested he wasn't raised in Texas, but perhaps Georgia or the Carolinas.

He was an older man and, befitting his age and situation, made a stately figure in his dark suit and snowy white hair. Austin felt poorly dressed next to the others. He and Jake had worn their Sunday best, but their clothes lacked the refinement and newness of that of the other men's clothing. Normally that wouldn't have bothered Austin in the least, but at the moment he wanted to make it clear to these men that he and Jake were equal to the task at hand and not simply some bumbling backwoods ninnies.

Weimer gave Austin a stern gaze. "Why don't you tell us about this matter, Mr. Todd."

Austin looked to Jake and then stood. "Gentlemen, I will endeavor to explain our circumstance and to address our needs in as concise a manner as possible."

For the next hour, Austin and Jake shared the information they could. The judge took notes and from time to time asked questions to clarify the details further. To Austin's relief, a man showed up about forty minutes into his explanation and provided a tray with glasses and a pitcher of sweet tea. The refreshment did its job and Austin found it easier to continue.

"Most likely," Austin said in conclusion, "the certificates and possible plates are still in Colorado. Even so, we don't know if Mr. Morgan is involved with the counterfeiting or if he's simply trying to regain the forgeries for the sake of protecting the originals. After all, the trouble came from his bank and makes a mark against his reputation. Unfortunately, he believes in threats and has caused Mr. Wythe grave concern for the safety of his family and for his own well-being."

"To what purpose?" the judge asked.

"To the purpose of obtaining Jake's assistance in finding those certificates," Austin replied, glancing at Jake. "Or to see Jake sent to jail on trumped-up charges."

After answering a few more questions, Austin took a seat. He felt exhausted from the detailed explanation and request for assistance. He knew the men at the table realized the importance of the situation, but nevertheless they talked amongst themselves as if trying to decide nothing more important than whether they'd buy the evening paper.

Last of all, the two Secret Service agents produced copies of several counterfeit bills. They pointed out some of the inconsistencies and mistakes.

"These are examples of some of the best," one of the men said and passed the bill around. Even Mr. Reiman agreed he wouldn't have known it wasn't a true piece of currency. The judge turned the twenty dollar bill over in his hands. His expression grew thoughtful.

"Gentlemen, I believe you make a good case. Mr. Wythe, I am of the opinion that your appearance here today lends support to your innocence. I consider myself a man of discernment, and I will afford you protection from prosecution in any way that I can. Not many men have inspired me to pledge as much, but I feel certain this is God's will. I have friends in the Denver area and will take this up with them, as well, should the need arise. They will be most eager to see this worked out, as am I."

"Thank you, your honor," Jake replied. "I appreciate that. And my family does, too."

The counterfeit bills were collected as final comments and suggestions were offered. Austin felt that their time together had been beneficial. The meeting closed and some of the parties went their separate ways, each man with his assigned responsibilities. All were determined to put an end to the problem of counterfeiting.

Austin arranged for a private audience with Carson and Deeters over supper. He'd already informed Jake of the plan but now worried that maybe his friend would rather do otherwise. "I hope you don't mind if we do business with our meal," he told Jake. "I figured this would be our only chance unless we stay longer in the morning."

"I don't mind one bit. I'm anxious to get home, but this is vital to my well-being, and even more so to Marty's. And to the Barnetts'. Might as well make the best of our time, and if that means we work while we eat, then so be it."

"I suppose we could head out after our

meeting. We could take the train from here to Cedar Springs. I understand there's a 7:45 this evening. It'd be difficult but not impossible."

Jake gave an appreciative grin. "You don't have to worry about me, Austin. I appreciate that you've been willin' to help us with this." He sobered considerably. "I figure we have to resolve this, or we'll always be lookin' over our shoulders. I can't live like that."

It was only a week before Thanksgiving, and Jessica felt the excitement of the season as well as the fact that tomorrow was her birthday. Her parents had always treated birthdays as a special event, but often Jessica's birthday got delayed and celebrated with Thanksgiving. She had no idea what her mother had planned this year.

"You're certainly quiet today," Mother said, motioning Jessica to raise her hands. She looped the yarn around Jessica's fingers and started to wind the yarn into a ball. "Is something wrong?"

"I've been thinking about Thanksgiving and then, of course, Christmas." Jessica glanced down at the dyed yarn. The rosy color would look nice made into a sweater for Johanna. At least that was what Mother had planned.

"And what of your birthday? It's tomorrow, or have you forgotten?" Mother asked, glancing up. "I can't believe my baby is going to be twenty-two."

"Me either," Jessica admitted. "All of my friends are married, and most have children, and I have nothing to show for my time on earth except myself."

"That is a matter of opinion. You've touched the lives of others and influenced them."

"Yes, but mostly in negative ways," Jessica replied. "I want things to be different from now on. I want this to be a new start."

Mother refocused on the yarn. "I think that's an admirable idea. But for now, wouldn't you like to know what I've planned for you?"

Jessica smiled. "Whatever it is, I will be content and happy."

"I'm glad to hear that," Mother said. "Since it's a Friday this year, I've invited a few people over to share dinner with us. The Barnetts and Wythes will be here helping to butcher hogs, so it seemed only right to have them stay for supper and cake. Lupe has already been hard at work to create one of her delicious coconut cakes."

"Who else have you invited?" Jessica

asked, quite curious. "Will the boys be home?" Her brothers had been absent for so long that Jessica feared they would make southern Texas their permanent residence.

"No, the boys won't be here. They've agreed to help build a church just across the border in Mexico. The minister of that congregation heard about the houses their teams had been building, and he begged them to help erect the church. It seemed they had some of the supplies needed but definitely could use more financial and physical help. We arranged some of the former, while the boys filled in the latter. Most of the other men had to return to their homes, but Howard and Isaac decided to stay — and with our blessing. What they're doing is important. So often people think of sharing God's love by preaching or reading the Bible to someone. More often, we can show people Jesus by demonstrating kindness and love in practical ways."

Jessica wasn't happy to know her brothers would remain in the South. It wasn't that she didn't believe they were doing good works, but she missed them and knew that Father needed their help with the ranch. "I knew they'd find some reason to stay. Sometimes I worry they'll never come back to ranching."

"Nonsense. It's in their blood. They'll be back. They're just enjoying their youth."

"They're older than I," Jessica countered. "Everyone is always telling me that I should already be settled with children. Why is it my brothers may continue enjoying their youth without correction?"

"That's how it is for a man. If he doesn't marry before he's thirty, people call him wise and laud him for his choice." Mother shook her head and reached over to undo a tangle in the yarn. "As for women, it's the opposite. A woman is supposed to marry young and have children. This is the way it's always been, and I doubt it will ever change. But, Jessica, I thought you wanted to be married. I remember your saying that with a wealthy enough husband you could see the world and all its splendors."

Jessica frowned. "That was the old me. The new me wants whatever is meant for me. I'm trying to understand what God wants. If it's marriage and children, then I believe I will be happy with that. If it's something else, then I will be content with that."

Releasing the yarn, Mother gave Jessica's knee a pat. "I'm glad to hear it. Wealth can buy only so much happiness. Real joy and peace come through knowing God's will and ways. Watch and listen for His direction."

Jessica knew her mother was right, but she couldn't really say she knew what was next expected of her by her heavenly Father. How did one learn to hear the voice of God?

"So do you want to know who else I've invited to share your birthday?" Mother asked.

Jessica had nearly forgotten that she'd asked. "Of course."

"Well, I gave it a lot of thought and even brought your father in on the decision. After we discussed it at length, I invited Aunt Laura and Uncle Brandon to come. And your father thought it would be nice to invite some of your . . . friends. Like Mr. Todd and Mr. Gable."

Jessica felt her face grow hot. Obviously her father and mother thought of Austin and Harrison as appropriate suitors for their daughter; otherwise they would never have considered such a thing.

"And did you invite them?" she asked, trying hard to sound as if she didn't care.

"I did. I am happy to say that both agreed to come."

Jessica glanced at the yarn in an effort to hide her delight. "I'm glad they can make it." She heard Mother chuckle and looked up to see her watching in amusement. "Why are you laughing?"

"You. You're trying so hard to convince me that it doesn't matter, but I know it does. I'm not so old that I don't remember the thrill of being pursued."

"You're not old at all, Mother. I heard Father say just the other day that you look as young and beautiful as when he first married you."

"His eyesight is failing." Mother smiled and continued with her task. "Still, I'm glad to hear he thinks I look the same. The evidence of the years is upon us both, and time is not always kind." She grew thoughtful.

"But I really can't complain. The years have been good, and the holidays are always such a special time. I remember your first Christmas. Goodness, but you were just a newborn — barely a month old. I was so happy to have another girl. I feared Gloria would be the only one, and she did so much want a sister."

"It must have been difficult, what with so many little ones," Jessica said, thinking back on stories she'd heard of her mother and father's early years.

"It was," Mother admitted, "but good things usually come at a price." Her expression was reflective. "You must remember that I had my sister close by, and Gloria was eight years old and a lot of help. We were also starting to do quite well for ourselves. Your father hired a girl to come cook and clean for us. She was Lupe's older sister." She shrugged. "I don't regret any of it. Your father always made me feel safe and well cared for. I was seldom afraid with him at my side." She paused in her work. "I want that for you, Jess. I want that more than I can say. I pray all the time for you to find the right man to marry. I know that God has a man for you."

Jessica heard the sincerity in her mother's voice. It touched her heart that Mother should care so deeply about her happiness. She supposed no one could ever love her as much as her mother and father, but Mother believed there was one man out there for her who would try. Jessica wanted to believe with all her heart that it was true.

"But what if He doesn't?" she murmured, doubt creeping in.

"What?" Her mother looked perplexed.

"What if God doesn't have a man for me? What if I'm to remain unmarried?" Jessica wondered if God would punish her in such a manner for her selfish years. "Some women do, you know. Look at Eleanor

Barnett. She prefers women's rights and politics to marriage and children."

"I know He has a husband for you, Jess. Don't ask me how; I just know it. One day you will marry and be happy. But don't take me wrong. Marriage will be work — the hardest work you'll ever do." Mother paused and smiled, adding, "And the most rewarding."

The next evening, Jessica found herself the center of attention. Well, at least most everyone's attention. Austin seemed rather distant, although he had made polite conversation and wished her well. On the other hand, Harrison was making somewhat of an annoyance of himself. He constantly sought to be at her side and whispered comments in her ear, as if they were already intimate. She couldn't help but thrill to his touch when he put his hand on her arm, but even so, it was Austin whose attention she was trying to get.

By the time supper was over and the birthday cake was served, Jessica found herself deep in thought. Harrison Gable was a stunningly handsome man with dark brown eyes and a gentle smile. He was obviously intelligent, having studied and practiced law with great success. He also had his eye on a future that included travel and living well. Austin, on the other hand, was equally handsome, but his features were completely different. Where Harrison's hair was brown-black, Austin's was a sun-kissed brown. Where Harrison had a bit of curl to his hair, Austin's was as straight as string. And to be sure, Austin was smart. He might not have Harrison's book learning, but he was nobody's fool.

"Do you like the cake?" Mother asked.

Jessica looked up and nodded. "It's delicious."

"And do you like the company?"

A smile crept across Jessica's lips. "Some of the best I've ever had."

Mother leaned in to whisper. "So who's in the lead?"

Jessica pulled back and looked at her. "What do you mean?" she whispered back.

"Austin and Harrison — who's winning the race to capture your heart?"

Jessica's confusion became feigned surprise. "Mother, really," she responded, her lips to her mother's ear. "You sound as if you're trying to matchmake. I thought we were just celebrating my birthday."

Her mother laughed and the melodious sound delighted Jessica's heart. She couldn't help but grin and give a little shrug.

■ ■ ■

Sunday morning dawned cloudy and cool. Jessica feared they might have to endure a cold rain on the way to church and was glad when her father brought around the enclosed carriage.

The weather, however, cleared a bit by the time they reached the church in Cedar Springs. Jessica was still reflecting on her birthday and how pleasurable her time had been with both Harrison and Austin present. She didn't even mind anymore that Harrison had acted so intimate with her in front of the others. She felt quite special and nothing was going to ruin her memories.

The Atherton family took their place in the family pew and awaited the beginning of the service. Jessica wondered if Austin and Harrison were in attendance but didn't want to look around for them. No doubt someone would see her and guess her mission.

The pastor offered a prayer and then invited the congregation to sing a hymn of praise. By the time they'd reached the fourth stanza, Harrison Gable had slipped into the pew beside Jessica. They exchanged a smile, but Jessica refocused her attention on the song. Then to her surprise as they started to sing the second hymn, Austin Todd appeared. He frowned at Gable but softened his harsh expression when Jessica met his eyes. To her surprise, Austin moved past both of them to take his place between Jessica and her mother. His nearness pleased Jessica, and his smooth baritone singing was most pleasurable to hear.

Jessica tried to keep her thoughts under control. This seating arrangement meant nothing. No doubt the other pews were full and the men had no other choice but to sit in her family's pew. Since her brothers were still away, it seemed the logical choice. Not only that, but Austin knew her parents better than he knew Mr. Gable. He most likely had made his choice based on the comfort of being with folks he knew. At least, that was her rationale.

As the music concluded and the congregation reclaimed their seats, Jessica had almost convinced herself.

The pastor offered another prayer and then encouraged the congregation to take out their Bibles. "In the second book of Corinthians, chapter five," he began, "the apostle Paul pleads the case for man to be reconciled with God. Let me share his thoughts." He leafed through several pages and began to read.

" 'Therefore if any man be in Christ, he is a new creature: old things are passed away; behold, all things are become new. And all things are of God, who hath reconciled us to himself by Jesus Christ, and hath given to us the ministry of reconciliation.' " He looked up from the Bible. "Make certain you understand. We are only reconciled to God through Jesus. There is no other way, and the Bible makes this clear."

Jessica felt as if he were speaking directly to her. She swallowed hard, suddenly feeling very uncomfortable. What was it about these particular Scriptures that made her uneasy? The pastor continued reading.

" 'To wit, that God was in Christ, reconciling the world unto himself, not imputing their trespasses unto them; and hath committed unto us the word of reconciliation.' " He looked up. "And here is the key: 'For he hath made *him* to be sin for *us*, who knew no sin; that we might be made the righteousness of God in him.' " Closing his Bible, the pastor stepped away from the small pulpit.

"Jesus made himself sin for us — that we might be reconciled to the Father in heaven. Jesus, who had never sinned, became the essence of sin that we might be saved. If that doesn't humble you, then something is wrong in the way you think."

Jessica's heart took on the full impact of the man's words. Reconciliation with God was something she'd not truly considered. In fact, she hadn't even been aware that it was missing. She'd never really felt the need to be reconciled with God. From the time she was small, church and its Christian teachings had been a part of her life that she took for granted.

"Paul urged people to be reconciled with God — to know the truth that comes to us through the Scriptures. Jesus is that truth. It is Christ and Christ alone who makes it possible for us — mere sinners — to be brought into right accord with the Father. It is nothing of ourselves and everything of Him who died to save us."

Jessica looked down at the floor. She was scarcely able to draw breath for the impact of the preacher's words. This was what was missing in her life. This was the oneness that she had longed for. It wasn't a husband or children. It wasn't wealth or new gowns. It was the need to truly belong — to be reconciled to her Father in heaven. It was Jesus whom she longed for. She couldn't make the past right. She couldn't change a single word or action, but she could become new through Christ.

The preacher continued to speak on the same passages, and by the time he concluded and asked if anyone in the congregation felt God's call upon their heart, Jessica could hardly sit still. She felt drawn as if someone were pulling her forward. Without any thought to what others might think, Jessica got to her feet, stumbled past Harrison, and made her way to the altar. She was becoming new — throwing off the old and the ugly, the sin nature that had done her no favors.

She wanted to cry and laugh at the same time. She was being reconciled, and it felt like a new birth.

CHAPTER 17

Sunday the sixth of December found Austin at the Barnett Ranch sharing the noon meal with the Barnett and Wythe families. Austin had found real love and acceptance from these people, and he didn't take that for granted. He had long since ceased to be just a man who inspected their cattle and agreed to patrol their new little town. He felt as if he'd been made a member of the family.

His mind warned him of the danger, but his heart craved the love they extended. Mrs. Barnett mothered him as his own might have done prior to his brother's death. Austin tried to force the memories from his mind and was grateful when Alice Barnett spoke up.

"Mr. Todd, I have something I'd like to show you. Robert said it might be useful to you in your investigation."

This surprised Austin, but he didn't show it. Alice was so like a little bird. She was lovely to look at despite the scar on the right side of her face, but she was easily spooked and unnerved by the things that were happening.

"I'd be honored to take a look," Austin replied, pushing back from the table. Already Hannah and Marty were beginning to clear the table.

"Well, I, for one, intend to take me a bit of a rest in the front room." Mr. Barnett looked at Jake. "Care to join me?"

"I would," Jake said, following Mr. Barnett from the room.

Austin started to get to his feet, but Alice bade him otherwise. "We can just stay right here. Hannah said it wouldn't be a problem. I'll go check on Wills and then bring the letters." She disappeared from the room, leaving Austin to turn to Robert.

"Letters?"

The other man gave a curt nod. "Correspondence between her father and mother, as well as business dealings. We were hopeful they might lend a clue to where Chesterfield might have put those plates and certificates."

Austin considered it a moment. "They very well might. I know the other two agents helping me in this are finding very little."

Alice reappeared just then, and in her

hands she held two stacks of letters. Placing them on the table, she took a seat and pushed one stack toward Austin.

"These are the writings of my mother to my father and a few of his letters to her that Mother saved. They were not pleasant to read, by any means. My parents were unhappy with each other, and my father blamed my mother for things that were clearly untrue."

"I'm honored that you would trust me to read them. I promise to be discreet about their contents," Austin assured her.

Alice took a deep breath and reached for the second stack. "These are business dealings, invoices, and such. Mother said she very nearly burned them, not seeing any real purpose for them, but she thought perhaps I would want them. Now I'm of a mind they may be of use to you."

"They just might," Austin said. "There haven't been very many clues, and Mr. Morgan hasn't appeared again to Jake. Reading through these might give us some idea of where to look next."

Alice looked to Robert. He squeezed her hand. "Mr. Todd will see this brought to an end."

She looked back at Austin, and the pain and fear in her eyes were almost his undoing. He wanted more than ever to help her — to help them all be rid of the demons that tormented their family.

"There's one more thing," Alice said, reaching into a small bag she had attached to her waistband. From it she pulled a small bronze key. "This was in one of the envelopes. There were no markings on the envelope, but this key was wrapped in a piece of paper and left inside." She pushed the key across the linen tablecloth and left it to Austin's scrutiny.

He picked the piece up and pondered its purpose. It wasn't a normal door key, nor did it look like one used for winding a clock. The key resembled a tiny violin or perhaps a banjo. One end had a solid round piece of brass by which to hold the key. The end resembled the tuning pegs on the neck of a stringed instrument.

"I've never seen anything quite like it," Austin admitted.

"Neither have we," Robert said. The envelope had no markings and there was no indication as to where the key might belong.

"I'll check into it," Austin promised. "It might very well be important."

"I hope so. I hope all of this proves to be of use," Alice said, her eyes seeming to implore him to assure her it would.

"Thank you, Mrs. Barnett. I'm convinced this will lend me a clue or two." Austin put the key into his pocket. "I presume I may take the letters home with me?"

"Of course. Keep them as long as you like," Alice replied.

Rather than linger, Austin took up the letters and made his way to the front door. He gave a wave to Jake and William. "Thanks again for dinner. If you don't mind, I'm gonna take my leave. I have a bit of reading that needs my attention."

"Good to see you again, Austin," William said. "I'm excited at the turn of events regarding the rail line, and as soon as the officials come to see me, I'll be in touch. We're just about to get the tracks started. The railroad is gonna be doin' more detailed surveying most of December."

Austin nodded and headed from the house. His horse awaited him in the barn, where Robert had given it fresh hay to enjoy while Austin ate with the family. He quickly added the letters to his saddlebag, then readied his mount. He made his way from the Barnett Ranch with every intention of heading home. However, when he came to the turnoff for the Atherton place, Austin couldn't help himself. He had seen Jessica in church that morning, and she was all he could think about. He'd given up trying to guard his heart and knew the painful truth. He was falling in love with her.

His inner warning still attempted to make him turn back. He thought again of Grace and how awful it had been to lose her. If only he wouldn't have insisted on their living in the country, away from the dangers of the city.

"She's in a better place — the baby, too," he told himself aloud. "She loved me and would want me to go on living." He knew it was true, but there was a part of him that feared being loved like other men feared death.

At the Athertons', Austin was eagerly greeted by Mr. Atherton. "Welcome, Austin. Come on in. What brings you our way?"

"I shared lunch with the Barnetts, and . . . well . . . I thought it might be nice to check in with you."

Tyler Atherton assessed him momentarily. "I think I know why you're really here. Jess is down at the springhouse. You might wanna make your way there. It'll give you a nice walk back — together."

Austin met the man's smile and nodded. "Thank you, Mr. Atherton."

"My pleasure. Just go around the house to the back and make your way down the path to the right. It'll lead you to the spring-house . . . and to Jess."

Austin nodded again, nervous. He left Atherton and did as he'd been instructed, making his way down the path. His hands felt clammy and he wiped them on his Levi's, all the while chiding himself for letting the stress of the moment get to him.

He spotted the springhouse and the stream of water that ran under and through it. What a prize to have a cold spring on their property. Smiling, Austin thought this a rather secluded and perfect meeting place for young lovers. Not wishing to startle Jessica, he called out.

"Miss Atherton, are you here?"

It was only a moment before Jessica peeked out the door. "Mr. Todd, I wasn't expecting to see you again today."

"I hope you don't mind. I didn't have a chance to speak to you at church."

"I was just putting away some things for my mother. I'm finished now, so we can talk all you'd like."

He watched her secure the springhouse door. She was dressed very simply in a dark brown skirt and calico blouse, which could barely be seen under the oversized coat she wore. Perhaps she had borrowed one of her brother's work coats to keep warm in the springhouse. She wore her hair casually pulled back with a ribbon. He recalled that in church it had been pinned up in an attractive manner with a little hat. Austin preferred it this way, however. In fact, if he could have been so bold, he would have released it all together. There was something very intimate about seeing a woman with her hair down.

Jessica joined him. He could see she was fully aware that he'd been assessing her. She smiled. "Would you like to walk while we talk?"

He grinned. "I kind of liked it back here. Seems pretty out of the way."

She laughed. "There is a very nice path to the orchard. I think you'll enjoy it. Come on."

Austin let her lead him. The couple remained silent until they reached the orchard. "The fruit has all been harvested," Jessica began, "but it's still a lovely place. In a few months this will all be in bloom, and the scent will be wondrous. I love springtime with everything coming to life."

Austin struggled to put his mind on the conversation. "Uh . . . it can be a troublesome thing, too. What with twisters and such. We never had many of those back in Virginia."

Her expression grew thoughtful as she looked into his eyes. "I wonder if I might impose upon you?"

Austin could only smile. "In what way?"

"I want to know more about you."

He felt his breath catch deep in his throat. He cared about this woman, and he knew there could be no future for them unless he told her of the past.

"All right," he said softly. "What would you like to know?"

"Tell me about your family. Do you have brothers or sisters?"

"I did," Austin said, trying not to betray his discomfort. "I had a brother . . . Houston. My mother's way of staying connected with Texas was to name us boys after beloved cities. I think I told you that she was raised in Texas but moved to Virginia."

"Yes. You said you *had* a brother. Does that mean he's passed on?"

Austin took off his hat and pushed back his hair. Replacing the hat, he squared his shoulders. "Yes. It was a tragedy that involved us both. It started a terrible cycle of death in my life."

She looked at him oddly. "Will you tell me about it?"

He had thought it would be difficult to share his memories with Jessica, but it wasn't. As he began to tell her the sad story, Austin actually found comfort in the telling. It was almost like a confession of guilt and sin. By confessing the past, perhaps he could be made clean.

"Houston and I both worked for the Secret Service. I had helped him to get the job, in fact. I had recently married." He paused to see if she was shocked by this declaration. She didn't appear to be at all.

"We worked well as a team, but one night things went wrong just as we were on the verge of breaking a big case and arresting the perpetrators. Somehow the men became aware that the law was closing in, and they took up positions to fight." The images were still clear in his memory.

"I found myself in trouble — boxed into a corner, which, of course, was exactly what my adversary wanted. That left me no choice but to shoot my way out. Houston found me and helped subdue the attackers by adding his fire power. We had them pretty well beat, and when the last man took off running, we knew we'd won. We figured the other agents would easily take them in hand."

"And did they?"

"All but one. One hid out in the darkness, in the brush. He jumped us as we made our way to join the others. I raised my gun to shoot him as he aimed his rifle at me. For whatever reason, Houston felt certain the man would kill me. He jumped in front of me and took the bullet."

"That was very heroic. He must have loved you a great deal. Did you get the other man, the man who shot him?"

Shaking his head, Austin felt sick at the truth of the matter. Could he really tell her? He drew a deep breath. "The other man managed to slip away because I attended to Houston. He died in my arms. Killed by my bullet."

"Your bullet?"

He gave a heavy sigh. "Yes, my bullet. I fired just as Houston jumped in front of me. The other man was out of ammunition. I learned that after one of the agents checked his discarded rifle. I'd killed my own brother for nothing."

Jessica shook her head vehemently. "Nonsense. It was a terrible accident and an act of supreme heroics by your brother."

"That's what Grace — my wife — said. But my parents didn't see it that way. My mother railed at me — blamed me and cursed me. She said it had been my responsibility to keep Houston safe, but instead I ended his life. She told me to leave and

278

never return. My father felt the same way. It was just too painful for them.

"Houston was engaged to be married, and I had to break the news to his fiancée. She blamed me, too. She pummeled me with her fists and hit me until she was weeping so hard she collapsed. Her father had the servants put her to bed, then told me it would be best if I didn't come back."

"I'm sorry. They were wrong to treat you like that. You didn't mean for him to die. They had to know that."

He shrugged. "I'd like to think they did. I decided to give them some time. This was the end of January, and Grace was due to have a baby the following month. I'd moved us out to the country the previous year. I felt she'd be safer there when I had to be away, which was often. I was wrong. I was in Washington, D.C., when she went into labor. There was no one with her, no one to help. The girl I'd hired to keep house and help Grace with the laundry and meals was sick and couldn't come. If she'd been there, things might have gone differently, but I can't blame her. That'd be no different from my parents blaming me for Houston's death."

"What happened to Grace?" Jessica asked. She reached out as if she might take hold of his arm, but hesitated and then decided against it.

"Something went terribly wrong, and she delivered a stillborn son by herself and then followed him in death. I found them there on the bed, the babe held close in her arms. I was beyond grief. I wanted to die and gave strong thought to ending my life. That was February."

"How awful," Jessica said. "To lose two people — three really — in such a short time."

"By June both of my parents had passed away, as well." Jessica gave a gasp, then covered her mouth with her hands as if embarrassed. Austin felt bad for having just blurted it out like that. "My father hadn't been well for several years. We were never sure what the problem was, but the doctor was of a mind that he had a weakness in his heart. My father died in May of a heart attack. My mother died a month later from some type of consumption that wasted her away. The doctor said it was mostly likely that she had lost the will to live. That was something I could well understand."

"Had you reconciled before their deaths?"

"No. They went to their graves hating me, blaming me." Austin looked past Jessica to the line of trees. "That was probably the hardest truth I've ever had to face. My parents had taught me about forgiveness and love, but when I needed it most, it was denied me." He hadn't meant to add the latter and gave a nonchalant shrug. "After that I came west. I couldn't bear to remain in Virginia. I needed a fresh start."

"I can imagine it was just too painful to stay." Her words were offered in sincere understanding.

Jessica reached out again, and this time she took hold of his arm. She gave a light squeeze and continued to hold on to him. "I'm so sorry that you had to go through such terrible loss. It's no wonder you always have a certain sorrow in your eyes."

That she had noticed touched him deeply. Austin took hold of her hands. She shivered, much as he'd seen her do when Harrison Gable touched her. The tiny reaction made him happy.

"The pain is less now."

She gazed into his eyes for a moment longer, then turned toward the trail, forcing Austin to release her hands. "We should probably head back," she said, smiling. "I wouldn't want Father to come looking for us."

"I agree," Austin said and easily caught up to her. "I hope I didn't offend you with my story."

"Of course not. I'm so glad you told me. As I said, I could tell you were a man of sorrows." She glanced up at him and smiled. "Perhaps that sadness can be laid to rest now. Perhaps in sharing the burden with another, you will find peace."

"The peace has come gradually," he admitted. "I longed for many years to be able to go back and undo what had happened. I thought God didn't care about me or my family, so I chose to ignore Him. Now I find He refuses to ignore me."

Jessica nodded knowingly. "He has done the same with me. You were there when I went forward."

"Yes, it was a very special moment."

"I hope you can have a moment of your own. God's peace is so much better than anything anyone else could offer you."

Austin felt the urgency to tell her how he felt, but the words stuck in his throat. Instead, he stopped her from walking and turned her to face him once again. Reaching out, he gently ran his fingers along her jaw. This time he felt the trembling go through her. Her eyes were fixed on his face, and Austin could see she had feelings akin to his own. The intensity frightened him, although he would never have admitted it.

Jessica was the first to look away. She pulled back and began to walk again. "Come," she said, her voice hesitant and shaky. "Mother . . . uh . . . we have some cake." She twisted her hands together but kept walking. "Yes . . . we have some cake. I think . . . you . . . you should have some."

He chuckled, feeling mighty pleased with himself over her reaction. "Cake?"

She kept her gaze straight ahead, but Austin could see that her cheeks were bright red. "Yes. Cake."

CHAPTER 18

Christmas was an occasion Austin hadn't celebrated in over five years, but this Christmas Eve the Barnetts had insisted he join them. In fact, Mrs. Barnett had commanded him to plan on staying the night so he could share Christmas breakfast with them before going to church. After that the Athertons had arrived, and Austin found himself most uncomfortable. Jessica hardly looked his way, and he wondered if he'd caused more problems than good by having told her about the past.

After supper he'd joined the family in the front sitting room. But like a coward, when the suggestion was given to play charades, he slipped down the hall to his temporary bedroom. Now he heard the family laughing and having boisterous conversations, and he'd never felt more alone.

A light rap on the door immediately caused him to stand at attention. Tyler

Atherton came in and smiled. "I thought I saw you head down this way. You're missin' out on the fun." He dusted his shirt and laughed. "Guess I got some powdered sugar on me when I tried to sneak a cookie and Hannah caught me."

Austin stretched his arms over his head. "I'm pretty worn out. Figured I'd get to bed early."

The older man gave a lopsided smiled and raised a brow. "You wanna try again?"

Austin looked at him in confusion. "What do you mean, sir?"

"I mean you didn't come back here because you were tired."

"Was it that evident?"

Mr. Atherton chuckled and pulled up a chair. "Why don't you sit and tell me what's botherin' you."

Austin reclaimed his chair and began to talk about the same things he'd told Jessica regarding his brother, parents, wife, and son. By the time he'd finished, Mr. Atherton was looking at him with an unreadable expression. Austin feared perhaps Atherton felt the same toward him that his parents had.

"Son, that has to be about the saddest story I've ever heard. What a heavy load to carry, and all alone."

"Well, sir, that's the problem. I'm not bearing it alone now. I told your daughter about it. I'm afraid I might have offended her."

Atherton shook his head. "Here I figured you were tryin' to work up the nerve to propose to my girl, when all the while you were sufferin'."

"I'm not really suffering," Austin admitted. "I've dealt with their deaths, but my folks died without ever forgiving me for my own brother's death. It's their anger and hatred that I can't seem to forget."

"Ah, Austin, good folks like you described couldn't have really hated you. They were grief stricken, and folks in grief often say things they don't mean. I remember during the war when I had to tell a young man that two of his brothers had been killed. I was his superior, but he looked me in the eyes and told me that if I'd done a better job of leading, his brothers would still be alive. Then he threw a punch at me, but I dodged it. Finally, he told me he was quittin' the war. He figured to head back here to Texas and break the news to his folks."

"What did you do?"

"I let him go."

"Just like that? I mean there would've been repercussions for desertion."

"Yes, if he had really deserted. He came back about an hour later, apologized, and said he was ready to take his punishment for what he'd said and done."

"But you didn't punish him, did you?"

Atherton smiled. "No. He was a good man, and I knew it was his pain talkin', not him. After that we were good friends. He even worked several years at my ranch after his folks passed and their place had to be sold to pay off debts."

"I wish my folks could have forgiven me. I never saw them again after that night. They refused my attempts to reconcile and told their house servants to turn me away. I wanted to make things right, to be back in their good graces." He shook his head. "They were God-fearing people who raised me to believe in forgiveness, but they had none to offer."

"Don't be so sure, son. I would imagine your folks had a load of regret that over-whelmed the forgiving act." Atherton scratched his jaw. "Regret is a powerful thing. A lot of times folks give in to it, and it eats them up. Unless, of course, they learn to give it over to the Lord."

"For them, I guess that was easier said than done."

Atherton got to his feet and fixed Austin

with a sympathetic expression. "I wasn't talkin' about them, son." He walked to the door and paused. "Come on back to the party. The gals will be breakin' out the Christmas cookies and candy, and I do not intend to miss out. 'Sides that, I'm bettin' my girl is wonderin' why you haven't been seekin' her out for conversation."

Austin was surprised, but he felt a sense of relief. He got to his feet and followed the older man back to the party. He'd no sooner rejoined the party when he spied Jessica stepping outside. Since it was already dark, Austin thought to see where she was headed.

He crossed the room, and those who were still playing charades roared with laughter as Jake did his best to act out something that looked rather painful to Austin. The feeling of happiness and family encircled him once again. If only it could last.

Stepping outside, Austin found Jessica standing on the porch just a few feet away. "I saw you come outside and thought maybe something was wrong."

"I just needed a little air," she said, smiling. "It was getting pretty stuffy in there."

"I thought maybe you were avoiding me." Austin couldn't help but remember the earlier dinner conversation. Jessica had referenced their being late because Harrison Gable had stopped by with a gift. "I guess you and Gable are getting pretty close." He tried to sound disinterested, even though he was dying to hear her response.

"Well, I must say he's certainly been attentive. He brought me a Christmas gift and told me how wonderful he thinks I am."

"And what did you tell him?" Austin knew it was a bold question, but he didn't apologize.

Jessica laughed. "I told him he wouldn't say those things if he really knew me. He only sees the me that has been fighting to change. He has no knowledge of the selfish, spoiled girl I used to be. I'm sure my former friends would be happy to inform him."

"That won't matter to a man if he cares for a gal." Austin didn't know why he had said anything in support of Gable, but he didn't intend to do it again. "And if it does, he's not worth your trouble."

She sobered. "I suppose that's true enough."

Her serious mood caused Austin some discomfort. He hadn't meant to cause her unhappiness. "I . . . uh . . . have really enjoyed sharing Christmas Eve with everybody. It's fun to see the little ones get so excited over lighting the Christmas tree candles."

"Wait until the ladies bring out the Christmas candy and cookies. They work for weeks on making them. Then they have to be very creative about hiding it all so the guys don't get into it before the holidays."

"And did you help in the making of these treats?"

She smiled. "I tried to help, but I'm not very good at such things. I always figured to have servants and didn't really care to learn. Mother mostly had me mixing ingredients together while she went to measure out a different recipe."

"So you decided to go back to the idea of servants doing it all?"

She shook her head and crossed her arms. "No. Now I figure I should learn all those things I put off — especially cooking. I don't know that I'll ever marry. After all, I am twenty-two, but if I do marry, my husband will probably want to eat." She gave a laugh, and to Austin it sounded like music.

"Most men do like to eat," he confirmed. "And twenty-two isn't all that old."

Jessica still smiled but said nothing for several seconds. When she did speak, she changed the subject. Now the focus was on him.

"I want you to know that I appreciate the things you shared with me about your family and the losses. As I told you that first time we met, I prefer that people speak their minds. I find that these days honesty is more important to me than just about anything else, and I know it wasn't easy for you to tell me."

"It wasn't as hard as I'd figured, Miss Atherton," he admitted. He could see in the glow of light from the windows that she was still smiling. "In fact, I find it kind of easy to talk to you."

Her smile widened. "Truly? Because I find it very easy to talk to you."

"Do you find it just as easy to talk to Harrison Gable?" He hadn't meant to speak the words aloud, but now that they were out, he couldn't take them back.

But Jessica wasn't offended. She seemed to really consider the question before answering. "Harrison is different from you. He likes to talk about intellectual and political things. He has all sorts of plans for his life that culminate in his becoming president."

"Really?" Austin tried to imagine even having the slightest interest in such an ambitious position.

"Yes. He told me he'd studied all of the

presidents in detail as well as our constitution and history. After doing this, he just knew that he could do the job better than most have done."

"Seems a little confident of himself."

"Well, I suppose, but at least he was honest about his feelings. Like I said, I prefer that."

Austin thought perhaps he should open himself up to her — tell her how he felt. But there was always the chance that she would spurn his affection. Especially if Gable had given her any indication of proposing. Surely a man — even a man like Gable — didn't do that without having a sense of the woman being willing.

Cheers rose up from inside the house. Jessica grabbed hold of his arm. "Come along, Mr. Todd. You have to see this to believe it."

He allowed her to lead him back into the house, where everyone had crowded into the formal dining room. Jessica made a place for them as best she could, and Austin stared down at the fifteen-foot table in complete wonder. Every square inch was covered with sweet treats of every kind. There were platters of cookies and tiny cakes, tarts and candy — candy of every flavor imaginable.

"You must try Mother's fudge and peanut

brittle. They are the best."

He could hardly hear her for the children's enthusiasm. They were all vying for the position of who would go first.

"Oh, be sure to get some of the divinity. Mrs. Barnett makes that, and it's very good."

"Anything else?" he asked with a grin. "Anything that you made?"

She met his gaze and shook her head. "I mixed those spicy oatmeal cookies, but they're pretty plain." She turned back to the table and motioned to him. "See those little sandwich cookies? My aunt made those. She calls them Melt Aways. She makes a little cookie with butter and cream and I don't know what else. Then she bakes those and makes a delicious frosting for the middle. You pop the whole thing in your mouth, and it just melts away. That's the cookie you really need to try."

He didn't get a chance to reply because William Barnett was tapping a glass with his knife to get everyone's attention. "If everybody will settle down, I'll announce the person who gets to start us this year. Austin, since you're our guest, I figure that job will go to you."

Austin was surprised by this, but the others seemed delighted and pushed him around the table to where the dessert plates awaited.

"I hope he hurries up. I'm starvin' to death for candy," Wyatt told his mother. Marty rolled her eyes, but Jake only encouraged it.

"Then maybe you'll need to go second," he teased.

Mrs. Barnett put a cookie in Austin's hand. "Take anything you like and as much as you like. There is plenty for everyone." She leaned in closer and said loud enough for everyone to hear, "But if I were you — I'd hurry." Everybody laughed at this.

Austin reached tentatively for a Melt Away. He looked up and saw Jessica smiling in approval. He moved on to a platter of white candy and raised his brows in question as he pointed to the divinity. She nodded. Then Mrs. Barnett handed Wyatt a plate, and the party began in earnest.

Jessica awoke on Christmas morning with a sense of peace and contentment that she'd never known. The evening before had been so much fun, and she'd very much enjoyed her private talk with Austin Todd. She knew she had come to care for him. She prayed for him constantly, knowing that his sorrow was great. Mother had reminded Jessica recently that Jesus had known great sorrow, and Jessica had been touched in a way she hadn't expected. Jesus could understand their hurts, their pain. What a comfort that was, and today was the remembrance day of His birth.

For Jessica, it was unlike any other Christmas. Before, she would have been concerned with what she might receive. She would lie in bed and imagine all the wonderful things her parents might have purchased for her. She had concerned herself very little with the true meaning of the day.

Mr. Barnett, however, had read the Christmas story the night before, and for Jessica it was like hearing it for the first time. He told of what Mary and Joseph each had to deal with. Mary was certain to face condemnation for having a baby before she and Joseph married formally. Joseph would no doubt have to deal with humiliation, as he would most likely be tormented and rejected by his friends, family, and the temple authorities. They both had to deal with the imposed taxes and the long trip to Bethlehem — an arduous trip that required them to travel a distance of nearly a hundred miles, mostly on foot, only to arrive and find that all the beds were taken and there was no room for them. There was nothing easy about the birth of Jesus.

Jessica found herself pondering the story for a few minutes more. Finally, she got up and dressed. The house was still quiet when she made her way downstairs. Feeling her way around, Jessica lit one of the lamps. She saw from the clock on the fireplace mantel that it was only four-thirty — not even light outside. But in another half hour her folks would be getting up. It might be Christmas, but the animals still needed to be fed. Several of her father's prized cows were due to calve most any time.

Putting fuel in the stove, she built up the fire and placed a pot of coffee atop. Next, she donned her brother's work coat, lit the lantern, and made her way to the hen house. The morning was chilly and she was glad for the warmth of the jacket. And for some reason it made her think of Austin. Perhaps because she'd been wearing it when he'd come to the springhouse. She smiled at the memory. It was funny, but she found herself thinking of him a lot.

It's just because he's had such a bad time in life.

The darkness outside seemed to wrap around her as she crossed the barnyard. Sunrise wouldn't come for another three hours, and the world seemed as silent as the grave. She shivered at the thought and picked up her steps. She wished Austin would show up, as he had done that day at the springhouse.

That was such a pleasant day, and I loved getting to know him better.

Harrison had promised to visit on Christmas Day, but Jessica wasn't sure she wanted him to come. The more she spent time with Austin, the less interest she had in Harrison. Besides, Harrison had already seen her the day before. He'd shown up without warning, bestowed a beautiful necklace upon her, and even brought a box of candy for her mother.

And all the while, I couldn't wait for him to leave so that I could see Austin at the Barnetts'.

Could this be love?

She shook her head at her own internal thoughts. She wouldn't know true love if it bit her. With all of her other beaus, she had only wanted to enjoy their company and the good time that could be had. But with her change of heart and desire to become a better person, she wanted more. And with Austin, she'd found that.

It must be love. I've never felt like this before.

She took up a basket that hung outside

the door. Humming a Christmas tune, she stepped inside to the flutter of the winged animals. Several rushed past her in a flash, no doubt hopeful to be first in line for the feed she would soon drop. Father had placed a hook in the center of the coop just low enough that Jessica and her mother could hang the lantern while they searched the nests. Jessica turned up the wick and then placed the long handle over the hook and settled the lantern. The room lit up and Jessica continued her tasks. First she took up the feed and stepped outside to the collection of chickens. Her mother had over thirty hens, and most were good providers. Those who weren't were noted and lined up to become fried chicken at Sunday dinner.

Outside, the hens were scratching the ground, and the rooster let out a crowing that nearly caused Jessica to drop the basket.

"Silly rooster," she chided. "It's not yet sunrise and it's Christmas morning. Be quiet and let my parents sleep."

He immediately stopped, as if he'd understood her command. Jessica tossed a handful of feed as a reward. She then gave the hens a liberal portion and made her way back into the coop to gather eggs. It didn't take long to fill her basket and head to the house. Mother and Lupe would be surprised that she'd taken on this duty.

I am resolved to make myself useful rather than ornamental.

Lupe was already hard at work. Jessica hadn't noticed when the older woman had come to the kitchen, but she had several lamps lit and was working down the dough she'd left to rise the night before.

"Merry Christmas, Lupe," Jessica said, holding up the basket. "I gathered the eggs and thought I might make breakfast."

"*¿Es verdad?*" Lupe questioned.

Laughing, Jessica put the basket on the counter. "Yes, it's true. I may need some help, but I think I can manage bacon and eggs. And I can slice some bread for toast."

Lupe smiled. "You do not need to do my work."

"I want to, though. I want to do something nice for Mother and Father . . . and for you. It's Christmas, and I think I owe it to all of you." Jessica paused and grinned at the older woman's surprise. "It's my Christmas present."

Chapter 19

With the new year came new information, and it couldn't have pleased Austin more. After going through the business correspondence of Alice's father, Austin had determined that one bank in particular might lend them an answer. The bank was in Colorado Springs rather than Denver, and furthermore, it was clear from Chesterfield's correspondence that he had been making some sort of quarterly payment to the institution.

A letter that arrived for Austin Todd explained why Chesterfield was storing a locked box in their vault. The man said that a previous manager had made the arrangements with Chesterfield and the new manager had long wanted the box removed. He made it clear that if Austin would come with a letter of permission from Alice, he would be happy to relinquish the property to

300

Austin's care.

Fingering the key Alice had given him, Austin felt confident that this would open the box. It wasn't like any key he'd ever seen, but even so he knew it must be the one. Why else would Chesterfield have kept it in his personal effects?

He looked at the bronze key a moment longer and then set it aside. Austin expected Robert at any moment. He'd stopped by the Barnetts' to tell them about the letter, but Robert and Alice and their baby had gone to visit Marty's family. Hannah had promised she'd send Robert over as soon as they returned. That was over three hours ago.

Tucking the key back into his pocket, Austin decided to put some coffee on to boil. He wouldn't say he made the best coffee, but it was pretty good. And on a chilly day the drinker might not be too picky.

With the coffee on the stove, Austin went in search of an extra mug and spied the cookies Tyler Atherton had brought him the day before. Jessica had baked them and wanted Austin to sample her very first batch. The memory made him smile. She was being true to her word on learning how to cook, and the outcome had been delicious. He couldn't remember ever having such delicious sugar cookies, and he wasn't of a mind to share them. Smiling to himself, he hid the remaining cookies in the cupboard. Robert got plenty of goodies at home, but he had a sweet tooth, and if he saw the treat he might be tempted to eat until they were gone.

After some time, Austin heard the distinctive sound of a horse approaching. He checked the coffee. It was ready. He took the pot from the stove and placed it on the table with the mugs. A loud knock sounded on the door.

"It's open. Come on in," Austin called, pouring coffee into each mug. He held up the pot. "Thought you might need a cup to ward off the chill."

"I do," Robert agreed. "Pa said it got down to thirty-five degrees last night." He rubbed his hands together. "And to make matters worse, I've lost my gloves . . . again."

Austin chuckled. "Maybe that was why you received so many pairs for Christmas." He couldn't help but think back to that morning and the family's exchange of gifts. There had been three for Austin. From the Barnett family he'd received a hand-knit scarf and a new shirt — both made by Hannah Barnett. The third present was a leather-bound copy of *The Time Machine* by

H. G. Wells from Jake and Marty. He cherished all three.

"Seems I set the gloves down and they walk off. Or maybe it's me who walks off," Robert said, discarding his coat. He hung it on an empty peg by the door and made his way to the table. "Jake tells me I don't know anything about the cold since I live in Texas, but I'm pert near frozen to death."

Remembering a time in Virginia when snow had blanketed their town, Austin gave a chuckle. "It is a whole different situation, and I find I prefer Texas."

Robert ambled over to the stove to warm his hands. "Ma said it was important so I came over straightaway. What seems to be the problem? Have you learned something new?"

"I have. Take a seat and I'll show you. You want cream or sugar for your coffee?"

"No. Just black is fine."

Austin produced the letter and placed it in front of Robert. He gave the man time to read while he took his seat at the table and sampled the coffee. He smiled in satisfaction at the taste.

"Do you think this might be where the counterfeit bills are hidden?" Robert asked, looking hopeful.

"That's my thought. You'll note that the

box is heavy, so I'm hoping that means the plates are in there, as well. I've contacted my superiors to see how they want to handle this. Most likely they'll have me travel to Colorado Springs to retrieve it."

"Then maybe all of this will be over with," Robert said, shaking his head. "Jake can tell Mr. Morgan and be done with it."

"Has he showed up again?"

"Yeah. We don't know where he was for most of the fall, but Morgan reappeared in mid-December and has been showing up from time to time, never planned or invited, but always persistent."

"Is he still threatenin' Jake with the authorities?" Robert asked.

"Not directly. When Jake suggested that perhaps Morgan himself was behind the counterfeiting and maybe he should take his suspicions to the authorities, Morgan changed his tune. He told Jake that he was just overstressed about someone forging certificates using numbers associated with his bank. Said he was worried about the effect it might have on the economy.

"Jake said Mr. Morgan was somewhat apologetic, like he expected Jake to understand it was his fear talking and not his reasoning. However, in the next breath, he muttered something to the effect that no one would believe he'd just handed Jake all that wealth and privilege. And, of course, there's really no one who can substantiate that Morgan did, in fact, give those things to Jake."

Robert considered this for a moment and took a long drink of the coffee. "It would seem Jake's comment threatened Morgan enough that he decided to move slower. Even so, I can't help but wonder if Morgan has a part in all of this. I have a hard time believin' he's just worried about the finances of the country."

"It's hard to say," Austin admitted, "but I tend to agree with you. I've gone over all the details given me by Alice, Jake, and Marty. I'm beginning to see a definite pattern. The one thing they all have in common is Mr. Paul Morgan. With that in mind, I've sent word to my associates in Washington to have him further investigated. I'm certain by now they've arranged for someone to look closer at his dealings. The man certainly lives above his means and did so even during the hardest times in '93 and '94."

"Well, he is related to J. P. Morgan. It is possible he's been subsidized by this distant cousin."

"I don't know. I guess that's just one more

thing to figure out." Austin picked up the coffeepot and offered Robert a refill. He gladly took it.

For several minutes the two men drank in silence. The wind picked up outside and made a moaning sound in the cabin. To Austin it sounded sorrowful.

"What's your plan, Austin?" Robert finally asked. "Is there anything I can do to help get this resolved?"

"Well, as I mentioned, I've sent a wire to my former boss. I figure he'll give me the go ahead to retrieve the box and open it. If it holds the certificates and plates, then that's good news. If not, we're back where we started."

Robert nodded. "I can help you with rail fare."

"Thanks, but when I agreed to take this on, the agency set up an account from which I can draw. I won't need financial help."

"So what kind of help do you need?"

Austin thought for a moment and without really meaning to he replied, "Spiritual."

Robert looked surprised, even confused. "In what way?"

Leaning back in his chair Austin shared something of the past. It seemed to get a little easier each time he told it. Robert listened patiently, making no comment while Austin related his story.

"I faced a lot of loss." Austin paused, uncertain he should continue. Robert was a good friend and appeared to be in no hurry to leave. Austin drew a deep breath and added, "It left me feeling that God no longer cared for me, that I wasn't of importance to Him."

Robert gave a hint of a nod. "Because you'd lost your family." It was more statement than question.

"Yes, mostly. In the aftermath I felt so alone — even spiritually. The church folk I knew didn't bother to check up on me. I had moved back to the city after Grace died. I couldn't bear remaining in that house." He blew out a heavy breath and fell back against his chair. "Even though I rented an apartment in the town's central area near my old church, no one came to call. It was as if I no longer existed."

"Perhaps they didn't realize you'd returned."

"Oh, they knew. I still owed the pastor for Grace's services, and when I went to pay him, I mentioned having moved and gave him the address. He didn't call on me or check to see why I wasn't attending services. Of course, it is a rather large church."

"Still, you would have thought someone would have come to see you."

"I think my parents scared them off. They probably told everyone that I was to blame for Houston's death, as well as Grace's and my baby's." He shook his head. "If only they knew how I still carry that burden of responsibility. I loved my brother. I loved my wife and son. For my parents to suggest or think otherwise broke me in a way I wasn't sure I could recover from."

"I can see now what you meant by spiritual help." Robert rubbed his chin. "I'm no preacher, but I do know that God doesn't strip away His love when we make mistakes. You never meant to cause your brother or wife harm, so there was no sin on your part. The responsibility and blame you heap on yourself really aren't yours. You've taken on a burden that never belonged to you."

Austin stiffened. "It was my bullet."

"What was the intention of your heart?"

"I was going to wound the counterfeiter."

Robert raised a brow. "You mean to tell me you weren't plannin' to kill him?"

"No," Austin said, shaking his head. "We needed the counterfeiters alive so we might learn if there were others involved on a higher level. It turned out there were."

"So the intention of your heart was to

capture this criminal and not to kill him."

Austin shrugged. "To tell you the truth, when I saw him aim his rifle, I feared for Houston and myself. I drew up my pistol, and like I said, the man moved to fire and I beat him to it. Unfortunately, Houston thought I'd be killed and jumped in front of me."

"Seems to me it was your brother's fault he got himself killed."

"That's a hard thing to hear. I don't look at it that way." Austin felt a sense of anger. "Houston was a good agent. He knew his job and did it well. We had always been a good team up until then."

"You were still a good team. In fact, I'd say his action proved that. He must have loved you dearly to sacrifice his own life for yours."

"He did." Austin's words were barely audible.

"And what about Grace? Was it your intention to kill her — to kill your son?"

Austin was indignant. "Of course not! But I took her from the city, fearing someone might try to hurt her because of my work. I thought I was doing a good thing, but the isolation proved to take her life."

"And you know for certain that had you been in the city, she would have lived?"

He thought for a moment. "No, but at least there would have been help available for her. Don't you understand? She was alone. I'd planned for someone to be there, but the woman wasn't able to come. So when Grace went into labor, no one was there to help her."

"Austin, women die in childbirth all the time. I feared I'd lose Alice, but she told me the sacrifice was worth anything to have a child."

For a moment Austin remembered Grace saying something similar. He didn't have a chance to think on it for long, because Robert continued.

"And with your folks . . . well, I think their deaths had little to do with you. No doubt they were grieved over the loss of your brother, but their own bitterness and the need to blame someone ate at them. We can't live under the pressure of hate and anger for long before it consumes us. It picks away little pieces of the heart day by day until there's nothing left — and a man can't live without a heart."

"My father died from a heart attack, and I believe Mother died in her grief — not anger at me."

"Which is my point," Robert said, getting to his feet. "This really isn't about you or what part you played. My guess is that your folks regretted what they'd said to you, but they didn't know how to make it right, so they just left it undone. They probably thought they had plenty of time to mend fences. But we never know how much time we have on earth, so it's best to treat each day as though it's our last."

Austin wanted to believe him. "And where was God in all of this?"

Robert never lost his smile. "God was there with your brother and you when a man threatened to kill you, and He took your brother's life instead of yours. He was there with Grace and your son when neither were strong enough to go on living. He was there with you when you found them dead. He was even there with your parents while they grieved and blamed you, and there, too, as they died in their sorrows and bitterness. He never left you, Austin. We are the ones who do the walkin' away."

Taking his coat from the peg, Robert donned it and opened the door. "Just think about it, Austin. Go look in the Bible and see if I'm not speakin' truth. That's the only place to go for confirmation. God will show you."

Austin followed him to the door and reached into his own coat pocket. "Here,

311

take these. I have another pair." He handed Robert his leather gloves. "Thank you."

Robert grinned. "I'm probably going to lose these, you know."

"That's all right."

Austin stared at the door long after Robert had exited. He reasoned through all that Robert had said and did his best to find cause to deny its truth. He couldn't. He shifted his gaze to the ceiling.

"Are you really here with me?"

Jessica kneaded her dough just as Mrs. Barnett had instructed. Mother had sent her over to Hannah Barnett for lessons on making bread and cinnamon rolls. She assured Jessica that Hannah made the best in the county — possibly the state.

"That's looking good," Mrs. Barnett told her. "Now we're going to roll out the dough. Once we have it stretched out, we'll slather butter on it and sprinkle it with cinnamon and sugar. Will likes me to be generous with the sugar." She smiled at Jessica. "After that, we roll it up, stretch it out a little to make it longer, and then we cut it in inch-wide slices all the way down the roll. We put them out on a pan and give 'em room, because they're gonna double their size when we leave them to rise."

Jessica fervently hoped she'd remember everything, because Hannah had mentioned she'd be heading to Marty's and be gone for maybe an hour. Alice would be there to help if she got stuck, but Hannah assured her that she'd be back in time to help Jessica get them into the oven.

Alice popped into the kitchen, as if the thought of her name had drawn her there. "The babies are asleep, so now I can get some of that ironing done."

Hannah Barnett looked at her daughter-in-law with such an expression of love, it stirred something deep in Jessica's heart. "I told Jess that she could come to you if she gets perplexed in finishing up here."

Alice gave her mother-in-law a nod. "I'd be happy to help. I'll be in the back room. Holler if you need me."

Jessica couldn't help but sigh in relief. She was glad they had become good friends. Alice was the only woman her own age who spent any time with Jessica, and clearly she wouldn't have had to. No one could have blamed her after the way Jessica had treated her in the past, but Alice was full of forgiveness.

I want to be like that.

The two women left Jessica to her work, and by the time she had placed the last roll on the pan to rise, she heard a loud knock on the front door.

"I'll tend to it," Alice called out.

Jessica took up some large flour sack towels, covered each of the trays, and put them aside to give the rolls time to rise. Grabbing more wood, she stoked the fire in the stove so the heated air would help the dough rise faster.

Since she'd heard nothing more from Alice, Jessica presumed that the caller was for her and went about cleaning up the kitchen. However, when she heard Alice cry out as if in pain, Jessica hurried down the hall as quietly as possible.

"I don't know where those certificates are. Let go of me."

The sound of her friend's fear caused Jessica to freeze in place.

"I know that you're a busy . . . mother," a man declared, letting the word fade. The unspoken threat was there all the same.

"I can't help you," Alice insisted.

Jessica wondered what she should do. There was a shotgun by the back door. Perhaps she should retrieve it. She didn't recognize the voice of the man, but he wasn't a friend.

"I know Mrs. Barnett has gone. We saw her leave in the buggy."

314

"We?" Alice asked, her voice little more than a squeeze.

This put Jessica into action. There was more than one man and that could mean trouble. More trouble than two young women could handle alone. The shotgun would make a good companion.

Jessica quickly retrieved the weapon, checked to make sure it was loaded, then made her way back as the stranger announced, "I think you know my friend." Alice gasped and Jessica stepped around the corner, shotgun leveled.

"I think you remember Mr. Smith."

Alice promptly fainted.

CHAPTER 20

Austin got home late at night after traveling that day to Dallas and back. He'd made the long ride to Dallas early that morning to meet with a representative of his old boss, Ellery Turner. The man took detailed notes of everything Austin had done and learned. Then he gave Austin a letter from Mr. Turner. Austin perused it quickly, happy to see that it contained official approval for him to go to Colorado Springs. Once there, he would meet with two other agents Turner would send. They were men he would know, so there would be no question as to their identity. The trio was then to retrieve the lockbox from the bank and return to the hotel. There were further instructions, but Austin decided to give them a more thorough reading at home.

Happy to have his orders, Austin had grabbed a very late lunch before seeing Judge Weimer in order to brief the man on what was happening. However, that had been hours ago, and now he didn't know whether he was more hungry or tired or cold.

The little cabin sat by itself under the starry sky. Nevertheless, the sight welcomed Austin and made him feel better. The wind had picked up in the last hours, chilling him to the bone. All he could think of was being warm, but eating and sleeping continued to run a close second and third. First he'd have to care for the horse's needs, so getting thawed out would have to wait.

Glancing overhead at the stars, Austin thought of Jessica and how much he'd enjoy looking up at the night sky with her by his side. The horse whinnied, as if agreeing with his thoughts.

"You like her, too? Well, that just shows you have good taste," Austin said in the stillness. He smiled and continued thinking about the beautiful woman. He also thought for a moment of Grace and knew she'd want him to be happy. She wouldn't have liked the man he'd become since her death — lonely and haunted by the past. She would want him to marry Jessica.

"I've done my best, Grace, but I intend to do more."

He rode around to the small pen Mr.

Barnett had made for the horse. There was a loafing shed with a suitable attachment where Austin could store his tack, and across the pen a trough of water sat by the main pump. It proved to be a good setup.

Once he'd finished with the horse, Austin made his way back around to the front of the house. It was only when he got to the door that he realized a note had been tacked to it. He pulled the paper off and took it inside with him.

Lighting a lamp, Austin turned up the wick a bit and read the missive. *Need to see you as soon as possible. R. Barnett.* Austin pulled out his pocket watch. It was nearly ten o'clock. Definitely too late to visit the Barnetts. No doubt Robert wanted to know about his trip to Dallas. He tossed the letter down on the table and yawned. Maybe he'd just wait until morning to eat.

Jessica could scarcely breathe. "Will I . . . what?"

"Will you marry me?"

She looked at the man kneeling before her. "This is rather sudden. We don't really know each other very well."

Harrison Gable got to his feet and pulled Jessica into his arms. "Believe me when I say that I want very much to know you and

318

know you well." He pressed a kiss against her left cheek and then her right. Jessica pulled away as his lips headed toward her mouth.

"This isn't right. My father would not approve of the way you're acting." She moved to stand behind her chair, hoping that it might keep Harrison at bay.

He threw her a leering glance and laughed. "Your father won't long have much to say on the matter. Marry me and we can slip away tonight. We'll go to Dallas, where no one knows you. I have friends there — a judge who can marry us right away." He paused and took a step toward her. Jessica backed up. This only caused him to smile once again. "Marry me, Jessica. You know that I can make you happy. I know that you have feelings for me. I've seen you tremble at my touch. Don't think me unschooled. I know exactly what I'm doing."

"I'm sure you do, but what you don't realize," she said, moving once again to expand the distance between them, "is that my father and mother are just in the other room. It wouldn't be difficult to draw their attention."

He stopped pursuing her and folded his arms across his chest. "So draw their attention."

He'd called her bluff, and Jessica knew she would have to act quickly. "I don't need them to fight my battles for me. I have no desire to marry you, Mr. Gable. I have considered the possibility and weighed it in the scales. However, you have been found wanting."

Her bold words seemed to surprise him. For several seconds he said nothing, but his eyes narrowed and his expression appeared angry. "It's Todd, isn't it? You fancy yourself in love with that sad-eyed lawman."

"It's really none of your concern to whom I give my love. Now, if you don't mind, it's getting quite late, and you promised my parents that we would only spend a few minutes alone. I believe we should now rejoin them, and you should bid them good-night." She headed toward the door with false bravado. Without looking back to make certain he followed, Jessica opened the door and stepped into the hallway.

She heard Gable follow and was pleased with herself. Maybe being strong and assertive wasn't always a bad thing.

"Mother. Father," she said, entering the larger sitting room. "Mr. Gable has to leave."

"It was way too late to come over last

night," Austin said apologetically. "I didn't want you to think I was ignoring you." He threw Robert a smile, but the man didn't return it.

"We've got a big problem."

Austin could see that Robert was more than a little agitated. "What's wrong?"

"Morgan was here. Worse still, he brought the same man who'd harassed Alice in Denver."

Austin twisted his hat. "Who was that?"

"He calls himself Mr. Smith. He always mentioned having worked for someone. We just didn't know it was Morgan. Alice is sick over the whole thing. She passed out cold. Lucky for her Jessica was here."

"Jessica Atherton?"

"The same." For the first time Robert smiled, but it wasn't joy filled. "She greeted the men with Hannah's double-barreled shotgun. She ordered them to leave, and I guess she must have looked menacing enough that they figured she'd shoot."

Austin couldn't help but laugh. "I would've liked to have seen that."

Robert lost a bit of his worried look. "Me too."

Austin could see that Robert was anxious to finish and sobered. "What happened next?"

"After they'd gone, Jessica bolted the door and put Alice to bed."

"Where was your ma and servants?"

Robert shrugged and began to pace. "Ma had gone to visit Marty. I guess everybody else was busy elsewhere. Jess said it happened in just a matter of minutes."

"So Morgan isn't just bothering Jake. Now he's after Alice. Well, I've got news that may change everything." A brilliant idea flashed through Austin's mind. "In fact, if you'll help me, I know it will."

"I'll do whatever I can to rid my wife of those men. I thought to track them," Robert admitted, "but my pa discouraged it. He said since you were now working on this, we had to lay low and give you a chance."

"I appreciate that," Austin said. "It'll help us with what I have in mind. I got the approval to go to Colorado Springs and retrieve the lockbox on behalf of the Treasury Department. All I need is a signed letter from Alice stating that I have been given the key and have her permission to remove the box from the bank and take it into my possession."

"I'm sure she will be happy to oblige."

"There's more. I will meet up with a couple of agents the department will send via express train. Barring any complications,

I should be able to be home in a week, maybe ten days."

"What will you do once you have the box?"

Austin pulled the key from his pocket. "I'll open it. I'm supposed to learn of the contents at the bank. If it's the forged certificates or the plates, we'll confiscate them and the agents will take them back to Washington. Otherwise, I'll bring whatever is in the box back to Alice."

Robert looked perplexed. "So what is it you need from me?"

"Well, the way I figure it, if Morgan and his Mr. Smith know what I'm up to, they'll follow me. They won't have any reason to stick around here once they know I'm headed out on the train and why. What I need is for word to get out about my plans. We need them to overhear what I'm doing and when."

"I'm bettin' you're right," Robert said, sounding hopeful for the first time. "I reckon they will follow after you."

"And that will take them away from your family and from Jake's." Austin considered the plan for a moment. "Since we don't know where they're staying or who they may have hired to keep watch on us, I'll have to make sure we have plenty of time to bandy the news about."

"How long do you think it will take?" Alice stepped into the room. It was clear she'd been listening from the hallway.

Austin didn't mind. "A day or two. I figure if we get enough folks talkin', Morgan is bound to hear about it."

"And you need me to write a letter?" Alice questioned.

Austin nodded. He could see the fear in her eyes. "I do."

"Then I'll get that for you now." She left the room without another word.

Robert stopped pacing and crossed his arms with a frown. "This had better work."

Jessica knew she would have to give her mother an account of her time spent with Harrison, but she wasn't looking forward to it at all. Thankfully, Father was off with William Barnett ironing out some final arrangements about the plans for the railroad.

At one time, what had happened the night before was something Jessica thought would make her the happiest woman in the world. But it hadn't. In fact, it had only caused her more problems.

"You have moped around here all day," Mother declared. "Now sit down and tell me what happened. Did Harrison get fresh with you? Did he try to take liberties?"

Jessica shook her head. "No. Well, yes, but not really." She sank into her favorite chair by the fire. "He proposed." Mother looked confused for a moment and then burst out laughing. Jessica frowned. "It's not funny, Mother."

"It is when you consider I feared something evil had happened. I'm relieved to learn it was just a proposal. So did you accept?"

Jessica met her mother's eyes. "No."

"Can you talk about it? You left so quickly for bed last night I was quite concerned."

With a sigh, the young woman began to share the details. "He wasted little time. With you and father otherwise occupied, I suppose he figured it to be the perfect time. So while we were in the sitting room, we made small talk about the evening and then without warning he asked me to marry him. I thought at first it was a joke."

"But he was serious?"

Jessica looked at her mother and nodded. "He asked me to marry him and to do so right away. He wanted me to run away last night to Dallas, where he has a friend who could marry us."

"Run away to marry? Didn't he know you would want a big wedding?"

"I don't think he truly knows anything about me, Mother."

"Goodness. I remember a few years back when you and I were dreaming about your wedding. We were looking at an article in one of the ladies' magazines about some royalty somewhere married in a lavish ceremony. It spoke of the princess wearing a gown embroidered with real silver thread. And her trousseau — do you remember what it said about that?"

Jessica shook her head. She longed to get back to her ordeal, but Mother seemed almost dreamy in her remembrance. "The magazine said her trousseau consisted partly of 'forty outdoor suits, fifteen ball dresses, five tea gowns, and a vast number of bonnets, shoes, and gloves.' I can still remember the exact number and wording, because it was so much more than anything I could imagine."

Jess gave a heavy sigh.

Mother seemed to understand her frustration and eased back against the sofa with a smile. "Sorry. I just think it unfeeling of him to expect you to give up a proper wedding."

For a moment neither woman said anything more. But Jessica couldn't leave the matter at that tentative point. "I don't love him," she confessed. "I don't have any feelings whatsoever for him. I thought at one time I might. He was thrilling and attentive, and I thought him very handsome."

"But someone else has caught your eye, or should I say your heart?"

"Yes."

Mother considered this a moment, looking thoughtful. "And you feel bad now? Perhaps you feel sorry for Harrison?"

"No. I'm afraid it's much more selfish than that." Jessica shifted uncomfortably. "I've tried so hard not to make myself the center of attention. I've tried to improve myself and be more focused on God, but . . . honestly, I'm worried."

"Worried about what?" This definitely had her mother's attention.

Jessica gazed upward, feeling unable to face her mother's reaction. "What if this is my only chance to marry?"

Mother lowered her gaze. Jessica thought perhaps her mother was disgusted with her shallow thinking, but Jess had to be honest. That was part of changing for the better. And, she'd always been one to say exactly what she thought.

"You can't marry a man you do not love," Mother finally said, raising her gaze to Jessica. "You told me that you don't love Harrison. Therefore, you did the right thing.

Whether or not anyone else proposes marriage is immaterial. If you married Harrison Gable, you would come to regret it, and then hate might very well build instead of love."

Jessica found her mother's expression sympathetic and not at all ashamed or disappointed. She felt her fears release. Mother understood.

"I want very much to marry. It's just that I want to marry someone else. Someone I love."

"But Mr. Todd hasn't asked?"

She wasn't surprised that mother knew. She'd done very little to conceal her thoughts of Austin Todd and had spoken quite favorably of him on more than one occasion. She sighed and didn't bother to deny it.

"He hasn't, but I wish he would."

"Maybe you should tell him that," Mother told her. "You said he liked the fact that you speak your mind. Perhaps he would find it acceptable if you did the proposing."

"Mother!" Jessica snapped, sitting up. "That's hardly proper."

Her mother's laughter was unexpected, causing Jessica to get to her feet. "If you think this is a joke, then I'm going to go to my room."

Mother stood and took hold of her. "I don't think it's a joke, my dear girl. I only want the very best for you. I don't want you to lose someone because of traditions and proprieties. If you love Austin, you must tell him."

"But what if he doesn't feel the same?" The thought of Austin's rejection made Jessica feel almost sick.

Mother was unconcerned. "What if he does? What if he's just been waiting for some sign from you?"

Jessica thought carefully. What was the worst that could happen? If she told Austin about her feelings for him and he told her he wasn't inclined to feel the same way, she couldn't possibly feel any worse.

Austin made his way home from the Barnetts', taking the road rather than cutting across their vast pastureland. He'd come this way on purpose — that purpose being he wanted to see Jessica.

Directing his horse to leave the road and head up the path to the Atherton house, Austin knew he needed to square things with Jess before heading to Colorado Springs. He wanted her to know that he had feelings for her, that he cared very much for her, and he wanted to marry her.

But what if she doesn't feel the same way about me? What if Gable holds her heart and I'm too late? The thought of losing Jessica to Gable made Austin sick to his stomach.

I know she feels something. She trembled at my touch — surely that's a good sign. But even as he thought about it, a troubling idea came to mind. Maybe she trembled because she was put off by his touch. Maybe it was abhorrent to her.

He nearly turned the horse for home at that thought, but he'd already reached the house, and Tyler Atherton was waving to him from just outside the barn.

Austin drew a deep breath and dismounted. Pulling his mount along with him, he walked to where the older man was washing up.

"Good to see you again," Mr. Atherton said. "I was just heading into the house for some coffee. Would you like to join me? Jessica has been baking again. I think she's caught on to it pretty quick. She made some of the most mouth-watering cinnamon rolls you could sink your teeth into."

"Sounds too good to pass up." Austin nodded toward the horse. "I shouldn't stay too long, however. There's a lot going on, and I have to make some preparations."

Atherton dried his hands and face on a

towel that hung nearby. "Well, let's get right to it, then."

Austin went along with the older man and soon found himself sitting at the long dining room table with Atherton. The ladies were strangely absent, and Austin found himself desperate to learn of their whereabouts. Especially of Jessica.

"Mmm, this is the best cinnamon roll I've ever had," Austin admitted. "And a perfect match to the coffee."

"I thought you'd enjoy it," Atherton said, then sampled his own roll. He ate for a moment and smiled. "Just as good as the first six."

Both men chuckled at the comment. "I know Jess will be pleased to know you've approved of them."

It was the opening he'd been waiting for. "Speaking of Miss Atherton, is she here?"

Tyler nodded. "She's helpin' her ma with one of the new calves. The mama won't nurse it, so my gals are seein' that it bonds with another cow. Carissa and Jess have always been good at that. But don't worry, she won't be much longer. I had just finished checking on them when you arrived." Then he quickly changed the subject.

"Say, that place we're building for you in Terryton is nearly done. I sure hope you won't mind havin' a jail on the front side of your house. We're building it with two cells and a small office. If we find we need more room, we can add some additional cells to the east and west walls. But your residence will be on the back side. We argued over whether to put an access to your living quarters from the jail or just have it on the outside free and clear. Will seemed to think you'd appreciate the internal access, and we fixed the door so you can bolt it from your side when you retire."

Austin didn't care where the jail or door was at this point. He thought perhaps he should just put his thoughts out there for Atherton to consider. It wouldn't be all that appropriate to ask Jessica to marry him without first stating his intention to her father. On the other hand, if he asked Atherton for his blessing, but Jessica had no feelings for him, then it would be for naught.

She has feelings for you. Stop being so bullheaded, his heart seemed to declare.

"Mr. Atherton, before the ladies join us . . . well . . . I wanted to talk to you."

"Oh? What about?" Atherton took up his coffee.

The laughter of women came from the kitchen. They were back already, and Jessica and her mother were definitely amused about something. The only problem was that Austin couldn't continue his conversation with Mr. Atherton.

"Ladies, look who's come to sample the cinnamon rolls," Jessica's father said as they entered the room.

"Oh, goodness, Austin," Mrs. Atherton said in surprise. "We'd have come sooner if we'd known you were here. We have a calf whose mama won't let him nurse. After we fed him we were watching his antics. Jess, you should take Austin out to the barn and show him."

Mr. Atherton looked at Austin and smiled. "I think you should go, son. The calf is quite the showman."

Popping the last of the cinnamon roll into his mouth, Austin got to his feet and followed Jessica through the house and out the back door. He loved watching the way her skirt swayed as she walked. Her hair hung down her back, tied with a single ribbon. A ribbon that wouldn't be at all difficult to pull loose. Austin felt perspiration form on his forehead at the thought of running his hands through her caramel and cocoa hair. He liked the way the sunshine lit glints of red amidst the browns.

"You're sure quiet," Jessica said, looking back at him.

They'd just reached the barn, and she swung the door wide. "Is something wrong?"

"Uh, no. Nothing's wrong."

"Well, you just seem . . . hmm . . . different." She grinned. "Not that different is bad." She smiled and motioned him to follow. "We have the calf over here." She led the way and stopped in front of a small pen.

The calf gave a pitiful cry. Jessica knelt down and reached through the rails, and he came to see if she had something to offer him. Austin thought the calf seemed surprised when all he found was her hand.

"He is a cute little fella," Austin said, giving the animal a quick glance. He'd much rather watch Jessica than the calf.

Austin wanted to say something more, but the words seemed to catch in his throat. How could he leave for Colorado Springs without telling her how he felt? If he didn't stake a claim, Harrison Gable might sweep her off her feet and carry her away.

"We will be pairing him with one of the other cows. Mother's been using a hide to put on the back of another calf. The scent will rub off, and then we'll put the hide on this little fella so that the mama cow will accept him. Mother feels certain she'll take him. He was just weak, but now he's doing better. Tomorrow we'll try to put them together."

Jessica continued talking about the animal, but Austin could only think of her and what he wanted to say. How could he just come out and declare his love for her? If he did that, would she think him too bold — too much the rogue?

Before he could answer that, however, Jessica got to her feet. Still facing the calf, she laughed. Having no will to stop himself, Austin reached out and plucked the ribbon from Jessica's head. The thick lustrous hair splayed out across her back.

In surprise, Jessica whirled around to face him, and without giving it another thought, Austin pulled her into his arms and kissed her soundly. He felt her melt against him with a sigh.

Maybe words weren't necessary, he thought, and deepened the kiss.

CHAPTER 21

Gasping for air, Jessica pushed away from Austin. "You kissed me!"

"Was that what it was?" he asked with a grin. "Well, I just might do it again." He stepped forward as if to follow up his words, but Jessica put her hands to his chest and pushed.

"Why did you kiss me?" she asked, searching his face.

"Why? You have to ask why?" Austin shook his head. "I've never heard of a woman having to ask why she was kissed."

"Well . . . I . . . I . . . don't understand. You've . . . never, I mean . . ." She stammered to find the right words, and finally she waved her hands in the air. "I don't know what I mean."

He chuckled and moved a step closer. This time Jessica didn't stop him. Her mind whirled with thoughts. Was this a declaration of love? Did Austin truly feel for her as she did for him?

"Look, Miss Atherton . . . Jessica," he said, reaching out to push her hair back, "I've been disturbed by you ever since I met you."

She regained her senses at this. "Disturbed by me? What kind of thing is that to say about somebody?"

He reached out again to touch her hair. This time, however, he toyed with the wavy strand as he'd once seen Gable do. "All right, you've been on my mind, and it's been almost torturous. I can't eat or sleep without thinking of you."

Inside, Jessica was cheering, but outside, she remained stoic. "Well, it sounds like you may be sick."

Austin looked incredulous. "I am sick. I'm love-sick. You've got me acting like a boy with his first crush."

She grinned. "What's so bad about that?"

He began to pace in front of her . . . only inches away . . . close enough that she could reach out and touch him if she chose to. With her heart racing and her breathing rather ragged, Jessica watched Austin's expression change several times before he stopped in front of her. His expression looked very much like an animal that needed to be put out of its misery.

"Well?" she asked, hands on hips. "What's so bad about being love-sick?"

"You know that I planned to never feel anything for anyone again. I told you about all the folks I lost . . . including my wife and son. I didn't want to go through that then, and I sure don't want to go through it now."

"And you figured that if you kept your heart as hard as stone you wouldn't have to. Is that it?"

"Something like that."

She shook her head. "It doesn't work. Believe me."

He put his hand to his face and rubbed his temples. "I just don't know what to do about it. One minute I'm sure I know what to say, and the next I feel tongue-tied. You've turned my world upside down and sidewise." He lowered his hand and studied her for a moment. "You are without a doubt the source of my disruption."

Jessica shook her head and started to speak, but Austin put his finger to her lips. "Hush. I know my words don't make sense. I know they sound harsh, but they're not intended to. Maybe I don't have flowery words like Harrison Gable, but I do have the truth."

She took hold of his finger and drew his

hand away. Jessica didn't release him, however. She continued to hold fast to his hand. "I don't want flowery words."

"I don't have his kind of money, either. Never will, most likely."

Jessica shook her head. "I don't need money, either."

Austin looked deep into her eyes. Jessica could see a longing in his expression that matched her own. "What do you need?" he asked softly.

"You," she whispered. "Just you."

Stepping back as if burned, Austin seemed to struggle for words. "I love you, you know."

"I didn't, but I guess I do now." She wanted to jump up and down and shout it out to the world. Why did young women have to act so composed when moments like this were begging to be celebrated?

His mouth clenched for a moment and then Austin asked, "How . . . how do you feel . . . about me?"

Jessica surprised them both by throwing herself back into his arms. She reached up to pull his face to hers. It was the first kiss she'd ever initiated, and she liked it very much. Pulling back, she smiled.

"I guess you feel the same as I do," Austin said, shaking his head. "Poor woman."

"So what are we going to do about it?"

He chuckled. "Well, I thought I'd talk to your father about marrying you. That is, if you want to marry me." She raised a brow, but said nothing. It wasn't the proposal she'd looked forward to.

He seemed to understand almost at once and dropped to one knee. Reaching up, he took hold of her hands. "Jessica, will you do me the honor of marrying me?"

Laughing like a young girl, Jessica thrilled to the question. She felt none of the dread she had when Harrison had proposed. "Here I thought I might never marry, yet I've had two proposals in the last twenty-four hours."

He frowned. "Gable?"

She sobered. "Yes, but I told him no."

"May I ask why?"

"Because I don't love him, silly. I love you."

Austin met her gaze. "So will you marry me?"

Jessica pulled her right hand from his hold and reached out to touch his face. A tenderness and love she'd never known filled her with wonder. "Of course I will."

A half hour later, Austin was asking Mr. Atherton for permission to marry his youngest child. Austin knew the man to be fair-minded but worried that he wouldn't want his little girl marrying a lawman. The life of such a man could bring danger upon his family, and Austin didn't want to cause the Athertons any grief.

"Do you love her?" Mr. Atherton asked. He watched Austin carefully as he awaited the answer.

Austin didn't hesitate. "I do. I love her very much." He looked to the floor, unable to take the intensity of the older man's gaze. "I never thought I could love again."

"I remember you sayin' you lost your wife and baby."

Drawing a deep breath, Austin raised his head. "Yes. It was in childbirth. Folks told me it was for the best . . . that if I had to lose the mother, it'd be better to lose both, since the baby would have had a hard time surviving without the mother. I never quite saw it that way, though."

Tyler nodded. "Sometimes folks don't know what they're sayin', and by the time they do, it's too late."

"Some even said that I wasn't to blame, but whether I was or not, I vowed not to let it happen again. Then I met Jessica and none of that seemed to much matter. I guess that's my heart trying to comfort me."

"Maybe it's God trying to comfort your heart. He does that, you know. The Holy Spirit is called the Comforter in the Bible. I reckon God wants us to find comfort and peace of mind, or He wouldn't have given us a Comforter."

"Even if we walk away from Him?" Austin asked.

"And did you?"

Austin blew out a heavy breath. "I didn't stop believing in Him, if that's what you mean. I just stopped believing He cared."

"And now?"

He wasn't sure what to say. His thoughts were filled with doubt. "Now, I guess I'm a little confused. I want to trust Him, but it's hard."

"For sure nobody ever said it would be easy," Atherton countered. "We've all had our demons to wrestle, Austin. I had mine in learnin' to forgive. See, I suffered loss when the Comanche killed my pa. I hated them for that and wanted to take revenge on them."

"What happened?"

"God had other ideas. He had Carissa and her little girl needin' me and me needin' them. Of course, I wasn't good to any of us with all that hate inside. I had the opportunity to face my demon in person, and

God made a way for me to lose my hatred and anger. I learned in that moment that I could let hatred have control of me for the rest of my life, or I could give up my rights to it and hand it over to God. I chose the latter, and I have to tell you, son, I haven't been sorry."

The older man's confession deeply touched Austin. "Guess I need to take it to God, as well."

Atherton pushed back his chair from the table. "Why not do it right now? I'd be honored to join you in prayer."

Austin hadn't expected this, but it felt right. It was time to set things straight. It was time to come home to His Father in heaven.

"Did you set a date?" Mother asked.

Jessica shook her head and fell back against her bed pillows. "No. I have to say both of us were so surprised by the proposal that we hardly spoke after I agreed to marry him."

"Well, no matter. I imagine you'll want to get to know each other better. Maybe a summer wedding would be nice."

"Summer? I don't think I'd want to wait that long," Jessica said, folding her hands together under her head.

"Well, you don't want to rush into anything. Getting married based on emotions alone is never wise. Make sure this is the man you want to spend the rest of your life with. Once you're married, there's no going back."

"Oh, I know that." Jessica didn't find value in her mother's warning. She felt as if she'd known Austin all of her life.

"So what kind of plans do you want to make for your wedding?"

"I'd like a big church wedding. I want a beautiful white wedding dress like we saw in *Peterson's Magazine.* You know, the one with the sweeping train and all the lace?"

"With the huge sleeves?" Mother asked.

"Goodness, no. It was the princess-style gown with the wide lace that came over the shoulders and made a V at the waist. It had no sleeves except for the lace hanging off the shoulder and over the top of the arms."

"Oh yes. I remember it. I suppose we shall need to find the pattern and have it made for you in Dallas."

Jessica nodded. "We could make a grand time of it. Just you and me." She was excited by the prospect. "And we could shop for shoes and maybe some new clothes." All at once Jessica sobered. She sounded just like her old self. Once again, she was focused on her appearance and the attention she knew she'd receive from having her mother to herself.

"What's wrong, Jess?" Mother asked, cocking her head to one side as she always did when assessing one of her children's health. Her eyes narrowed slightly in scrutinizing her daughter. "Are you ill?"

"In a way. I'm sick of myself. I hate that the first thing I think of is a grand wedding and new clothes. I've been working hard to put the old me away and let the new me take charge."

"It's really better if you let God take charge. I find that when I try to be in control, I lose control."

"But I'm trying so hard," Jessica replied in exasperation. "Why can't God just make me be unselfish."

"It would be nice if we could snap our fingers and become better people instantly." Mother sounded sympathetic. "Unfortunately, change is a journey we must take one step at a time. Give it over to God and rest in Him."

"I am — at least I'm trying to give it over. Then something like this happens, and I feel as though I go back ten steps." She paused and shook her head. "I'm sorry, Mother. I didn't mean to get carried away.

The idea of planning my wedding just makes me giddy," she said, smiling.

"Jess, I don't think you're selfish to be happy about your wedding. Every girl dreams and fusses over it. I did. When I married Gloria's father I had a beautiful wedding with all the trimmings. That turned out miserably, and I was widowed with a baby. When I married your father, it was different. I wore a simple gown of white Indian muslin over yellow cotton, and we married at the Barnett Ranch so that Hannah could be there. She'd just given birth to Sarah, and William wasn't letting her go anywhere." Mother smiled at the fond memory.

"When I think of all the money my father spent on my first wedding and how badly it ended up, well, I know what it is to be selfish and demanding." She met Jessica's gaze. "You are neither one. Now go to sleep and have pleasant dreams." She turned the lamp down until it went out, leaving just the light from the hallway.

Jessica snuggled down under the covers, feeling much like a little girl again. She gave a contented sigh and closed her eyes to dream of wedding gowns and flower bouquets.

CHAPTER 22

Two days later Jessica was still contemplating the kind of wedding she hoped to have when she glanced outside and saw Harrison Gable show up unannounced. She had no desire to see him and quickly ducked out to the kitchen to see if she could help Lupe with anything. Peeking around the arched entry to the kitchen, Jessica heard her mother's soft voice.

"Good morning, Mr. Gable. What brings you here today?"

"I am hoping to speak with your daughter."

Jessica contemplated running for the back door. She had nothing to say to Harrison Gable. She'd refused his proposal and clearly wanted nothing more of his desire to court. She glanced back at Lupe, and the older woman shrugged as if to say, *"It's your problem."*

Mother was telling Harrison that she'd go

347

in search of Jessica if he would just have a seat in the front sitting room. Jessica drew a deep breath to steady her nerves and brushed her sleeves for any hint of lint. Mother came down the hallway smiling.

"You have a visitor."

"Yes, I heard," she replied in a whisper. "I wish I didn't have to speak with him. I don't want to hear his comments about how I should be marrying him instead of Austin."

Mother put her hand on Jessica's hand. "Don't make more out of it than it has to be. Just be kind and polite and let the matter resolve itself. Maybe he's come to congratulate you. After all, someone is bound to have mentioned your engagement by now. Your father was mighty excited about it — maybe even more than I was."

"I suppose he's been telling everyone in Cedar Springs," Jessica said, frowning.

"Just stop worrying. There's nothing Harrison can do about it. You love another."

She knew Mother was right, but it was so hard to ignore her feelings of anxiety. She wanted to celebrate and enjoy this wonderful feeling of happiness. Instead, Jessica knew that trying to explain the situation to Harrison wouldn't be easy.

"I'll go," she finally said.

"I will pray for you, Jess."

The words comforted Jessica. The thought of her mother taking time to pray about something as trivial as her encounter with Harrison touched her. She patted her mother's arm. "Thank you."

Smoothing down the front of her blouse, Jessica slowly made her way to the front sitting room. She felt rather like someone going to her execution. *I won't bring up the engagement unless he does.*

"Ah, here you are," Harrison said, getting to his feet. He gave her a broad smile, which revealed his almost perfect teeth. "And how lovely you look today."

Jessica bristled at his compliment. "Thank you. I wasn't expecting you, and I am rather busy."

He nodded knowingly. "I do apologize for coming so early in the day, but I felt I had to. Please sit down and I'll explain."

He motioned to the sofa, but Jessica took her place like a queen in her favorite chair by the fire. "All right, please continue."

Harrison pulled up another chair to sit directly in front of her. "I wanted to apologize for my actions the other night. I know I surprised you with my proposal of marriage. I realize we haven't done much in the way of courting, but I thought to do more of that after you accepted my proposal."

Jessica started to say something, but he held up his hand. "Please let me get this out. You see, I care very much for you, and because of that I felt it important to speak to you privately about this. It has to do with Austin Todd."

"Why would you come to me about Mr. Todd?"

Gable actually looked uncomfortable. "I've heard it said around town that you have accepted his proposal of marriage."

Jessica stiffened. "I have."

"I also heard about his plans. I thought you might be upset. I mean, there's no way of knowing whether he'll return."

Her eyes narrowed. "What are you talking about?"

"Oh dear, you don't know. I was afraid that might be the case." He gave the look of one who truly felt bad. However, Jessica knew it was a lie. "I've heard folks talking all over town about Mr. Todd leaving on the morning train tomorrow. He's going to Colorado, they're saying. I really don't know why he is heading there in particular, but I feared for you, since he didn't seem to have plans to return. He didn't buy a round-trip ticket. I knew you two had just become engaged, and I feared this would leave you in great shame."

"Colorado?" she murmured. Why hadn't Austin told her about this?

"I thought perhaps with his leaving, and it being uncertain that he would return, you might need the comfort of a good friend." He reached out to touch her hand. "I know you have no desire to marry me, but my offer does remain on the table. Truly I am only here as a friend."

Jessica felt momentarily sickened at the thought that Austin had skipped out on her. Surely this was a mistake. Even if it weren't, however, she didn't want to give Harrison the upper hand. She had to have faith in Austin — in their love.

"Austin will be back. He loves me and I love him. That's something I couldn't share with you. Austin no doubt has to go to Colorado on business."

But rather than appear surprised or even angry at her declaration, Gable seemed even sadder. Shaking his head, he gave her a look of pity. "Poor woman. No doubt he lied to you, especially since he hasn't bothered to let you know of his plans. What a savage thing to do to one so innocent."

Jessica squirmed in her chair and hoped Harrison Gable wouldn't notice how uncomfortable he'd made her. "Really, Mr. Gable, I hardly see why any of this is your business."

He threw her an apologetic look. "Of course you are right. You are the one he's made a fool of, but this isn't my business. I shouldn't be causing you more pain with the telling of that cad's actions. After all, you are my friend, and I don't wish to hurt you."

"He's not a cad!" Jessica jumped up from the chair. "He's a good man, and I intend to marry him. Now, if you'll excuse me . . ." She started to leave the room, but Gable crossed the room in a flash and took hold of her.

He dropped the façade. "I can give you a better life than he can. I would care greatly for your comfort and happiness." He pulled her closer, and though Jessica tried to push him away, he held her in an ironclad grip. "I know ways," he whispered against her ear, "to make a woman happy — and keep her that way."

She put the heel of her boot down on his foot. Yelping, Gable dropped his hold, and Jessica flew from the room, passing Mother on the way. She knew her mother would question her about what had happened, but at this point Jessica only longed to put some distance between herself and the vulgar Mr. Gable.

Seeking the sanctuary of her bedroom, she slammed the door shut behind her and locked it. The memory of Harrison's declaration gave her a tight feeling in her chest. Why hadn't Austin mentioned that he was leaving for Colorado? She didn't want to give doubt room to grow, but what was he doing? Was he truly not planning to return?

Jessica paced the room and tried to make sense of it all. She calmed a little as she remembered something she'd said to Harrison about Austin's trip. It might very well be that the Rangers needed him to travel to Colorado. Perhaps they'd asked him to bring back cattle rustlers for trial. Or maybe he was helping another Ranger. She frowned, running out of reasons for Austin to abruptly leave town without telling her. Suddenly, nothing made sense.

Having spread the word that he was headed to Colorado Springs on important business for the Secret Service, Austin felt certain word would get around to Mr. Morgan and his cohort. Robert, too, had helped spread the news, and it seemed to be all that folks were talking about.

Austin smiled to himself as he made his way to the Atherton ranch. "Let 'em talk," he said to the twilight. He would leave on the morning train, and he wanted to make sure that Jessica knew about his plans.

It was nearly suppertime when Austin arrived. He knew Mrs. Atherton would invite him to join them for the meal — at least he was counting on that. He gave a firm knock on the door, then dusted the tops of his boots off on the back of his Levi's.

Mr. Atherton answered the door with a smile. "Austin. Good to see you, son. Come on in. We were just sittin' down to supper. Can you stay?"

"I'd like that, sir. I was hoping to speak to Jessica after the meal."

"Of course. I think that's more than acceptable. Maybe I'll find an excuse to help her ma with the dishes. 'Course, I don't want her thinkin' it might become a regular thing." He chuckled and put his arm around Austin's shoulders. "Come on, son. I think the ladies will be pleased to see you."

When Austin entered the dining room, he found Mrs. Atherton and Jessica sitting before their empty china settings at a table laden with delicious-smelling food. He remembered just then that he still had his hat on and quickly remedied the situation.

"Look who I found at the door. I told him he needed to join us for supper."

"Of course," Mrs. Atherton said, getting

to her feet. "Let me get another place setting. Austin, why don't you sit there beside Jess."

"Here, I'll take your hat," Mr. Atherton said. "It'll be on the coat-tree by the front door."

Austin moved to where Jessica sat and pulled the chair out. She didn't look at him, and it bothered Austin greatly. Why this sudden cold shoulder?

Mrs. Atherton placed the dishes and silver in front of him and asked if he wanted coffee or tea. "I've made both, so you have your choice. Either one will warm you up."

"Coffee's good for me," Austin replied, still concerned about Jessica's silence.

With the coffee poured, Mrs. Atherton retook her seat, and Mr. Atherton offered a short prayer. As the meal progressed, Austin's curiosity mounted. Jessica hadn't turned once to look at him, and it was starting to be quite annoying.

"So what brings you out this way?" Atherton asked. "Were you just hopin' to spend some time with Jess, or did you have other pressin' business?"

"Actually, I came to let you all know that I'm going to be gone for a while." This brought Jessica to attention.

"And where are you headed?" the older

man asked.

"Colorado Springs. I'm helping the Barnetts and the Wythes with a matter." Jessica's tight shoulders seemed to relax just a bit. "It shouldn't take long," Austin added. "Probably no longer than a week or two. Either the item I seek will be there and be what we expect, or it won't."

"Does this have somethin' to do with the man who's been pesterin' Jake and Alice?"

"Yes," Austin replied, relieved that Atherton had been apprised of the situation.

The rancher nodded and cut into his meat. "I hope it will put the past to rest and give them the peace of mind they seek. William told me it was quite the conspiracy."

"It would appear that way," Austin said.

"And why are *you* going in particular?" Mrs. Atherton asked, a forkful of food midway to her lips. "Why not Robert?"

Austin had figured on this question. "I used to work with the Secret Service. As a part of the Treasury Department they deal with counterfeiting and fraud. I presume you know that this is part of the problem at hand."

"We know all about it," Atherton replied. "A big mess, if you ask me."

"It is indeed, but I'm hoping to put an end to it. My old boss asked me to come in on the investigation because I've had experience with this type of crime, and I am friends with the folks involved."

"I'm sure that put William's mind at rest," Jessica's father declared. "I know it would mine. We'll certainly be praying for you."

"Is it dangerous?" This came from Jess's mother, and Austin couldn't help but sense Jessica's tensing once again.

"No more so than anything else," he said with a smile. "I don't expect problems. And if there are any, I'll have the support of two other agents, who are even now taking a fast train to Denver and then to Colorado Springs. They're good men — men I know and have worked with before."

The conversation continued, but Jessica only spoke when her parents asked her something directly. Austin remained puzzled at her attitude. She almost seemed angry with him. Once supper concluded, Mrs. Atherton shooed the couple from the dining room, and Mr. Atherton made good on his suggestion to help wash dishes when Jessica protested.

"I'll help your mother. You two go on and enjoy the fire I started just before we sat down. That front parlor ought to be nice and warm for you now."

Jessica didn't so much as look at Austin

but nodded and headed from the room. Austin followed after her like a puppy after his master. He figured it would be an uncomfortable evening of silence, since something had clearly disturbed Jessica. He was wrong. The moment they were in the parlor, Jessica turned on him to demand answers.

"Why is it that I'm the last to know of your plans? Harrison Gable said you were leaving me high and dry."

"And you believed him?" Austin frowned. "Besides that, what were you doing with him?"

"Oh, don't try to avoid the question." Jessica put her hands on her hips. "He told me that it was all over town about you heading off. Harrison said you were most likely not coming back, and since he'd heard that we were engaged, he thought he'd come and comfort me."

"He heard about our engagement, eh?" This made Austin smile. "I'll bet that was a sucker punch to his pride."

Jessica shook her head. "He pitied me. He told me in a most sympathetic way that I'd been a fool."

Austin's voice softened. "Jess, why would you believe him over me?"

"Because you weren't here. You hadn't

told me before telling the entire town that you planned to leave. I don't want you to go — especially now. I want Harrison Gable to eat his words."

Stepping forward, Austin reached out to take Jessica's hands, but she refused. With a shrug, he continued. "I can't go back on my word, Jess. Not for you or for anyone else. I gave the Barnetts and Wythes my promise to see this through."

"But it's dangerous, and don't tell me it's not. If it weren't, there wouldn't be a need for additional Secret Service men."

"All right, it's dangerous, but I've been trained to handle situations like this."

"You're making me the laughingstock of town."

"Hardly that, Jess. Be reasonable." Austin decided it might calm her if they sat. "Come sit with me, and I'll explain."

She sat but folded her arms across her chest and fixed Austin with such a stare that he knew this wouldn't be easily resolved.

"No doubt Harrison will spread the news of my situation all over town, and everyone will laugh about how I've been duped."

Austin shook his head. "You haven't been duped."

Jessica's eyes widened. "But that's what everyone will think. If you leave me now, people will think that you are running away from our engagement. Especially if Harrison Gable has his say."

"Since when have you cared about what other people thought? Since we first met you've been unconcerned about others and what their opinion of you might be."

"That isn't true. I didn't use to care, but now I do. I don't want to shame my parents, and I don't want . . ." She let the words trail and fell silent.

"Jessica, I'm not leaving you. I'm simply doing a job. You have to understand that my job requires me to travel. Eventually, I'll be marshal of Terryton and stick close to home, but right now I have an important mission, and I'd like to go to it knowing I have your blessing."

"Well, you don't," she declared, getting back to her feet. "I don't want you to go. I won't come in second to your job. If I can't come first as your wife and friend, then maybe you should leave and not come back."

Austin realized that in her anger, they weren't going to accomplish anything. He rose and headed for the door. "I'll be back as soon as I can."

"Don't bother!" Jessica turned away from him and fixed her gaze on the fire.

Austin knew she didn't mean it. Grief, but that girl could work up a rage. He smiled to himself as he collected his hat and left the house. *I like a gal with spit and spirit. Grace was always so sweet and quiet. Like sitting in a beautiful garden.* Austin chuckled to himself. *Life with Jess is gonna be like riding in a runaway wagon.*

He rode back to the cabin and settled in for the night. He had already determined he would pen Jessica a letter. He wanted to make sure she knew his intentions were to return and bring a wedding ring when he did. That ought to give her something to think about.

Jessica couldn't sleep and tossed and turned most of the night. She regretted her anger and the words she'd hurled at Austin. She knew she'd acted inappropriately, but she had been so enraged that Harrison was right about Austin leaving that she hadn't been able to control her temper.

It was just the thought of being pitied by people who thought she'd been deserted. Jessica couldn't stand to be in that position. It was even better when folks didn't like her, but to pity her was more than she could bear.

You're being foolish. Even if they pity you,

they'll see when Austin returns that they were wrong. It was little comfort, but she knew in her heart that Austin had spoken the truth. He would return.

But now he'll go away, and his last memories of me will be of anger and worry. She chewed on her lower lip. *I have to apologize. I have to see him before he goes. I have to tell him that I believe him and that what other people think doesn't matter.*

But how was she supposed to do that?

When light streaked the horizon, Jessica gave up on sleeping and dressed for the day. She had only one thought. She would ride into town and meet up with Austin before he caught the train. She would apologize for her actions, and then she would let him go.

"I have to trust that God will take care of him," she murmured.

She waited until she saw a light in the bunkhouse and then slipped out the back door and went in search of Osage. The old man was already putting a pot of coffee on to boil when Jessica found him.

"Osage, I don't mean to be a problem to you, but I need to ride into town."

The old man got slowly to his feet. "That's no problem, little gal. How soon do you want to head out?"

"Right away, if we can. I'll let Lupe know, and she can tell Mother and Father. I know they'll understand. I wasn't very kind to Austin last night, and I can't send him away without apologizing."

"Startin' to care for the fella?"

"More than that," she replied. "I've agreed to be his wife."

Osage chuckled. "Well, I'll be a three-legged cat." He motioned to one of the other cowboys. "You see to this coffee. Miss Atherton and I have to ride to town." He turned back to Jessica. "I'll have Peg saddled and ready to go in ten minutes."

"Thank you, Osage," Jessica said, surprising the old man with a kiss on the cheek. She could hear him whooping it up as she exited the bunkhouse. His enthusiasm made her smile.

The ride didn't take long. For an old man, Osage was still amazingly limber and able to sit a horse as well as he could when Jess had been a little girl. They didn't run the horses all the way but covered the distance in walks, trots, and gallops. By the time Jessica and Osage entered the city limits, the sun was up and the cool air was warming. Jessica went immediately to the train, only to learn she was too late.

"What do you mean he's already gone?"

Jessica asked. "The passenger train doesn't even arrive for another forty minutes."

"Now, Miss Jessica, don't go gettin' all put out," the stationmaster admonished. "The schedule changed for the winter. But don't worry; he left you a letter. I was supposed to get it out to you today."

He rummaged around the papers on his desk and handed a folded piece of paper to Jessica. "I didn't snoop in it. I figured it was private." He grinned. "But I wanted to look. I heard you two were gettin' married."

Jessica nodded and took the letter. She thanked the stationmaster and hurried back to where Osage stood holding the two horses. "He's already gone," she said, opening the letter.

Jess,
    I'm sorry for the way things went last night. You had a right to be upset. I didn't handle this well. For that I apologize, and I hope you'll forgive me. I never meant to make you the last person to know about my plans. The only reason the word was sent around to the entire town was because we're hoping it will aid the case. I can't really explain in this letter, but will tell you everything when I come back. And I *will* come back.

I love you, Jessica, and I know that you love me. I don't plan to be gone any longer than I have to, and when I come home, I plan to bring you a wedding ring.

Love, Austin

She looked up at Osage and gave a heavy sigh. The old man cocked his head to one side. "That letter resolve everything?"

She smiled and tucked the letter into her jacket and let her worries fade away. "Yes. I suppose it does."

CHAPTER 23

Austin remained on guard throughout the trip to Colorado. He had established on the first day out of Cedar Springs that both Morgan and a man he presumed to be Mr. Smith were aboard the train. Neither man had made himself visible during the day until around five o'clock, when the elusive Mr. Smith joined Austin's car. Of course, he hadn't known for sure that it was Smith, but the man acted suspicious and seemed to be watching Austin closely.

Later that night Morgan and Smith had apparently thought him to be asleep when they met toward the back of his car. Austin happened to be facing the same direction, and though his hat was pulled low, he could still see from just under the rim. Morgan had appeared, now with his beard shaved off, only for a brief moment to notify his partner to follow him. Austin supposed they might be headed for the smoking car. Austin didn't know if Morgan's change of appearance was for the purpose of throwing Austin off Morgan's movements, but if so, it didn't work.

He was glad that the two men had learned of his plan and followed him. He'd worried they might not have received the news or had chosen not to follow him. It was good to know they wouldn't be pestering the Wythes or the Barnetts. When the train stopped in the next town to refuel, it allowed the passengers time to disembark for a short while. Austin took advantage of his time off the train to send a wire to Robert to let him know that the men were following him. He knew the information would help Robert to relax his watch and get back to the tasks at hand.

January in northern New Mexico made Austin realize his suit coat was hardly heavy enough to ward off the cold. By the time they reached Raton, he felt numb from the winter winds. There had been a blizzard just hours before, and the trains were delayed in getting through until the snow-drifts could be plowed from the tracks. This took a special rotary snowplow, the likes of which Austin had never seen. The huge machine was put on the front of the locomotive engine and pushed forward to remove the snow with its whirring blades.

Austin sat shivering in the poorly heated passenger car while one plow was used on the tracks about twenty yards to the east of them. He saw the blades cut through the snow, which was blown out a chute over the top of the engine. It was quite interesting to watch, but it only served to make Austin feel all the more chilled.

Once they were finally on their way, it was slow going and caused Austin no end of anxiety. He wanted to see this investigation through, and do so quickly. He was anxious to return to Jessica and make plans for their marriage. If she'd still have him.

By the time they rolled into Colorado Springs, it was the following evening. Austin made his way to the nearest hotel and settled in for his first good night's sleep in a week. The delay on the train had given him a sore neck and backside. He could sit in a saddle for days on end, but the hard seat of the train car made him miserable.

He saw Morgan and Smith momentarily in the depot but had no idea where they might have decided to stay. Austin wasn't concerned that they might lose track of him, so rather than expend his energies keeping an eye out for them, he would let Morgan and Smith worry about keeping Austin under surveillance. After all, this was just as important to them as it was to him. For now, all he wanted was to sleep in a bed.

The following morning Austin awoke to even more snow. He felt chilled to the bone and longed for Texas . . . and for Jessica. He reminded himself over and over that there was a job to be done and it shouldn't take him long to retrieve the box and see if it held what they were looking for. If it did, then they could finally put this case to rest.

Dressing, Austin gave serious thought to buying a heavy coat. He quickly decided against it, however. The extra money he'd brought was going toward a wedding ring for Jess. He could bear a little cold. Besides, he'd have no need of a heavy coat in Texas.

But Texas seemed like a million miles away. Austin went to the window. The shop roofs were covered in snow, as was the rest of the town. At least it seemed that it had stopped snowing, and for this Austin was grateful. Hopefully he could accomplish everything in just a few hours and be back on the next train headed south. Then again, he might have come for naught and would find nothing in Mr. Chesterfield's box. He quickly shook off that thought.

"I can't let myself borrow trouble," he said

aloud, noticing his breath fogged the window.

Dropping the draperies back in place, Austin checked his pocket watch. It was too early for the bank to be open, and he was hungry. A good meal seemed most important at that moment. Just then there was a knock on the door.

He frowned. No one knew where he was — not exactly. Unless, of course, they had managed to get the clerk downstairs to reveal his room number.

With great stealth he moved closer to the door. He was about to question the person on the other side when a youthful male voice called out. "Morning paper?"

Austin opened the door and nodded. "I'll take one." He flipped the kid a coin and told him to keep the change.

The boy's eyes lit up. "Thank you!" He hurried to the next room and began the routine again.

Austin tucked the paper under his arm and made his way to the hotel dining room, where the temperature was much warmer. He supposed it was because of the busy kitchen and the room full of guests. Despite the fact that he was still chilled to the bone, Austin chose a table by the window in order to keep an eye on both the entrance to the hotel and the street.

"Would you like to order?" A young serving girl smiled at him most generously.

"Yes. I need to thaw out, and a hot meal might just do the trick," Austin replied. "I wasn't at all prepared for winter weather."

"You weren't? Where are you from, mister?" She eyed him carefully. "Don't you have a warm coat?"

"I'm afraid not." Austin gave her a grin. "I'm from Texas, and we're not used to this white stuff." The girl giggled. Austin figured her to be about seventeen.

"Would you like some hot coffee?"

Austin nodded. "Lots of it. Maybe a bathtub full." He settled back against the wooden chair. "That might finally thaw me out."

She giggled again, but then appeared to get an idea. "I can seat you closer to the kitchen. Sitting here by the window is bound to be colder."

Austin appreciated her thoughtfulness but shook his head. "Nah, I'm all right. The coffee will do the trick. Oh, and I'll need a nice big breakfast."

"We have two breakfast specials," she declared. "Biscuits and gravy on one order, and eggs, bacon, and toast on the other."

"I'll take both."

The girl's eyes widened in surprise. "They're really generous with the portions here. Are you sure you want both?"

"Yup, I'm sure. I'm half starved." He'd not eaten much on the train. The prices were high, and he'd heard from other customers that the food was not that good. Short of buying some jerked meat and apples during one of their stops, Austin had eaten nothing.

The waitress disappeared into the kitchen. Austin busied himself with the newspaper he'd bought earlier. The *Daily Gazette* had very little of interest to Austin. Nevertheless, he forced himself to read the paper and sip the hot coffee his waitress brought. He didn't want to appear anxious to anyone who might be watching — especially to Mr. Morgan. As far as he was concerned, Morgan needed to believe Austin completely clueless to his presence.

When the girl brought two plates of breakfast with most wonderful aromas, Austin wondered if perhaps his eyes had been bigger than his stomach. Nevertheless, he thanked the young woman and put the paper aside. He offered a short prayer of thanks, then straightened and plunged his fork into the biscuits and gravy. A first taste revealed heaven on earth, and Austin quickly inhaled another two forkfuls. It wasn't quite as good as he'd had on the Barnett Ranch, but very nearly.

He continued to eat, pretending to be completely absorbed in the food while keeping an eye out around him. He wasn't worried about Morgan or Smith actually presenting themselves, but he figured they'd hire someone for the job. Morgan had to know that Austin would recognize him, and Austin doubted that he'd allow his henchman to get too far away from him. They'd no doubt pay some dim-witted ninny to watch him and report his movements.

By the time he'd finished the biscuits and gravy and started in on the eggs and bacon, Austin was fairly certain his hunch was right. At the far end of the restaurant, an older man, looking rather weathered, worn, and out of place, sat eating a huge meal as if he hadn't had food in a month. The man was dressed in layers that he began to shed as time passed. Whenever Austin looked his way, the man quickly returned his gaze to his plate.

Smiling to himself, Austin ordered more coffee and relaxed at the table. The bank wouldn't be open for another half hour, and he still needed to make contact with the Secret Service agents who were to have arrived in town prior to Austin. They had agreed to send him word as to where they should meet before Austin made his way to the bank.

He picked up the paper again and nodded to the girl when she offered more coffee. Just as he started on his fifth cup, Austin noticed two well-dressed men enter the dining room. They were impeccable in their appearance and furtively studied the room from hooded eyes. Austin knew them immediately. Five years hadn't changed them much. Marcus Kayler and Sam Fegel were two of the department's best men. They would get a message to Austin without anyone being the wiser. It was exactly what he'd been waiting for.

Austin decided it would be best to remain at his table, and when the waitress appeared to ask him if he wanted anything more, he decided on something else to eat. "Do you have any cinnamon rolls?" he asked, remembering how good Hannah Barnett's had been.

The girl grinned. "I can't believe you're still hungry, but yes, we have cinnamon rolls. My mother made them, in fact, and they're as big as plates."

"Sounds good." Austin delayed her just a moment longer. "So is this your family's restaurant?" He continued to glance toward his two friends.

The girl nodded. "My uncle owns the hotel. He's my pa's brother. They set this up when the Cripple Creek Mining District was formed a few years back, and the family's been here ever since."

Seeing the men move his way, Austin decided he'd give them the perfect opportunity. "Well, it's a mighty fine place. I can't remember ever eating this well on the road. I do believe I'd like to have a cinnamon roll and some more coffee. And if you could hurry, that would be great."

The girl seemed amused by his order. She whirled on her heel to head toward the kitchen and ran headlong into Marcus Kayler, just as Austin had planned. In the flash of a moment, Kayler steadied the girl while Fegel slipped a note to Austin. It happened so quickly that Austin was sure no one was the wiser.

The girl flushed in embarrassment, giggled nervously, then hurried for the kitchen. Austin thought of Jessica and imagined her in the same position. His Jessica would have probably berated the men for not watching where they were going. Austin couldn't imagine Jessica being nearly as giggly as this young woman. He frowned. The last time they'd been together, Jessica had been anything but giggly.

The thought of her still holding a grudge was most disconcerting, but Austin had prayed she would receive the letter and understand his heart, even if she couldn't accept his actions. He missed her so much, and had it not been for his promise to the Barnetts, Austin might have given up the job, turned the key over to the Secret Service agents, and headed back to Texas. He let go a heavy breath.

I gave my word.

Austin didn't have a lot in this world, but he still had that. He had his fledgling faith, as well. He knew God was with him, but the old memories fought against him like some kind of plague. How was it that he could lay Grace to rest and learn to love again, but he couldn't free himself of the guilt he felt over his brother's death?

"Here you go," the girl announced, putting a plate in front of him. On it sat the biggest cinnamon roll Austin had ever seen.

He stared at the roll for a moment and then looked to the server. "This is just one roll?"

She giggled. "I warned you. Ma believes in filling folks up. She said for me to tell you that this one's on the house."

"How come?" he asked. It seemed most unusual for a restaurant to give food away.

"Ma said that if you were hungry enough to eat both of her specials in one sitting and still want more, then you deserve to have it on the house." She picked up some of his empty dishes. "I'll be back with the coffee. Should I leave your check?"

"Yes, thank you."

The girl shifted the dishes with one hand and reached into her pocket with the other. She glanced at the check and then handed it to Austin.

"If you'll wait," he called loud enough for everyone to hear him, "I'll pay for this now."

The girl took his offered payment as well as the paper on which she'd written his total. "Now, you keep the change," Austin told her. The girl's eyes widened at the generous tip. He could see that she was more than pleased.

"Thank you, mister." She hurried away, as if needing to show someone her good fortune.

With the girl gone, Austin raised the newspaper and retrieved the note he'd slipped under there earlier. He kept the paper folded and pretended to read an article, all the while working to open the note Fegel had slipped him. After several attempts he managed the task and read the content of the message.

Will meet you in alleyway behind jewelry store across the street from bank. There's a place we can meet without being seen. We've arranged with the store to allow you access to the back from inside the store. Just go into the place and ask for Mr. Mitchell. Tell him you've always wanted to see his famous gold nugget but you haven't the nickel for a ticket. He'll show you to the back.

It was signed *Kayler* and *Fegel.*

Austin managed to tuck the note into his vest pocket before the girl returned with more coffee. She asked if he needed anything else, but Austin assured her he was fine. He looked across the room to where the man who'd been watching him sat. Again the man quickly looked away. This gave Austin a moment to look at the two agents and nod. The game was now afoot.

Getting to his feet in a slow, methodical manner, Austin gave a bit of a stretch and headed back to the hotel lobby. He wasn't surprised when the weathered old man followed him after a couple of minutes. Austin made it easy for him by heading up the lobby stairs slowly. He would return to his room, wait a few minutes, and then head down the back stairs, which he'd scouted out before coming to breakfast. Hopefully the old man would think Austin still in his room and continue to wait in the lobby.

This, Austin hoped, would throw off anyone's ability to keep him under surveillance. He didn't mind that Morgan knew he was in the area, but he wanted him to only know as much as Austin deemed necessary.

At the appointed time, Austin made his way to the jewelry store. He couldn't see that anyone had followed him and breathed a little easier. No doubt Morgan had already snooped around to learn the whereabouts of the bank Austin had come to find. Still, Austin hoped he might have time to go to the bank and retrieve the box before he had to encounter Morgan and his man.

The jewelry store owner looked up when Austin entered. There was no one else in the place, but still Austin felt it necessary to speak softly and maintain his cover. He browsed around the store for a minute before the owner approached.

"Welcome to my store. May I help you, sir?"

Austin rubbed his chin. "You're the

owner?"

The man gave a tight smile. "I am."

"Well, I was hoping to see your famous gold nugget, but I'm afraid I don't have a nickel to spare — for the ticket." His voice was low, but nevertheless the man's eyes widened, and he gave a quick glance around the room as if fearful that someone had overheard.

"Come right this way," the owner said upon ensuring they were alone.

He led Austin through a door and into a small stockroom. He pointed out the back door somewhat hidden behind a stack of boxes. Austin made his way to the door while the owner returned to the front of the store.

The two agents were awaiting his arrival in the alley. Austin gave each man a nod. "Did anyone follow you?" he asked.

"No," one of the men replied. "You?"

Austin shook his head. "I took the back stairs and a nondirect way here. If anyone followed me they did it in a very skillful manner."

"Well, it would seem to me these folks are full of skills," Marcus Kayler put in. He extended his hand. "Good to see you, Austin." Austin ignored the hand and the two men shared a hardy embrace. After giving

Austin a slap on the back, Marcus laughed. "Wasn't sure we'd ever get a chance to work together again."

Sam Fegel likewise gave Austin a slap on the back. "I thought old Mr. Turner had gone daft when he told us we'd be working with you again." He shook Austin's hand and gave him a brief embrace. "I thought you were done with us."

"Yeah, well miracles do happen." Austin pulled out his pocket watch. It was nearly time for the bank to open. He shivered from the cold wind and snapped the lid shut.

"What's the plan?" Kayler asked.

"I'll go to the bank and retrieve the lockbox. If it is what I think it is, then I'll hand it over to you at the hotel. You'll be able to catch the afternoon train and head back to Washington."

"Sounds like a plan," the man replied. "We can keep watch from the store. If you have the box when you come out, then we'll know you have retrieved the contents. We'll head straightaway for the hotel."

"If the box is too large or heavy for one man but is what we've come for," Austin told them, "I'll step outside the bank and walk away without putting my hat on."

"Got it. If you're quick enough, a trolley will be there at half past the hour. It will take you on a route that passes the hotel. No one should try anything while you're so clearly in the company of others. If you miss it, another will be by at the top of the hour."

Austin nodded. "I guess that takes care of it. I'll see you at the hotel either way." He gave the men his room number, then headed back into the jewelry store. The owner looked at him with a worried expression. No doubt he feared the stranger's presence might bring problems for his store. Despite this, Austin paused for a moment at a case that held wedding rings.

"Are you looking for something in particular?" the owner asked.

Austin looked up with a grin. "A wedding ring. I promised to bring one back with me."

The man opened the case and pulled out the tray of rings. "We have many to choose from, as you can see."

Austin picked up a beautiful ring of gold with two tiny blue sapphires. "This one caught my eye." He held the piece up to catch the light from the window. "How much?"

The man quoted him a price. Austin arched a brow. "How much?"

"Well, I might be able to take off five percent."

"Still seems mighty high," Austin told

him. "How about twenty percent?" He knew full well the man would never agree to such a large discount, but this way they could dicker to the percentage Austin expected to get.

"I should say not," the man replied, sounding most offended. He seemed to forget all about the covert reason Austin had come in the first place. "I could go maybe as high as seven percent."

"How about fifteen? I mean, that's me coming down five percent." Austin grinned. "And it's for a good cause. I have the prettiest gal waiting for me in Texas."

The man stiffened. "Ten and that's my final offer."

Austin pretended to be uncertain, even though ten percent was exactly the discount he was seeking. "I suppose if that's your final offer then I haven't got much of a choice. I'll take it."

The jeweler seemed surprised when Austin pulled out the cash and handed it to him. "I'll take it with me."

"But sir, what about the size? Will this fit your young lady?"

Austin looked at the ring and thought of Jessica's slender fingers. "I think it'll be fine. If not, we can take care of the matter in Texas." He tucked the ring into his vest pocket and bid the man good-day.

Pulling up the collar of his coat, Austin stepped outside and squinted against the morning sun. The light glinting off the snow all but blinded him. He drew a deep breath and felt the cold air sting his lungs. How in the world did people live in this frozen land? Without another thought he dodged a couple of men on horseback and crossed to the bank.

The bank was an older redbrick building that held a sort of warm grace in contrast against the snow. Austin had already been informed it was one of the local banks that hadn't needed to close for long during the recent financial crisis. Hence, they'd been able to keep Chesterfield's box locked in the vault until they could once again reopen. Austin walked into the building and pulled off his hat. Looking around the room, he saw tellers already busy receiving customers. Unfortunately, it wasn't much warmer inside than it had been outside.

A man at a desk to the left of him glanced up and smiled. "May I help you, sir?"

"I'm here to see the bank manager, John C. Espry."

The man stiffened. "Do you have an appointment?"

"Of sorts. I think when you let him know

I'm here, he'll be more than happy to meet with me."

The man gave him a look of disbelief but nevertheless got to his feet. "Who shall I say is calling?"

"Austin Todd."

The man gave a curt nod and hurried to a closed door near the back of the bank. It was only a moment before he returned. "Mr. Espry will see you immediately." The man looked to be surprised by this turn of events but said nothing more. He showed Austin to the office and closed the door behind him.

"Mr. Todd," the older man said, getting to his feet. "Thank you for coming today. I received your note last night and am quite anxious to see this matter attended to. The president and owner of this bank wants it cleared up right away. He is making plans for changes in the future and feels this needs to be settled."

"I'm happy to oblige," Austin replied. "Here's the letter I've brought from Mr. Chesterfield's daughter, Alice Chesterfield Barnett, giving me permission to receive the lockbox and its contents."

Espry took the letter and, without even bothering to read the contents, instructed Austin to follow him. "The box is being kept in a private room. I'll take you there," he told Austin, glancing again at the letter. He tossed it to his desk. "Frankly, even without the letter, I was instructed to hand it over to you."

The older man pulled a set of keys from his pocket. "Come with me."

He led the way out a back entrance to the office and down a long narrow hallway. When they reached a back staircase, Austin thought they might be headed up. But Espry took a sharp turn to the right and led Austin to a large wooden door. Espry inserted a key and the lock opened. "It's just in here," he said. Espry turned on the lights and escorted Austin inside. Austin couldn't help but sneeze several times in a row. The room smelled musty. The cloying scent of cigars seemed to permeate the draperies and carpets. Espry seemed embarrassed and apologized. "This room was used just yesterday to hold a board meeting. I am sorry that we didn't think to air it out."

Despite sneezing, Austin assured the man it was of no concern. "I'm here for the box. I've endured worse smells than this." His glance went to the table where a black box sat. "Is that it?"

Espry looked to the table. "Yes, this is the box left with us by Mr. Chesterfield."

Austin stepped forward. The box was most unusual. It looked to be about twelve by twelve by twelve. Austin ran his hand over the ornate black lacquered piece and noted obvious Oriental touches to the box. He pulled the strange key from his pocket and inserted it in the lock. The moment of truth came as the key turned and the box opened.

CHAPTER 24

The contents of the box were better than Austin had hoped for. Not only were the counterfeiting plates within, but so too were the certificates, papers for additional certificates, and several bottles of ink. He snapped the lid closed quickly as Espry stepped forward to see the contents.

"Thank you," Austin said and relocked the box. Looking up, he could see that Espry was disappointed Austin hadn't shared the look inside. "I'll take this with me." He hoisted the locked box to his shoulder. "You've been a great help, and I know Mrs. Barnett appreciates your cooperation in this matter."

The bank manager seemed hesitant. "And the contents . . . were they what you'd expected?"

"Exactly so," Austin replied, heading out of the room and back down the narrow hall.

He didn't waste any time. Making a

straight path through the bank, he exited the front door, knowing that his cohorts would see him and the box. The trolley was just approaching, and Austin quickly signaled with a wave and jumped aboard the crowded conveyance.

The box wasn't all that heavy, but its value was enormous. The contents could have easily caused massive problems with the monetary system. He would need to make a closer examination, but it was clear why this had cost Alice's father his life.

As the trolley reached the area of Austin's hotel, he paid the fee and jumped down from the steps. He shifted the box to his left shoulder and made his way into the hotel. The clerk looked at him in surprise and called out before Austin could make his way to the stairs.

"Sir, would you like a bellman to help with that?"

"No thanks," Austin said over his shoulder. "I've got it." He bounded up the stairs, as if to prove his ability, and quickly made his way down the hall to his room.

Once inside, he deposited the box on his bed and returned to the door to lock it. The room was warmer than it'd been downstairs, and sunlight shone brightly through the window. At last Austin was starting to warm up.

Taking the banjo-shaped key from his pocket once again, Austin inserted it in the lock.

Pushing back the lid, Austin reached into the box and began pulling out the contents. There were plates for the gold certificates, as well as plates for pressing twenty dollar bills. Austin carefully examined each item, marveling at the work that had gone into putting together such a kit. The work was exquisite and no doubt done by one of the best in the business.

A knock on the hotel door brought Austin to attention. That would be his friends Kayler and Fegel.

"Just a minute," he called out and placed the items back into the lacquered box. He didn't bother to close the lid and lock it, but went to unlock his door.

"I'm glad you guys are here," he said and quickly realized it wasn't the agents at all, but rather Morgan and his man.

"We're glad to be here, as well," Morgan said, pushing Austin back.

Austin felt like ten kinds of fool for having let his guard down. He had been more than a little foolish to feel safe in his hotel room.

Morgan headed to the box and peered

inside. "It's exactly as I had hoped. You've saved me a great deal of trouble, Mr. Todd."

His holster was hanging at the top of the bed. Austin moved slowly toward it. With a little luck, he hoped to pull his revolver without the men noticing. But even as he tried, Morgan's partner pushed Austin back and took the gun from the holster.

"You won't be needin' this." The man's icy blue eyes narrowed, and his expression seemed to dare Austin to fight.

Morgan looked up to see what had caused the exchange. "Glad to see you're on the job, Mr. Smith. That could have set us both back had Mr. Todd managed to get his weapon. I'm afraid I wasn't very observant, since I had my mind fixed on other things."

He went back to rummaging in the box while Austin tried to figure a way he might overpower the tall lanky Mr. Smith.

"I'm glad to see that Chesterfield was careful with this." Morgan looked at Austin and smiled. "When he told me he no longer planned to help me in my endeavors and that he planned to go to the police, well, I feared I might never again see these."

Snapping the lid in place, Morgan turned the key. "But now they are safely back in my care."

"You do realize that the Treasury Department is well aware of these plates and forged certificates. They've put more men than me on this case, so you can't hope to get away with this."

"I don't hope to get away with this, Mr. Todd," Morgan said, fixing him with a blank stare. "I've already gotten away with it. For some time before Mr. Chesterfield got cold feet, I had gotten away with it. Chesterfield caused me a most uncomfortable delay, especially in light of the financial difficulties of '93. However, now that my property has been returned to me, I shall endeavor to make up for lost time." He looked to Mr. Smith and shrugged. "I suppose the first thing we need to do is dispose of Mr. Todd."

The henchman stepped closer to Austin and put the revolver to his head. "That won't be no trouble."

A knock on the door startled the two thieves. With his eyes narrowed to slits, Smith lowered the gun to Austin's midsection.

"Austin, it's us. Open up."

Morgan moved to Todd. "Say nothing."

"Come on, Todd, we haven't got all day if we're going to catch the train to Denver."

Austin shifted uncomfortably from one foot to the other. He had to warn the men of what was happening, but how? Smith punched the barrel of the gun into Austin's stomach. Doubling over in a grunt, Austin managed to back into the nightstand. The lightweight piece of furniture toppled over, and all the contents on it spilled noisily to the hardwood floors.

"Fool!" Morgan exclaimed as the hotel door was kicked in.

Austin straightened just as the agents attacked. A gunshot rang out and Austin felt a burning sensation run through his body. Even so, he pushed forward to disarm Smith. The other agents were busy with Morgan, who had drawn a revolver of his own.

Austin kicked Smith in the shins, but the man held fast to the gun. The taller man had the advantage and held his ground. Forcing Smith's arm upward, Austin tried but failed to make him drop the weapon. Instead, as Smith's arm lowered, he somehow managed to get his finger on the trigger once again. The sound of the gun being fired was all that Austin heard as blackness overtook him.

It had been two weeks since Austin had headed to Colorado. Two weeks and no word. Jessica paced most unhappily through the house, wringing her hands and fretting

393

about what might have gone wrong.

Perhaps Harrison had been right and Austin had changed his mind about returning. But even as the thought came to mind, Jessica did her best to take it captive, as the Bible directed. Her mother and father knew how worried she'd become.

"You're not helping yourself any by fretting," Father said when Jessica made her way back through the front sitting room.

"I know, but I can't put aside the feeling that something is wrong." She went to where her father sat and knelt. "Papa, can't you send a wire or contact someone who might know what's going on?"

Her father reached out and patted her hands. "Sometimes these things take time."

"But this has already taken far more time than Austin believed it would. Not only that, but he promised to wire as soon as his task was completed. He should have been able to send us a message, something telling us he was all right."

Gazing at her with a sympathetic look, Father reached up to gently take hold of her chin. "I hate to see you so worried. You're not eatin' or sleepin' properly, and your mother is beside herself. I guess I'd better do what I can, or she'll have my hide." He gave her his classic lazy smile, which eased Jessica's mind just a bit. "I'll check with Will and see if they've had any word."

Jessica threw herself against her father's seated frame. "Oh, thank you. Thank you. I'm so afraid of what might have happened. I can't rest until I know."

"I figured as much," her father declared. "If you'll get up off me, I'll go right now."

"Can I come with you?" she asked, her voice pleading. "Please, Papa, I promise to do whatever you say, and no matter what news we hear . . . I assure you I can bear it."

"Very well. Have one of the boys saddle our horses, and I'll let your mother know what we're up to."

The ride to the Barnetts' seemed to take forever. Jessica wanted to run Peg all the way, but Father wouldn't allow for such abuse. "We've plenty of time, Jess."

When they finally arrived, Jessica drew her leg up and over the horn of her sidesaddle as she kicked out of her stirrup. Without warning, she jumped to the ground.

"You trying to kill yourself?" Father asked. "Next time wait until I can help you down."

"I'm sorry. I'm just so anxious to know what's going on."

"I realize that," he said, tying off their

horses, "but if you're dead, you won't get to know anything."

Jessica knew he was right, but she trusted her mount. Peg was used to her mistress taking chances. Father took hold of her arm, and together they made their way to the porch.

"Let me do the talkin'," Father said. "In your state of mind you won't make a lick of sense."

Jessica nodded but knew it would be hard to say nothing. Even so, she'd do her best. When Robert appeared at the door, she fought the urge to pounce on him and demand answers.

"Mr. Atherton . . . Jess," Robert said with a grin. "We weren't expectin' you to come visitin'."

"We came to see if there's been any word from Austin."

"Come on in." Robert moved away from the door. "I haven't heard anything since the wire tellin' me that Morgan and Smith were on the train."

"Jess is worried. I guess I am, too. He hasn't come back, and he hasn't gotten in touch with Jessica. I figure since the man plans to marry her, he'd at least let her know when he'd be back."

It was the first time Jessica realized that

her father was just as concerned as she was. She looked to Robert. "Do you suppose your father has had word or maybe Jake and Marty?"

Robert shrugged. "It's possible, but Pa would have told me if he knew anything. As for Marty and Jake, I couldn't say. I haven't seen them in a couple days. The kids have been down sick, and they weren't at church yesterday, as you know. If they've had a letter or telegram in the last few days, I wouldn't know about it."

"I have to think that if they'd had any word," Father countered, "they would have let you know."

"We have to do something!" Jessica exclaimed. "We can't just keep waiting."

"Waiting for what?" Will Barnett asked, coming from the hallway.

"Howdy, Will. Jess and I were just trying to learn if there had been any word from Austin."

"None that I know of." He frowned. "And you've heard nothing?"

"Not a word."

Jessica stepped forward to the man who'd been a sort of uncle to her. "Please help us. We have to find out what's happened. I'm afraid something is wrong and Austin is in trouble."

"We could send a telegram to his old boss in Washington," Robert suggested. "What was his name?"

"Ellery Turner," Jessica replied without a breath. "Can you go immediately?"

Robert smiled and put his hand on Jessica's shoulder. "For you, I'd do most anything. Let me tell Alice, and I'll head out."

"You'll stop by the house as soon as you know something?" Jessica asked.

"Sure will. Just remember, it might take days to get word back."

Jessica nodded, knowing full well those days would feel like years.

Austin opened his eyes to a sight he'd never thought to see again. His brother Houston was perched on his bed, grinning at him like he'd just beat him at checkers.

"You're dead," Austin said, shaking his head.

"Well, from the standards of life as you know it — yes."

"Does that mean I'm dead, too?"

Houston chuckled. "Nope. It means you're dreamin'."

Austin looked around the room. It all seemed so real, so clear. How could it be a dream, a trick of the mind? "Where am I?"

"Does it matter?" his brother asked.

"I suppose not." Austin looked at his brother for a moment. "I've wanted to talk to you for a long time."

"I know," Houston replied, his smile fading. "You're wondering if I blame you for what happened, 'cause you blame yourself, and it's become a difficult burden to carry."

Austin nodded. "Yes." He tried to sit up, but pain caused him to fall back.

"You always were too focused on yourself," Houston said, shaking his head. "My dying wasn't your fault. It was an accident. I put myself in harm's way. You didn't make me do anything."

"But you were protecting me, and it was my bullet that . . ."

"That killed me?" Houston shrugged. "Didn't much matter if it was yours or his. I knew what my odds were, and I took them. I didn't want to see you die. Grace and the baby needed you."

"They didn't need me long. They died."

Houston nodded slowly. "I know. The folks, too. You've been alone for far too long."

Austin felt a rush of sadness. "But there wasn't even time to tell you good-bye. You died so fast. I watched the life go out of you, and there was —"

399

"Nothing you could do." Houston finished the sentence with a sigh. "I know. There still isn't. Moping around and feeling like you do won't bring me back. You need to stop letting this control you. You need to fight for yourself now. Fight to live."

Austin felt so very tired. He closed his eyes. "I don't know if I can."

"But you have a gal waiting for you back in Texas."

"Jessica." Austin opened his eyes.

Houston nodded and bent toward Austin. His brown hair fell over his left eye, causing him to reach up and push it back in his habitual manner. "She's a good woman. I think you two will be happy." He paused for a moment and smiled. "And that's what I want for you, Austin. I want you to be happy. Let the past rest." Houston got to his feet. "It can only hurt you if you allow it to. Let it go like the Good Book says. Let *me* go."

CHAPTER 25

Austin awoke to abdominal pain and a blinding headache. He felt as if every muscle in his body had gone to mush, and when he tried to move his arms, he found it nearly impossible. Rather than fight, Austin relaxed as best he could and closed his eyes again. He couldn't help but think of the dream he'd had. It had seemed so real. Houston seemed so happy and free of accusation. Had God used the dream to send him a message? Or had Houston's spirit appeared to him? Did God do that kind of thing? A memory came to mind of reading about Jesus and the appearance of Moses and Elijah, who had died long before.

"With God all things are possible," he murmured. But even as he contemplated whether or not the dream was real, peace like he'd never known settled over him. His brother was in God's care — as were Grace and his son and his parents. Somehow, he just knew they had come to realize his part in Houston's death had simply been an accident. A terrible, tragic accident.

Opening his eyes again, he stared up at the gray ceiling. The lighting seemed different. Had he fallen asleep again? Why was he here, and exactly where was *here*? It was obviously a hospital, but he didn't remember coming to it or why.

"Good afternoon, Mr. Todd. I'm glad to see that you're still among us."

Austin looked at the older man and gave a weak smile. "I'd shake your hand and make your acquaintance if I had any strength."

"I'm Dr. Kirkland. You were brought to my care nearly a month ago. You were in pretty bad shape, and we didn't expect you to live."

"A month? I've been asleep for a month?" Austin found it impossible to believe. Why, just yesterday he'd . . . he'd . . . His mind was blank. He strained his memory to search for what he last remembered.

"I remember I took the train . . . somewhere." He thought hard. "Colorado."

"Yes, that's right." The doctor picked up Austin's chart and studied it while Austin continued to search his mind.

"I live in Texas. I know that much."

"And are you married?"

"No. But I'm going to be." An image of Jessica came to mind. "She's the prettiest girl in all of Texas."

The doctor looked to Austin and chuckled. "I'd say then that you're remembering the most important things in your life."

"How did I end up here?" Austin shook his head. "Why does my head hurt so much? And my gut. I feel like I've been ripped apart."

"You suffered two bullet wounds, Mr. Todd. The first one was more serious. It entered about here." The doctor put his finger on his own body. "It pierced your small intestine and narrowly missed your kidney on its exit. It caused considerable damage. We operated on you twice. The other bullet grazed your head but didn't cause serious damage. However, you lost a great deal of blood and suffered an infection, as well. Now you're showing signs of recovery, and we are all most happy to see that."

"And you say this happened almost a month ago?"

"Yes. You've been a very sick man. It wasn't until a couple of days ago that we had real hope of your survival."

"I feel like a wrung-out dish towel," he said, trying to rise up. Intense pain ripped through his body, and now his back hurt as much as his gut. Austin felt as though his neck could barely support his head and fell back against the pillow. "Am I going to be like this forever?"

"No. You'll need time to recover your strength. You've been flat in bed for a month, and we performed the second surgery just four days ago. You aren't just going to jump up and do everything you used to do, but in time you will regain your abilities. Of that, I feel certain. Now, I plan to have the nurse give you something to help with the pain, but first I'd like to know if you feel up to some visitors. They've been here for a couple of days."

Austin nodded. "Who are they?"

"Let's see if you remember them," the doctor said, going to the door. "I'll be right back."

Austin frowned, trying to force his memories to return. He kept thinking about a box. A black lacquered box. What did it mean? He tried again to sit up but found it impossible.

Frustrated by his own weakness, Austin relaxed against the bed, determined that he would beat this. He'd do whatever the doctor said to do, and he'd recover.

"Austin!" A woman rushed into the room

and to his bedside.

"Jess," he whispered. He remembered her.

She sobbed and took hold of him. "I was so afraid. When you didn't send us a telegram, I knew something must be very wrong."

Jessica hugged him tightly, and Austin's pain increased, but he said nothing. His joy at seeing her again and remembering who she was overcame any concerns about the pain.

"I don't remember what happened."

"Your Secret Service pals filled us in on that," a man declared.

Austin looked past Jessica to see Tyler Atherton. At the mention of the Secret Service, Austin had a flicker of memory. "I was working for them, wasn't I?"

Mr. Atherton came closer, and Jessica released her hold. "You were," she said. "You were trying to catch counterfeiters who were blackmailing Jake and scaring Alice. Remember?"

He considered this news for a moment and let the pieces fall into place. There had been someone bothering his friends. Austin could remember talking to Jake and Alice's husband, Robert. "I remember some. I took the train here, right?"

"You did," Atherton replied.

"That's all I remember. I don't remember getting here or what happened afterward."

"This kind of assault on the body often blocks the ability to remember," the doctor told them. He looked to Austin. "Your memory may return in time."

Austin hadn't realized the doctor had rejoined them. "I hope you're right, Doc. I sure don't like this feeling of not knowing what happened."

"Your friends said that you met them and were in agreement that you would go to the bank and retrieve the box belongin' to Alice's deceased father." Atherton paused a moment. "Do you remember that much?"

"The box. I was after the box." It made sense now why he kept pondering that black lacquered box.

"Yes, you were followin' a lead that brought you to Colorado. It was thought that perhaps the box contained the missing gold certificates and even some plates for makin' 'em. And it did. You took the box from the bank back to your hotel, where you were waylaid by Paul Morgan and his man, Lothar Hale. He went by the name Mr. Smith when he was stirrin' up trouble with Marty and Alice in Denver."

The story was coming together, and though parts of it remained veiled in a fog,

Austin could finally recall his mission and the agents. They were Marcus Kayler and Sam Fegel. He'd worked with them in Washington.

"Were Kayler and Fegel hurt?"

"No. They heard the ruckus as they stood outside the door to your room. They rushed in and took Morgan and Hale into custody. Then they realized you'd been shot. The police arrived to assist them, and they got you to the hospital."

"Were they able to retain possession of the box?"

"Yes, and all the contents. There were certificates and plates and papers for making additional certificates, as well as ink and stamps and a few other things."

"They were all the working tools of Mr. Chesterfield, given to him by Mr. Morgan," Jessica added. "Apparently Mr. Morgan has been making counterfeits for a long time."

"It's all still rather foggy to me," Austin admitted.

"In time it may well clear for you," the doctor assured him. "You may retain some memory loss, but otherwise I'm hopeful you'll have a full recovery."

Austin gave Jessica a weak smile. "Then we can be married."

She began to cry again. "I'm so sorry for

the things I said before you left. I didn't mean them. I love you." Jessica reached down to touch his cheek. "I love you dearly. Please forgive me. I'll never doubt you again."

"I don't think I remember much of anything bad being said," he replied, "so I hardly see the need for forgiveness. I love you, too, Jessica, and even if we had words, I know your love is true. It's a matter of heart." He smiled as she once again bent low to hug him. He remembered the argument in full, but he wasn't about to hold it against her.

She pulled back and wiped her tears with the back of her hand. "Yes, and my heart is full of love for you."

The doctor stepped forward. "These things were in your pockets when they brought you to the hospital. He handed a knotted handkerchief to Jessica.

"Open it," Austin said. "Maybe it will help me remember."

Jessica did as he said, and when she spread back the pieces of cloth, she gasped. Austin could see her expression was one of surprise but also of happiness.

"What is it?" he asked.

She held up a gold band with sparkles of blue. "You promised me a wedding ring."

"Do you like it?" He struggled to remember exactly how it had come into his possession, but he trusted God would return the memory in time.

"I love it. It's perfect." Her eyes welled again with tears. "I will cherish it."

"I know it's a bit extravagant, but I figure you're worth it. I wanted you to have the best." He knew that much was true. He also remembered where the money had come from. "I took my savings and brought it with me. I knew I was going to buy you a ring." He said the words more as an account of his agenda, hoping it would recall to mind the details.

"Austin, I don't need an extravagant ring," Jessica said, meeting his gaze. "I just need you. And you need to get well and come home. You need to forget the past and move forward. Your brother and Grace and I believe even your parents wouldn't want you to linger in guilt and sorrow. After all, your folks loved Jesus. They're with Him now, and they know the truth of what happened. They don't blame you anymore."

"Maybe you're right," Austin replied, feeling more tired than he could remember ever being.

"I believe my patient needs to rest," the doctor declared. "We're going to give him something to help him do so."

Jessica stood. "There's a pocket watch, some money, and your Ranger badge in this cloth. Shall I keep these things for you?"

Austin nodded and closed his eyes. "I'd feel better if you did. I don't know how long I'll have to be here, but as soon as I'm able to return to Texas, I will. I'll have the Secret Service wire me money for the trip home. They owe me that much."

"They're also paying for your hospital stay," the doctor added. "And all fees associated with your injuries. Your friends said that this was the wish of a Mr. Turner."

Austin smiled. "Sounds like him."

Jessica hated leaving Colorado Springs when Austin was still in such a weakened state, but she knew her father had to return to the ranch. Howard and Isaac were returning after a long time away, and Father wanted to be there when they arrived home.

"It won't take him any time at all to recover," Father told her as the train pulled out of the station. "And you will be so busy plannin' the weddin' that you won't have time to miss him."

"I doubt that is true, but I will endeavor to focus on my duties," Jessica replied. She grew thoughtful, almost fearful. "Father,

410

you don't think things could go wrong now, do you?"

"With the weddin'?"

She shook her head and peered past her father to the window. "No, I meant with Austin's recovery. He couldn't get . . . well . . . sicker, could he?"

"The doc said he was strong and in good shape. He thought it would take a few weeks but that in time Austin would recover fully. I don't think he figures on Austin failin'. And if I know that boy, he'll recover in half the expected time."

"Why do you think that, Papa?"

Her father laughed. "Because I was young once, too. If I had a pretty gal like you waitin' for me to take her down the aisle . . . well, I wouldn't be abed for long. Injuries or no injuries, nothin' would keep me from my beloved."

Jessica smiled and put her head on her father's shoulder. "Thank you, Papa. Thank you for bringing me here and for encouraging me."

He slipped his arm around her and pulled her close. Jessica relished the warmth of her father's embrace. She tried hard to think of a hot Texas summer rather than the cold that nipped at her face and fingers.

■ ■ ■ ■

"It's so good to be back in Texas." Jessica sighed. "I don't care if I never leave here again. It was so cold in Colorado." She glanced in the shop windows of Dallas's finest shopping district. She and her mother were making purchases for Jessica's wedding and having a wonderful time together.

"Before long the temperatures will be unbearable, and we'll be saying how much we hate it. Then you'll find yourself wishing for the cold," her mother said with a smile. "Oh look, here's the glove shop the dressmaker mentioned. I hope they have what we need."

Jessica followed her mother into the shop. She looked at the various sets of gloves Mother chose and tried on a couple of them. Mother wanted her to have full-length white gloves to wear with her wedding gown, since the dress was without sleeves.

"I think these with the tiny pearl buttons are perfect," her mother declared, once Jessica had donned the exquisite pair with silver embroidery vining along between the pearls.

"I do, too, Mother. I think they're the most beautiful gloves I've ever seen. But, you know, I don't really need them. I would probably never wear them again."

"Nonsense. You might attend the opera or the symphony and need them then. Many brides wear their wedding finery again on their first anniversary. Now, let's see what else you might need."

They spent a productive day shopping, and before they retired to their hotel room, Jessica and her mother shared supper in a restaurant a block away.

"When did you say Austin is due back?" Mother asked.

Jessica sampled the lemonade the server placed on the table. It was sweet, but not overly so, just as she preferred it. "He said he should be back by the middle of March."

"Are you sure you want to go ahead with the thirty-first for the wedding? That will give him only a couple weeks to get his affairs in order for the ceremony. Wouldn't you rather wait until next month? April is such a lovely time for a wedding in Texas."

Jessica shook her head. "I would have married him in his hospital bed if I'd thought I could get away with it. No. He wants us to go forward with the thirty-first. He's even arranged to buy a wedding suit in Colorado. The tailor has already come to measure and fit him there in the convalescent home. He'll be ready, Mother. Never fear."

Her mother laughed. "I suppose I should have guessed that much. Your father would have been the same way."

The waitress brought them veal cutlets and fried polenta with cheese. There were cooked greens on the side, as well as fresh dinner rolls. It was a veritable feast, and Jessica savored the aroma as she slathered butter on her roll.

Mother offered a prayer, and Jessica found herself thanking God for all that He had done in her life. She wasn't yet completely transformed, and some of the old selfishness still rose up in her occasionally. *I'm not perfect,* she mused, knowing that she would never be so . . . on earth. She would continue to work hard, however, to change her bad habits and selfish ways. She was determined on that point.

After a good night's sleep, Jessica dressed with Mother's help and accompanied her to breakfast and then to a final bridal gown fitting. As Jessica nervously stepped into the satin and lace gown, she couldn't help but gasp. The reflection in the mirror made it all seem the more real. She was truly getting married.

The dressmaker's assistant worked at pinning the gown until it met the approval of her employer. The dressmaker herself walked around and around, critically reviewing the work and looking for flaws. Jessica felt rather like a pin cushion as they reworked a piece on the bodice. Oh, but it was a lovely dress with its beautiful train — the stuff of little-girl dreams and big-girl hopes.

"I think you've done a beautiful job," Mother told the dressmaker. "And you say it will be ready in a week?"

"Yes, there isn't that much left to do. We will reduce the waist and adjust the buttons in the back, then sew the final pieces of lace to the bodice and smooth some of those seams. Do you still wish for me to ship the gown to you?"

Mother nodded. "Yes. Have it delivered to the depot at Cedar Springs in care of the stationmaster. He has already been instructed about it, but I will remind him that the dress is coming."

"Very good. I shall endeavor to have it on the train within the week."

Jessica looked once again at her reflection in the mirror. *It's really happening. I'm going to marry Austin Todd. I'm going to be his wife — the mother of his children.* She cast a quick gaze heavenward, scarcely able to believe it.

Thank you, Lord. Thank you so much for all that you've done to make this happen. I haven't always understood why my life took the turns it did, but I can see your hand in everything that has taken place.

Austin performed the exercises suggested by the doctor and felt his muscles growing stronger each day. He was anxious to return to Texas but wanted to do so as much a whole man as he could be. The doctor had told him he might struggle with pain for the next few months, but that it shouldn't be serious or last for long. Already the pain associated with the bullet wounds was so much better that Austin felt certain he could deal with anything that came his way.

March in Colorado wasn't as warm as he'd hoped. And because it was still just as likely to snow as it had been in February, the doctor had loaned Austin a coat for those times when he sat outdoors in the fresh air. For now, most of the snow had pretty much melted, thanks to several warm days. One of the nurses had informed him that the Farmers' Almanac suggested an early spring, with warmer temperatures than normal. If this was warmer, Austin didn't think much of it.

"Mr. Todd, you have a visitor," a young

student nurse announced.

Austin felt a momentary hope that it might be Jessica. However, when Ellery Turner walked through the door, Austin was just as happy to see him.

"Mr. Turner, I never expected you to come to Colorado."

"It was necessary for some of the work related to the case against Mr. Morgan. I thought, why send someone else when it would benefit me to see you." The two men shook hands.

"Well, by all means have a seat." Austin motioned to the only chair in the room. "I'll sit here on the bed. So tell me everything. How goes the case?"

Turner sat and crossed his legs. "It goes very well. The evidence is vast, and as we've been able to uncover more details, the case has strengthened."

"Good," Austin said, knowing this would be good news to the Barnetts and Wythes. Not to mention everyone else. "I'm glad it's working out that way. I hope this won't be too big of an embarrassment to his family. J. P. Morgan has been most helpful in getting the country back on its feet."

"No need to worry. This Morgan isn't related in the leastwise to J. P. Morgan. He only told people that in order to win their trust. He was quite good at convincing people of his powerful connections."

"I'm glad you've been able to resolve this. I hope the courts send Morgan and his cohorts to prison for a very long time."

"We never would have had that chance if you hadn't gotten involved. That's another reason I've come. I'm hoping to convince you to rejoin the department. We need men like you, Austin. I know that business with your brother was devastating, but hopefully you can put that behind you and move forward."

"I am doing exactly that, but I'm afraid it won't be with the Secret Service." Austin noted the disappointment in the older man's expression. "I plan to be a town marshal in Terryton, Texas, with a wife and a passel of young ones. You see, God has sent a very special young woman into my life, and while I was certain I could never love another, He's given me that gift, as well."

Turner smiled. "I'm so glad to hear it, Austin. I can't say that I'm not disappointed, but I'm also very happy for you. However, if you should change your mind in the future, there will always be a place for you in my department."

"Thank you, sir. That means a lot to me."

CHAPTER 26

"You look so beautiful," Alice told Jessica as she put the final touches on the bride's hair.

"Thank you for saying so and for doing this. I know I could never have made such an intricate arrangement on my own."

Alice smiled. "I used to dress Marty's hair when I worked for her. It was my favorite part of the job. I love being creative and adding beauty to the world." She tucked one last piece of baby's breath into Jessica's hair.

Jessica watched from her seat in front of the dressing table. She had waited so anxiously for this day, and now that it was here, she could scarcely breathe. It was like holding her breath, waiting to see if all would go well.

"There. I think we're done. Is it what you'd hoped for?"

Jessica looked at the curls pinned high atop her head. "I think it's perfect. The veil will sit just right."

"We can see about that in a moment. But now we need to get you into your gown," Marty Wythe announced.

With a slight tremble, Jessica got to her feet. She couldn't help but wonder about the man who was awaiting her arrival at the altar. What would their life be like now that the railroad was finally building the spur line and Austin was acting marshal of the up-and-coming town of Terryton?

Marty smiled and helped Jessica step into her dress. "You are going to make a beautiful bride, Jessica. I've never seen anyone quite so radiant as you."

"It seemed like this day would never come, and now that it's here, well, it seems to be going by much too quickly." Jessica stood stock-still while Marty and Alice helped secure the skirt of the gown. Once this was done, Marty held up the boned bodice and helped Jessica to slip her arms through the lacey material. Alice immediately went to work pulling the bodice in place. She and Marty worked quickly to do up the thirty-some covered buttons. When this task was complete, the women set about straightening any wrinkles and repositioning the lace to lie properly.

"I think our work is done," Marty said,

stepping back.

"Except for the veil," Alice declared, bringing it forward from the wardrobe where it had been hanging.

The hand-crafted lace and tulle veil crowned Jessica's head in a most elegant manner. The lace edging matched that on her dress and flowed so neatly against it that it appeared to blend into the gown itself as it extended down and past the train. Jessica thought she had never seen anything quite so lovely as her headpiece, which was adorned with a silvery band trimmed with white camellias.

Alice secured the flowery tiara while Marty helped Jessica into her gloves. "Be sure the slit on the ring finger offers easy access," Jessica reminded her.

"I have it perfectly placed," Marty assured her.

"I'll need your help to pull the blusher veil over her head to cover her face," Alice told Marty.

The two women worked perfectly together and adjusted the tulle to cover Jessica's face. "I'll get your flowers, and then we will finally be ready." Alice hurried to the table and retrieved the bouquet. She handed the exquisite arrangement of white jasmine, camellias, and very pale lavender lilacs to the bride.

Jessica felt butterflies in her stomach, and she bit her lip to keep her teeth from chattering. She knew she was being silly, but her anxiety was getting the best of her. What if she wasn't a good wife? What if Austin saw her and changed his mind? What if he hadn't even arrived at the church?

Stop it. Austin loves you, and he's waiting for you.

She looked to the young woman whose scar she had once thought ugly. It had faded over the years, and now seemed far less noticeable. "I'm ready."

Alice smiled. Dressed beautifully in a new but simple lavender gown, Alice stood ready to act as matron of honor — the only attendant Jessica wanted. Alice's husband, Robert, would stand as best man to Austin. Jessica was grateful to both for having put aside her former transgressions. She planned for them all to be great friends for years to come.

"Shall we go?" Marty asked. Both Jessica and Alice nodded. "Very well, then. I'll go take my seat and signal the organ to start the wedding march."

Alice followed her out the door with Jessica slowly coming behind. As she exited the room, she found her father waiting to take her arm.

"My, but you take my breath away," Father declared. "I've never seen you prettier, Jess."

"Thank you," she whispered. "I'm afraid I'm feeling a little nervous."

He patted her gloved arm. "That's normal. I thought I might faint dead away when I married your ma."

Jessica didn't believe him. Her father had always been a pillar of strength. It was impossible to imagine him feeling weak in the knees over anything.

"You know, Jess, when I first held you in my arms all those years ago, I couldn't imagine this day. I never wanted to give you away to anyone because you were so special. You were the completion of our family, and a blessing to all of us."

"Papa, you'd best stop or I'll be in tears." She looked up to her father with a smile. "I love you."

Father smiled at her in return. "I love you, too, darlin'. But there's a young man waitin' for you who thinks he loves you even more. I guess we'd best go meet him at the altar."

Jessica nodded and held fast to her father's arm. "I'm ready."

Organ music filled the entire church as Jessica's father led her down the aisle.

Although Austin stood waiting at the front of the church, Jessica couldn't lift her head to glimpse his face. She feared if she did, she might become overwhelmed, so she watched the church floor instead.

When her father stopped, she knew they'd reached the altar, but still she struggled with her nerves and refused to look up.

"Dearly beloved," she heard the pastor begin, and after that the words were something of a blur. She rallied when her father gave her over to Austin. His strong grasp on her arm felt reassuring.

When the time came to repeat her vows, Jessica did so in a hushed whisper. Her mouth seemed as dry as cotton, but somehow she managed to get the words out. When Austin prepared to put the ring on her finger, all Jessica could think about was the first time she'd seen it in the hospital.

Austin had been so pale, so wracked with pain as he lay on the hospital bed. But even in that condition, Jessica had seen in his eyes the love he held for her. It gave her strength, and Jessica raised her face to gaze into Austin's warm brown eyes as he found her finger and slipped the ring on.

He smiled and Jess couldn't help but smile back. What they were doing felt so right — so perfectly ordered — and Jessica's fears drained away. It truly was a matter of heart, and her heart told her that they would share a lifetime of love, and that made the future seem perfect.

When the pastor announced they were man and wife and that they could share a kiss, Jessica waited in anticipation as Austin carefully lifted her veil.

"Hello, wife," he whispered, his lips close to hers.

"Hello, husband," she replied, then fell silent as his mouth claimed hers.

ABOUT THE AUTHOR

Tracie Peterson is the award-winning author of over a hundred novels, both historical and contemporary. Her avid research resonates in her stories, as seen in her bestselling HEIRS OF MONTANA and ALASKAN QUEST series. Tracie and her family make their home in Montana. Visit Tracie's website at www.traciepeterson.com and her blog at www.writespassage.blogspot.com.